—THE—
Stoned
APOCALYPSE

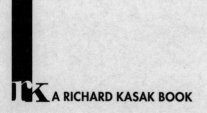

A RICHARD KASAK BOOK

—THE— Stoned

APOCALYPSE

MARCO VASSI

First Richard Kasak Book Edition 1993

First printing October 1993

ISBN 1-56333-132-2

Cover art by Amy Melson

Cover Design by Steve Powell

Manufactured in the United States of America
Published by Masquerade Books, Inc.
801 Second Avenue
New York, N.Y. 10017

FOR RICHARD CURTIS—MINISTER AND MIDWIFE

I truly attained nothing
from total unexcelled enlightenment.

—Gautama Buddha

Life is an omen.

—Frank Gillette

INTRODUCTION

Were the Sixties put on earth so that Marco Vassi could happen? Or was Marco Vassi put on earth so that the Sixties could happen? To read his classic works of erotic fiction and his masterpiece of autobiographical fiction, *The Stoned Apocalypse*, is to realize that the man and the era were created out of the same fire and primordial elements. It is not, however, enough to say that Marco Vassi was a child of his age. It could just as accurately be said that the age was Marco Vassi's fantasy, a fantasy so intense and compelling that it is impossible to read any of his books in one sitting: one must either jump into a cold shower, relieve oneself sexually, or go for a long contemplative walk to reflect on the profundity of his insights into human behavior.

Vassi had done many things before he became a writer, but writing was not one of them except for some translations from Chinese and critiques of manuscripts submitted to a literary agency where he was employed for a few years. He had also tried numerous identities on for size as he acted out and lived out the experiences that were to pour from his mind like water raging over the spillway of a dam. When in the late 1960s "Fred" Vassi announced that he was embarking on a journey, his friends knew that it was not to a place but to a state of mind.

The state of mind was what came to be known as The Sixties, and anyone seeking to live in that state must enter it through the vision of the author of these works. In cartographic terms it was a journey from the East Coast to California, a trip that resonates with meaning for every student of The American Experience. Speaking metaphorically, however, it was a trip into the heart of life, love, laughter, horror, and sweet pain. Fred Vassi came back Marco Vassi, having recreated himself in the name of the intrepid voyager to the ends of the known world hundreds of years ago.

Heart fecund with all that had happened to him, he started writing the work that was eventually to become The Stoned Apocalypse, a book that captured in coruscating words what others of his generation were capturing so brilliantly in music.

With no source of regular income he tried his hand at what were then popularly known as sex novels, a genre of tame pornography that pandered to the fantasies of repressed males still mired in postwar inhibition. With the wide-eyed innocence and self-deprecating humor that characterized every venture he undertook, he showed them to me, his friend and a fledgling literary agent. He merely hoped to raise a few dollars with them. I told him that they were the most incredibly arousing works of erotic literature since Henry Miller, and arranged for them to be brought out by Olympia Press, Miller's publisher. Critics and reviewers confirmed my assessment. What distinguished his books from the rest of the pack was the application of Vassi's intelligence. He knew that the mind is the most erotic organ of all. He termed this fusion of mind and sex organs "Metasex."

For Marco Vassi, the liberation of sexual emotions, paralleling the liberation of so many others in the late 1960s and early 1970s, promised a new age of beauty, love, and honesty, and he lived his vision to the hilt—quite literally. For a long while it seemed to him impossible that this vision did not rest on the bedrock of reality.

But, in the words of Robert Frost, nothing gold can stay. The bloody hand of Vietnam and the corrupt fist of the Nixon presidency crushed the fragile beauty of the flower generation. The unbridled commercialism that became the 1980s captured and exploited the butterflies of Woodstock, enriching half of them and killing the other half with sex, drugs, and rock and roll. Finally, the horror of a new scourge, AIDS, visited death upon the bodies of those who had dreamed of eternal love, irresponsible fun, and self-realization. It was then that Marco Vassi awoke from his dream of The Sixties. When he did, the virus had entered his blood. The first malady of any consequence to come along, in this case pneumonia, conquered his defenseless immune system and made short work of him.

Marco Vassi's body died, but not the body of his work, which lives again in these new editions. Like a rainbow over a bleak landscape, his dream of The Sixties shimmers above the depressing, sordid, and tragic decades that succeeded his. And ultimately, it triumphs over them.

—Richard Curtis

1.

"Are you...searching?"

For a moment I thought she might be mocking, but her eyes were clear. Her name was Joan, and she was the secretary to the director of public relations for *Encyclopedia Americana*. I was immediately intrigued. I leaned back in my editor's chair, appraised her in my best astral Valentino, and said, "Yes, you might say I am searching."

"Ah," she said, and walked out of the office.

She was the most interesting woman I had ever met in an office. Of all the workers there, she was the most totally self-possessed, seeming always on the edge of some amusing secret. I felt an uncomplicated animal passion for her, and for several months had been ravishing her up and down the corridors of my imagination, flinging her across my desktop, ripping her skirt and blouse to shreds, forcing her with my throbbing manhood, until the fires of refusal in her eyes liquefied into yearning.

Outside of my fantasies it was nothing like that. I was the editor of a sixteen-page piece of baroque reportage called *Encyclopedia News,* and each month I filled the space with exhortations to SELL MORE!, and inspiring stories of salesmen who had sold six sets in one week! I was housed in a private cubicle on the nine-teenth floor of the piss-yellow Americana Building which squats over Lexington Avenue on Fifty-first Street. And at night I read the literature of alienation and suffered the psychic suffocation which came with contemplating my current condition, the daily lie to myself which told me I ought to go to work, the death-in-life subway ride, the overwhelmingly oppressive air and vibration of midtown Manhattan.

I was a slum kid on the rise, fulfilling my parents' expectations of college degree and respectable office job, escaping the eight hours of daily manual labor my father had spent forty years at. But there had always been something occult in the way I went about things, for I was always ready to give as much weight to the potential as to the actuality of any given circumstance, knowing intuitively that the environment is as much defined by my perception of it as by any objective qualities it may possess.

Three days later, Joan came into my office again. She waited until I put down my pen, had turned to face her, and then spoke. "Do you know…Gurdjieff?" she said. I wanted to impress her, but all I knew about Gurdjieff was a short jumbled conversation Bob Wellman and I had had one night, during which he referred to Gurdjieff as a Russian mystic. "Oh, yes," I said. "He's a Russian mystic, isn't he?' Her response was sheer silent disdain. I trembled inwardly. She arched one eyebrow and said, "Well, actually, he's neither Russian nor a mystic. But no matter." And quickly turned and walked out of the office.

The window blind slipped a gear and came crashing down to the sill, in the process decapitating a small cactus plant I was growing there. That night I went to Washington with Conrad, a fellow editor who was going on a tour of the southern territory; I was to spend three days going out with salesmen to get a feel of how they actually worked, supposedly to make my writing more realistic for the men. I spent a night with an old Estonian pirate named Peter, and the evening was highlighted when we moved in on an Italian tailor, who spoke almost no English, and browbeat him and his wife for over an hour. The man had a two-year-old daughter, and Peter was trying to convince the cat that unless he bought a set of encyclopedias, he would be condemning his little girl to a life of ignorance and poverty. He pulled out all the stops, and did the entire pitch including a ten-minute résumé of man's recorded history and climb up from savagery to the conquest of space. He grew so eloquent that I was ready to buy a set myself. The tailor understood very little of the account, but being Italian, he was swept away by the sound of the rhetoric. He wrung his hands and vowed his eternal desire to buy a set of encyclopedias but pleaded, "I don't have enough money." Peter then proceed to show him that it would only cost "pennies of day." They wrestled for a long time until, with a gesture worth of Verdi, the man strode to a table piled high with clothing and shouted, "I have to work all night just for food enough for my family. Please, I can't buy the books."

Peter leveled him with a cold glance. "All right," he said, and in his voice I heard defeat. "All right, if you won't make the sacrifice for your child..." And he gathered up all the charts and contracts and sample volumes, packed slowly and deliberately, and walked out without a backward look. I followed him out, and no sooner were we five feet from the house than his shoulders straightened, his step got brisk, and his face lit up. "Well," he said, "every one you lose means you're that much closer to the next sale."

One can desire only that which one has tasted, and while I was desperately sick of my job, of the city I lived in, of the entire flat, tedious round of meaningless daily existence, I didn't know what else to do. Everything I tried was only a minor variation on the theme, a palliative for the moment. New York has many toys for its slaves to play with. And yet, there had to be more. For my entire life, I have known that there was more. Not in the way of possessions or life style, but in the way of understanding, of knowing. At the time, the psychedelics were beginning to hit the public eye, and the phrase "expanded consciousness" was filtering through society. But I wasn't ready for LSD; it frightened me.

When I returned from the trip to D.C. I found a slip of paper on my desk. It was from Joan. It read, "*The Psychology of Man's Possible Evolution,* by P. D. Ouspensky." I bought the book on Friday, and read it on the bus to Bennington, where I was having a pornographic love affair with a very romantic and slightly nymphomaniacal girl of nineteen. I was, at the time, working desultorily toward an MA in psychology at the New School, going three nights a week to take notes and scream inwardly at the cosmic obtuseness of the teachers there, each of whom scurried like a white mouse down the end corridors of some inane specialty, getting to know "more and more about less and less until finally they knew everything about nothing." I was coming to the great realization that the study of psychology could not take place apart from an understanding of life as a whole, and to talk about theories of projection was not worth a thousandth of a single insight during which one fully and materially experienced the fact of how one projects. So when Ouspensky began by dismissing all of Western psychology as childish, I felt that I had found my man.

I understood the book merely on the intellectual level, except for one experiment he recommends, which is simply to look at the second hand on one's wristwatch for two minutes, all the while maintaining a single awareness: the fact of one's existence. Of course, I couldn't do it, and the lesson was not lost. "You are asleep," Ouspensky was saying, "and your so-called waking life is the blind stumbling of a sleepwalker. You prate about consciousness, and internal unity, and will, but you are as far from these as an ant is from the snow-covered mountaintops."

"I'd like to know more," I said to Joan when I saw her next. She looked at me approvingly. "Can I go to bed with you?" I asked. She smiled and I couldn't tell at all what the smile indicated. "Try this," she said, and wrote down, "*Meetings with Remarkable Men,* by G. I. Gurdjieff." I picked up the book that night, and expected a rush of high-level intellectual force, for this was, after all, written by the Master. Where the Ouspensky book had merely piqued my interest, this work blew my mind. Gurdjieff came across as a drinking, brawling, ballsy madman. In a flash I saw the difference; it was the Jesus–St. Paul split all over again. Gurdjieff's ideas were epiphenomenal to his life, while with Ouspensky, who was a Russian, life was just the stage upon which ideas could develop. I communicated my enthusiasm to Joan, and after I had waxed out for a few minutes, she took a deep breath (her breasts rising beautifully on her chest) and said, "You're ready for *In Search of the Miraculous.*" For a moment I thought she was going to clasp my hands, but she seemed to restrain herself. "If I read this, then can I go to bed with you?" I said. This time her smile was encouraging.

Within a hundred pages of Ouspensky's Gospel, I saw the light. Once again I was converted to a system. The man had the gift of unerringly articulating every one of my secret visions and half-felt intuitions. I became a true believer, and could hardly wait to get to work the next morning, to see Joan, this oddly disguised Beatrice who was introducing me to a strange journey through myself. "It's fantastic," I shouted when I saw her. She retained her cool. "I want to know more," I said. "What do I do next?" She seemed to come to some deep resolve inside herself and then said the words which were to permanently change my life. She said, "I'll speak to my guru."

Now, this was at a time before the term "guru" had become associated with the Maharishi, Satchidananda and Yogananda Brothers Psychic Circus. The word struck a chill in my heart, and I conjured images of austere old men in Tibetan caves, whose eyes burned with the unbearable vision of truth. Since I rarely study a thing unless it has some fervid following in one circle or another, I had no knowledge of the Eastern semantic, and had no precise understanding of what a guru was, or did.

My knowledge of the East came from the three years I had spent in Korea and Japan, working as an electronic spy for the U. S. Air Force. I had, after drunkenly enlisting one afternoon during the doldrums of my sophomore year in college, been sent to Yale's Institute of Far Eastern Languages for a year to study Chinese in an intensive course. For seven hours a day, forty of us raged and giggled our way through the Mandarin lexicon, learning to hear spoken Chinese at a faster and faster rate, and finally in dialect and through heavy static, so we could spend the following few years hunched over radio receivers, trying to hear obscure messages being passed by inscrutable pilots winging over the mainland of China. The advantage was being able to spend all that time actually living in the Orient, learning about the civilization through osmosis.

The drawbacks inhered in the work. Since what we were doing was ostensibly a secret—although huge radio antennas sprouted from every square foot of the compound—we could have no uncleared guards working to protect us from raids, which from time to time did occur. At one point I found myself on a low hill on an island in the Yellow Sea, on the 38th parallel and just two thousand yards from the North Korean shore, standing for four hours, with the winter wind whipping down from Manchuria at thirty degrees below zero, staring into pitch-blackness past the glare of searchlights and over a barbed-wire fence. I held a rifle which had frozen to my fingers, and each second I wondered whether there might be an "enemy" just about to put a bullet into my forehead.

Four days later, Joan approached me. "My guru has asked that you write her an autobiography."

I was bemused. "How long should it be?" I asked.

"As long or as short as you wish," she replied. Suddenly, I saw her lying on her back on a red rug, her fingernails digging into the fur, her face screwed up into a mask of pleasure-pain, her legs straining to open wider and wider while her cunt surged toward me. I became momentarily dizzy. "Do it as quickly as you can," she said.

I wrote a one-page sketch of my life that was a masterpiece of fatuousness, although I thought it was quite clever at the time. I assumed an Olympian stance and described the major incidents of my life as though they were diversions I had chosen for my pleasure. I gave it to her and waited a week. I spent a lot of time wondering whether the guru might be impressed with what I had written. It seemed to me that I was a most interesting and unusual person, and that if the guru were worth her salt, she would immediately welcome me into the inner circle, whatever that happened to be. Part of me was also amused that the guru was a lady. I had come across the phrase "male chauvinism" in Engels, but hadn't yet realized how much of my attitude was embedded in that particular posture.

The day came. "She will see you," said Joan. She handed me a slip of paper with a name and phone number. It read, Mrs. R. 688-4319. Joan said, "Call her," and walked out.

The first five phone calls I made were exasperating. At times she sounded drunk; at other times she seemed not to remember who I was; and then she would surprise me by sounding outrageously intelligent. Her mood would change from politeness to irascibility. Once she said she didn't have time to talk to me and then hung up. By the sixth time I was genuinely angry, and when she attempted to put me off again I shouted, "Well, you're the one who asked me to call. When can I see you?" She answered in a calm, reasonable tone of voice. "Come on Tuesday morning at 10:30." And she gave me the address.

Oddly enough, on the day she agreed to see me, I received a call from a man called Sweeney, who wanted to offer me a job with the *Reader's Digest*. Although I despised the publication, and saw it as the final step in the ultimate degradation of thought in our time, receiving the offer turned me on. He invited me to the Princeton Club for lunch, and I went through all the changes involved in working my way up a stream of absolutely superficial people. In my forty-dollar Howard suit and sixty-nine-cent tie, my dollar-fifty haircut, and inability to understand much of what was written on the menu, I was clear game for the doorman and deskman and *maître d'* and waiter. Sweeny spent almost two hours pumping me of every bit of information I had concerning *Americana*'s educational division. I saw fairly quickly that he was less interested in my qualifications than in what I could tell him about a rival's mode of operation. But I was disgusted enough at myself, and pissed off enough at *Americana,* to tell all. This was a scene that was to be repeated later when one of the senior vice-presidents of a large ad agency, who happened to be the father of a friend of mine, asked me to find out all I could about *Americana*'s advertising scene, since he was going to make a bid to steal the account. That time I spent a number of hours late at night Xeroxing documents and rifling through correspondence. Once again, my sense of drama obscured any business advantage, and my payment was no more than a lunch at the Four Seasons, during which I handed over the documents.

The fantasy machine went into overdrive, and I saw myself as an editor on the *Reader's Digest.* The salary was to be twelve thousand a year, and I would be expected to live in Pleasantville, and I would receive Blue Cross and paid vacations and bonuses and wholesome meals in the company cafeteria. It was interesting that I could simultaneously see such a step as one more nail in the coffin of my personal stultification, and as a step up in some vaguely defined social hierarchy. My soul would die, but my mother would be pleased.

When I arrived at Mrs. R.'s I suffered a further disillusionment. She lived in one of the ugliest, stuffiest buildings in the Seventies on the West Side. It was one of those apartment houses that seem as though they would much rather be hotels, and was guarded by a lackey at the door, bowing obsequiously to well-dressed visitors and residents, and glaring suspiciously at any odd types who wandered in, such as delivery men, freaks, and anybody with dark skin. "How can a guru live in a place like this?" I thought.

I gave the doorman my name, and he buzzed the information upstairs. A voice rasped back over the speaker: "Tell him to wait." I sat in the lobby, doubly mortified. I consoled myself with the fact that this is the way Zen masters are reputed to treat those who come seeking assistance. I reasoned that she wouldn't know that I was hip to the game, and this gave me an advantage in the coming encounter. I smiled as I imagined how I would wrestle the guru down and force her to admit my superiority. Then, having shown my strength, I would humbly ask for her guidance.

Almost three quarters of an hour later, she had me sent upstairs. I went to the door, and stood there a moment, marshaling my forces. I rang the bell and almost stumbled backward when a plain, pleasant, middle-class woman, with friendly eyes and a dowdy dress opened the door to greet me. I stepped into an ersatz Victorian living room, calling to mind the line that Marilyn, my Bennington star, had delivered in relation to Gurdjieff. "Somehow," she had said, "that entire scene reminds me of overstuffed furniture with thick cloth slipcovers." The woman stepped back and motioned me inside. "Take off your coat," she said. "And sit down."

I dropped my coat on a chair and walked into the next room. She turned off down a hallway and disappeared. I waited for another half hour. I passed the time by casing the joint. There was a well-chosen collection of books, a ring of Third Avenue antique store furniture, and several original Modiglianis and Renoirs. I began to smell the contours of wealth, and a subtle dimension braced my perceptions.

She came back in bustling, and arranged herself tidily on the couch. For a moment we sat in silence, she smiling, and me "sitting on a cornflake waiting for the van to come."

"Well," she said, "tell me about yourself."

I hesitated, but couldn't find anything to hang the hesitation on. I took a breath and proceeded to give her about two hours of my best rap. Shortly, I went into a kind of hypnotic state, lulled by the sound of my own voice, and presently was no longer aware of what I was saying. I must have appeared like some mechanical doll which had been wound up and was letting out a mindless spiel. At one point, I noticed that I had stopped talking, and snapped to. I became aware again that I was in the room, with this woman watching me, blandly, openly. I sat back and waited for her reaction.

Without changing the expression of pleasant attention she had worn for the entire time, she said, "I think you are such an utter fool that if you have acquired, by the age of forty, the courage to kill yourself, it will be the one significant act of which you are capable."

I stared at her in disbelief. I waited for some indication that she was joking, or offering the line as some sort of gambit. But she looked at me levelly, without malice or judgment. She had simply been making an observation and seemed not to have the slightest interest in how I received it. Very slowly a feeling of horror crept over my body. I began to feel worthless and somehow vile. I felt as though I had committed some kind of nameless sin, and was now being called to task for it. Except that the sin was the sum total of how I had lived my life up to that point. She remained pleasant.

For a long time I waited for something to say, and then collapsed inwardly. I was a punctured balloon, and could do nothing but bow my head to receive whatever punishment she wished to mete out. She stirred. "Nonetheless," she said, "there are some barely salvageable features about you; you are not an entirely broken machine." She appraised me with a long look. "Perhaps something can be done," she added.

I squirmed with pleasure. A wave of gratitude washed over me. Involuntarily, I smiled. She was playing me like a mannequin.

"Begin by getting rid of that foolish grin," she ordered. "I haven't decided to take you on as yet. There are some things you will have to understand first. You cannot fool me. Anytime you try to fool me, I shall know about it. You are to speak to no one about what goes on here. And you shall have to obey me utterly. Can you do that?"

I was eager to please. "Yes," I said, "I think so."

"Nonsense," she barked. "You can do nothing."

"That's right," I said, "I can do nothing."

"Stop parroting me, you idiot," she yelled.

"Excuse me, I'm sorry," I mumbled.

"Very well. Now, sit up straight in your chair. You might at least act as though you had some pride in yourself."

With that she showed me a simple exercise for centering the self and gathering a fine grade of psychic energy. I was to do it every morning, simply sitting quietly, letting my body awareness move from my feet, up through my legs, through my torso and arms, and into my head. Nothing fancy. Simple body awareness. She put me through the paces a few times, and it was one of the most astounding experiences of my life. I wasn't feeling my body; my body was aware of itself, and the "I" which I usually identified with became a kind of shadowy presence. "Try that for a few weeks, every morning, and then call me again," she said.

When I left, I was having acid flashes, although I hadn't yet dropped acid and didn't recognize the experience. It was as though everything I saw was washed clean, as though the entire world had just been formed that day and I was seeing it with newborn eyes. I was filled with hope, exuberance, and a roaring sentimentality. Much like the early Christians who bore the Eucharist through the streets among hostile Romans, I clutched my experience to my breast and walked warily to the subway. I resolved that I would change totally, that I would obey all of Mrs. R.'s directives, that I would do my morning exercise without fail. To paraphrase Orwell, I loved Big Sister.

For the following several months, I was treated to a similar routine. Every three weeks I called the guru and went to her apartment, where she politely asked me about my progress. I dutifully reported my activities, describing the results of my morning awareness exercise. It was an odd period, for I received neither encouragement nor blame from the lady. It was like treading water, and I found myself becoming slightly bored. It seemed to me that I should be learning all sorts of esoterica and being initiated into mind-boggling rites.

During that time, I quit my job at *Americana*. I had reached a point of near suffocation, and three weeks before Christmas, I handed in my resignation. With their usual lack of grace, they promptly rescinded the Christmas bonus I was to receive in the next paycheck. Infuriated, I wrote a four-page diatribe and left it on the president's desk, and then went back to my office and gathered up all the correspondence and every back issue of the magazine, leaving nothing for any future editor to work with in continuing to put the book out. I waited until seven o'clock, and then piled everything into four cardboard boxes, took a cab to my pad, and threw the entire lot down the incinerator. I would have preferred dynamiting the building's foundations but I didn't have the means to match my fantasy.

My next job was as managing editor for Avant Publications, hearty publishers of *Escapade, Caper,* and a small library of sex-cartoon books. The editor quit shortly after I got there, and willy-nilly I found myself running a suite of offices and six employees. Suddenly I had a huge office on Fifth Avenue and Forty-fourth Street, with two phones on my desk, a receptionist, a secretary, and a salary in five figures.

The work consisted mostly of finding more or less palatable

material to fill up the sixty-six pages of each eighty-page issue that weren't covered with shots of naked women—nipples and buttocks exposed, pubic hair forbidden. During the five months I worked there, I looked at over five thousand sets of photographs of women without clothes.

One afternoon, up to my elbows in editorial confusion, I received a phone call from Joan, whom I hadn't seen since leaving *Americana*. She and her husband, Douglas, wanted me over for dinner. This surprised me since Mrs. R. allowed no unauthorized fraternization among her students. But I was glad at a chance to pick up information.

They lived in a perfectly decorated apartment in the West Fifties. Douglas was an industrial designer, almost forty, and wore a great bushy moustache à la Gurdjieff. In keeping with the fact that Gurdjieff loved to drink and Ouspensky was down on drugs, they packed away a lot of booze during the evening and spoke disparagingly about marijuana. "I used to smoke charge," Douglas said, using a term that hadn't been current for fifteen years.

They were quite stern in refusing to answer any of my questions about Mrs. R. but spoke quite freely about themselves. "I first read Ouspensky ten years ago," Douglas said, "and I knew I had to follow that path. So I came to New York and sought out the Foundation. I've been with them ever since."

He was utterly committed, without a doubt concerning the rightness of his way of life. It was simultaneously admirable and infuriating. I noticed with them what has often been noted about people in the Work by those outside of it: that they never seemed totally at ease, they seemed always somehow to be watching, to be acting from some privileged platform. There was the unmistakable aroma of orthodoxy about them. Later, I was to understand that, as Brendan Behan notes about the Irish, the Gurdjieffites "are quite popular among themselves"; and their approach to life, despite its peculiarities, lends itself to a sanity and sobriety which contrasts sharply with the collective insanity of the species.

The evening may have been a screening of some sort, for the next day Mrs. R. told me that I could attend group meetings. "This doesn't mean I have decided to take you on as a student," she said, and continued with a lecture that made my back teeth ache. "You must be serious about the Work. It can chew you up.

I will tolerate absolutely no nonsense from you. You can fool everyone in the world, but you can't fool me. Also you'll be asked to pay a fee." The fee turned out to be twenty-five dollars a month, about which her comment was, "You'd have to pay twice as much for an hour with a mere psychiatrist and not begin to get what you'll get here.

The meetings were held in a renovated brownstone in midtown off Park Avenue. The ambience was that of a Los Angeles funeral parlor. Everyone walked around being terribly aware. Conversations were held in whispered tones. Seriousness seeped from the walls.

The major activity during each group was the reporting of observations each of us had made of ourselves during the week. In Gurdjieff's regimen the student spent perhaps several years simply taking mental snapshots of basic behavior: posture, gesture, facial expression, movement, and tone of voice. This is considered necessary to rid the individual of all sorts of preconceptions, misconceptions, and fantasies he may have about himself.

About thirty of us sat in five or six rows of chairs facing the front of the room. Everyone maintained a totally still pose and a zombie-like silence. The point, I imagine, was to re-collect ourselves to be ready for the guru when she entered. But there was something about the enforced behavior which was oppressive; there was no ease or spontaneity, no joy of the moment. The mood was one of psychic constipation.

Usually she had us sit there for over an hour past the appointed time. And when she entered, it was with one or another form of put-down. "Well, what have you been doing while waiting for me? Dreaming? Dozing? What have you been doing this week? Who has some observation to report? Come on, come on. Speak!" And then, when someone would begin with, "As I was observing myself this week..." she would interrupt with, "You mean, as you were *trying* to observe yourself this week. You know as well as I do that you stumble around in sleep most of the time. How often did you remember yourself this week? Two times? Three times?' And the offending victim would bow his or her head and say, quite meekly, "Yes, Mrs. R."

The first week I said nothing. I spent my time learning the protocol, for it became obvious that any breach of etiquette would be summarily squashed. At the second meeting, I was ready. During the week I had had a stunning experience. I had taken to doing my morning exercise sitting on the john in the office because I couldn't get it together until I was up at least two hours, had drunk some coffee, and let the dregs of the night's dreams settle. I was bringing my awareness, as instructed, up from my toes, to my legs and torso, and then to my head, when suddenly my brain felt itself as an organ. Up to that moment I had thought of what happened in my head as "mind," due mostly to the aberrational training I received at the hands of the Jesuits when I was young. Now, at once, I understood the fact of "brain," and the realization of its existence staggered me. I became aware that my thoughts were simply the way my brain felt when it exercised itself, in the same way that the sensation of stretching was how my muscles felt when they moved. And further, I realized that there was an awareness within me which transcended thought; that thought was a fairly low-level activity, and not to be at all confused with intelligence.

When she asked, "Does anyone have anything to report?," I raised my hand and addressed her in the proper self-effacing format. "When I was trying to observe myself this week," I said, "I experienced my brain as an organ, as a physical entity." She looked at me through squinted eyes. "I didn't expect you to report so soon," she said. "But it appears you may be an adept. Continue."

An adept! My ego inflated like a blowfish. I was flushed with success and the rest of my report came out distorted. "Well," I said, "I felt as though I were trapped inside my own skull, and…"

"ENOUGH!" she thundered. "That's pathology. Don't bring that garbage in here to infect the minds of the other students. There will be no more of that here."

I felt the collective condemnation of the room. She turned on the others with equal fury. "Take your attention away from him. I have told you countless times you have nothing to learn from one another, you can only confuse yourselves. Turn your attention here."

I was grateful for having the heat removed from me, but I was smarting as though from a blow. I felt chastised and a slow fury began to grow in me. My anger centered largely on the fact that, despite the inaccuracy of her formulations, she was absolutely correct in her attitude. But I refused to admit this to myself.

So, I began to cheat. In the weeks that followed, I started smoking grass again. I began to tell my friends about the trip. Of course, they couldn't understand why I found the Work valuable, and they put it down. Being suggestible, I felt the impress of their cynicism on my mind. The only person in the world who could understand exactly where I was at and could help me with it was Mrs. R., but she was an irascible old bitch to whom I had no access. I began to harbor resentments, to play head games with the situation, to take freaky risks with my morning exercise.

After two months of the routine, I began to fall apart. My leg began hurting, and I had to wear a support bandage around my calf. I began an affair with a German model who could come only if I whipped her with her brassiere. I started classes in hatha yoga with one of those benign imbeciles who get tired of holy obscurity in the hills of India and come to seek fame and fortune in New York City. Finally, I was introduced to a Gestalt therapist by the head of the Sexual Freedom League in the city, and spent nine sessions complaining to him about my guru. He was one of those brittle Englishmen whose humor is always at the razor's edge. His entire therapeutic approach involved reminding me to breathe, and laughing at my woes. He thought my problems with Mrs. R. were uproarious, and one day I exploded and demanded that he take me seriously. He smiled and said, "Look, your precious guru sounds like a silly old lady with a dry cunt. The next time you see her, ask her if she's good enough for you, and not the other way around."

I never told her that, but the emotional content of his message burned inside me. Secretly I felt I was as good as she was, that she had no right to treat me like a slave. But she had the Indian sign on me, and there was no way for me to bring my feelings to the surface. True to her word, she saw that something was going on, and she told me not to come back to the group any more. "I'll see you privately in a week or so," she said.

The next time I went to her home, she racked me up cold. For the first time, she let the shades off her eyes, and began zapping me with megavolts on the astral plane. The words she flung at me were enough to wipe me out, and they were coupled to a force that had me literally wincing. She seemed to be reaching into my mind and heart and bowels, destroying any last bit of security or strength I thought I had. She catalogued all my weaknesses and sins, she openly mocked every trick of personality I had been using to manipulate my way through society. She forced me to see all the ways in which I lied to myself, cheated myself, fooled myself. At one point, I felt my perceptions go hazy, and her face became a ball of glowing light. I was forced out of my chair and pushed out of the room, simply by her sheer presence. I stumbled backing up, and almost knocked over a lamp. I apologized profusely. I was sweating. The effect of the woman was overwhelming. She was being pure woman, without any of the social artifices and cringing attitudes, without the coyness and seduction, without the strident self-assertion that gets mistaken for strength. She was letting me have it, the frank femaleness of her, and I couldn't take it. I started to leave, almost literally bowing and scraping, when she barked out, "And you don't even have the sense to thank me for what I'm giving you." I looked up bleakly. What else did she want from me? Then she softened and said, "You're right. There can be no thanks for this kind of Work."

The following week was hectic. In the last issue of *Escapade* I had done a story on the *East Village Other,* and as part of the piece had run a photo of one of their covers, which pictured a bearded man holding a sign which read: FUCK HATE. The distributors refused to deliver the magazine to the wholesalers. Hypocritically prudish to a man, they were willing to distribute millions of photos of naked women, but balked when the word "fuck" appeared in print. There was panic. Some two hundred and fifty thousand copies of the magazine were stacked in warehouses, and hundreds of thousands of dollars were about to be lost. My job hung in the balance. The publishers wanted my head to roll, until the boss's son-in-law got a bright idea.

The magazines were owned by a printing firm that had been founded by a shrewd Italian who arrived in America some thirty years ago, with no money and no knowledge of English. Within that time, he became a multimillionaire, and now owned nine-tenths of a small Connecticut town, including the printing plant, the supermarkets, the theater, the bowling alley, and the rest. The town was largely Italian, and he ran it like a feudal kingdom. The old man's son-in-law had every last copy of the issue brought back to the town, marshaled some three or four hundred of the girls who worked in one or another of the old man's enterprises, and set them to work with magic markers. Within three days, using an assembly-line technique and working with coffee and sandwiches around the clock, every last FUCK had been covered over with black ink. And within the week, a quarter of a million copies of *Escapade* moved once more onto the newsstands of America, with the offending picture bearing the one permissible word: HATE.

It was at that time that I began to get the first flashes that I had to leave New York. I didn't know to where, or how; but things were closing in. And I decided that I had to settle things with Mrs. R. My humiliation had transmogrified into pride, and I squashed all impulses to be honest with myself. I just wanted to attack and destroy, to get the guru monkey off my back. And so, one afternoon, amidst the stacks of photos of naked women and the sign over my desk which read HELP STAMP OUT FUCK, I called the lady and demanded an appointment. To my surprise, she said, "Very well, come up now."

I took a cab to her apartment. Some tension had been resolved in me, and I was ready to let it all hang out. I no longer cared whether she threw me out or not, although deep within myself I felt my losing contact with the Foundation might be an error I would regret all my life. Yet, I took all my doubts and hammered them into the point of the warhead I was aiming at the guru's citadel. I would force her to recognize my worth, to stop treating me like dirt.

I stormed past the doorman with an angry glance, daring him to attempt to stop me. I rode to the fifteenth floor, my anger now having obscured whatever good sense I may have had. It felt good to be so mad. I rushed to her door, and stopped cold when I saw that it was a few inches open. Deep inside me a warning bell went off as my animal nature instinctively recognized a trap. But fools rush in, etc.

I took a giant step inside and shut the door hard behind me. I walked to the entrance of the living room and saw her, sitting quietly, smiling faintly, watching me. I wasted no words. I drew my sword, flung back my cape, and charged toward her. Instantly I became a horde of furies, an army of avenging knights. I felt invulnerable, eternal, mighty. I got halfway across the floor when she said, very gently and firmly, "The rug."

I froze on the spot. Rug? What rug? What did that man, the rug? The koan transfixed me.

The she said, "You kicked over the edge of the rug."

I looked back. Sure enough, one edge of the rug was turned over, perhaps a few inches of it. I swung my eyes back toward her, my glance holding a steel-edged condescension. "I came here prepared to confront you on something vital," I said, "and if all you can notice is something as trivial as a rug..."

Without moving, she set off her explosion and derailed the train. "If you can come into my home," she said, "kick over the edge of a rug, and *not even realize that you have done it,* then what sort of confrontation can you hope to have with me?"

And with that, she threw me out.

For a few weeks I maintained a state of self-righteous indignation. And then slowly, I began to realize that I had not distinguished myself in the relationship, that despite all the esoteric jargon, despite all the circuitous maneuverings, the Foundation had something that I desperately needed and wanted. They were people who were dedicated to waking up, to dispelling the hypnotic trance which continually leads the species into stupidity, into war, into misery. And they eschewed all the mystical claptrap, the pseudo-religious trappings. They valued critical intelligence highly, although, to this day, I am not sure to what degree they were free of their own sociological conditioning. At one time I received an invitation to see a filming of sacred dances performed at the Gurdjieff Foundation in France. The work performed there exhibited the highest level of intelligence I have ever seen, a profound reverence for the mystery of existence coupled with an uncompromising understanding of that portion of the universe which can be known. But once again, the people who attended all looked as though they had pokers rammed up their asses. The film showed at one of the East Side movie houses and was attended by most of the Gurdjieffites in the Western Hemisphere. The movement puts some stress on wealth, for a person must have enough means to move about to wherever he needs to be at any given time. I felt as though I were at a convention of psychic closet queens. The head of the Work was there from France, a superbly manicured woman wearing a sable jacket. She was fawned over as though she were royalty. And I saw that above all else the Work is an excuse to form another clique, a group of people among whom complicity was the chief virtue. They had all agreed to play life according to a similar set of rules, and within that matrix, were more or less successful.

Of course, the esoteric aspect of the Work is the crystallization of a spiritual body, one which will continue, at a different level of consciousness, after the death of the physical body. The goal is immortality within the limits of the solar system, with immortality being understood in a special sense. Yet, despite all the hush-hush high-level work on awareness, there was for me the suspicion that the only thing Gurdjieff was saying was to wake up and enjoy life, its total joy and terror, its mystery and its revelations.

The entire affair concluded shortly thereafter, when I took LSD for the first time. The experience of the drug cannot be communicated through words. I went through the usual cycles, flavored by my own conditioning. My guide was freaked out on *The Tibetan Book of the Dead* at the time, and she kept reading me snatches from that hoary comic book. Oddly enough, Gurdjieff's system is derived from the same sources as the Tibetan, and in fact, he learned much of his scene from the Tibetans while he was smuggling guns past the British into Asia. Among other things that night, I reenacted the tragicomedy of Abbott and Costello, and then sailed off into a full-blown Jesus trip, complete with glory, agony, death, and resurrection. Finally, I rose from the dead, resplendent in golden rays, and floated off into the heavens.

But at the height of my victory, with all the earth at my feet, I looked down and saw dumpy old Mrs. R. walking down the street. With a voice like trumpets I shouted, "Mrs. R. Look at me, I'm Jesus Christ." Without so much as looking up, she muttered. "You're Marco Vassi, and you're still a fool." At that moment I may have become the first person to blush on the astral plane.

The next day I was down from the drug, and called her. "I took acid yesterday," I said, "and I want to tell you that I am ashamed of the way I behaved." She paused a long time and then said, "Oh, I suppose you'll have to do the whole drug thing now. Call me when you're finished with that foolishness."

I never saw or spoke to her again. Her phone number mysteriously disappeared from all my records one day. She stayed in my consciousness as a living force for some time. There was little I did during that time which she didn't actively super-ego. Her influence reached into my deepest core, and I had hardly got to know the woman!

Some time later I ran across several renegade Gurdjieff groups on the West Coast. John Klaxon led some two hundred people in bizarre psychic orgies each week. And a number of people who had read Gurdjieff but not come into contact with any teachers were using his ideas to put together their own syntheses of mind control. The most interesting person was Mr. F., however. His wife and he had both been members of the Foundation, and she stayed on while he broke away to form his own school. He claimed that the New York school had been overly Ouspenskyite in its orientation, and he called for a return to pure Gurdjieff. Old G. had hardly been dead a score of years, and already high-level factions were forming, complete with defections and purges.

I walked into one of F.'s groups carrying a copy of *Search* before I knew what the score was with them. One of the people came up to me and said, "Reading Ouspensky, eh?" And suddenly I felt like I had carried a copy of Trotsky into a roomful of Stalinists. My reflexes went into overdrive and I immediately dug the scene. "I find him...interesting," I said. He nodded. "Yes, he says some valuable things. But one mustn't be misled by him." It reminded me of my days in the Party. The same guarded tones, the same innuendoes, the same air of complex intrigue.

Almost two years later, on a chill night in the desert outside of Tucson, with some fine Southwest grass coursing through my brain, I woke up simply to the fact of existence. And at that moment, Mrs. R. ceased being an influence and became simply one of the many people I had known in my life. I was returned to myself, and I knew that, paradoxically, I had found the place Gurdjieff talks about, without being a Gurdjieffite. Of course, I fall in and out of enlightenment, as I fall in and out of all the states which compose the human condition. After all, cosmic consciousness is just a part, and is no more or less than a fart.

For a long time, before coming to myself, I was haunted by the visions I had while under her influence. The fact that almost every human being I meet is actually asleep, dead to himself or herself, walking in a world of illusion, created a loneliness that was almost crushing. And from time to time I still suffer night horrors, haunted by that insight into existential aloneness. I find that having a woman nearby, some cold beer in the refrigerator, and a copy of *Ecclesiastes* by the bed, however, go a long way to counteract the influence of Turkish fairy tales.

Shortly after dropping acid, I dropped out. I left the girlie book publishers. And I began to get even more restless. My journey to find myself started to take on a geographic bent, and in the classic manner of every American who seeks to know himself, I began to look west, toward the fabled land of California.

But before the final resolve to leave, one more event was to fill my paranoia quotient to the brim. With the wounds from my encounter with Mrs. R. still bleeding, one sunny afternoon, I walked into the Hotel Martinique, and into the arms of the Scientologists.

2.

I have never had any luck with organizations. I began life between the Mafia and the Catholic Church, in the enclave of East Harlem in upper Manhattan. The neighborhood had the ambience of feudal Italy; it composed a fief with clearly marked boundaries. It was bounded by the East River on one side, a large park on another, with Park Avenue and 125th Street marking the divisions between it and the stretches of black Harlem to the northwest. Just about everyone over thirty had been born in Italy, and I remember asking my mother at what age I would begin talking Italian, since it seemed that all the young people spoke English while the older ones reverted to the more ancient tongue. To say that we were sheltered is to miss the depth of isolation from twentieth-century America that blessed and blighted us. I didn't meet a non-Catholic socially until I was seventeen; and at the age of fifteen, when one of the neighborhood girls dated a Protestant from the YMCA which stood in benign neglect at the fringes of the kingdom, we all swarmed around her after she returned, asking her what Protestants were like, how they looked, what they said. For all practical purposes, for the first decade and a half of my life, my picture of Protestants was a vicious lampoon of Martin Luther and legions of godless heretics. Jews were simply landlords and the people who had killed Christ, while Negroes stood in relation to us the way the Gallic tribes were viewed by Republican Rome. Our only natural enemies were Puerto Ricans, and by the time I was thirteen, more than twenty boys had been killed in a series of escalating gang wars.

Since I couldn't make the ethical choice between the racketeer whose money came from heroin and prostitution, and the priest who gave him social standing by loudly accepting his money gifts, I became an introverted fanatic, that is to say, a mystic. While still very young I was having visions of statues weeping and wondering why baby kittens died such horrible deaths in the cellars which became our natural playground. At eight I read the life of Don Bosco, and decided I would mortify my flesh in his example. I didn't know how to make a hair shirt, so one night I put five hundred marbles in my bed, thinking to spend the entire time in prayerful anguish. Of course, the marbles merely made a deliciously erotic hard-soft stimulus between the mattress and my body. I was rewarded for my intended sacrifice with a most memorable wet dream, and the next morning found my mother standing by the bed demanding to know what the marbles were for. "It's a thing for school," I said, and my parents, having neither the ability nor the desire to explore the complexities of their son's mind, wrote it off as yet another aberration to be patiently endured.

The tale of my infatuation, disillusionment, hatred, return, and final renunciation of Catholicism is too stereotyped to warrant detailing. It ended with my making peace with the fact that, although I had discarded the entire content of Catholic thought, the structure of my mind was forever imprinted in a hierarchical fashion. In everything I perceive, I compensate for that, much like putting psychic english on my eyeballs.

Before coming to terms with my organizational conditioning, I joined everything from social fads to occult societies to utopian schemes, and finally, to that modern paradigm of Catholicism, the Communist Party.

When I left medieval Italy at nineteen I went into the Air Force—another joining—and after the training at Yale, found myself in Japan which, being feudal itself, seemed natural and comfortable to me. I quickly learned as much of the language as was necessary to do what I needed to do, which in those days was mostly to fuck, travel, and get stoned on the entire phenomenon of Japan. The total and thorough civilization of the place staggered me, as did the way in which the whole social structure was perfectly mirrored in the pyrotechnics of the language.

I got to see things very clearly from the Japanese viewpoint, and it took no time at all before I saw the role of the United States there. The Americans were using Japan as a base from which to headquarter their entire Far East operation, from keeping Korea divided in the north to keeping Vietnam divided in the south. Japan was also the Rest-and-Relaxation center for the brutalized Army men on the Korean peninsula, and, finally, the tip of the sword aimed at China, depending on whether the right-wing elements in the government could get Japan to become a nuclear power or not. In return for all this, the United States allowed Japan to use it as a vast market upon which to practice, and later to master, the entire field of electronics. At home, disgruntled businessmen were either being silenced, satisfied with the maintenance of a high European tariff, or being promised a piece of the pie somewhere else, notably the Middle East and South America.

With this vision, and the Gothic tale of horror which comprised the U.S. occupation of Korea, when I returned to this country I was ripe for revolution. Having had no real contact with America at large, and having been out of the States for three years, I had no idea where the real revolution was taking place, and with a burst of naïve fervor, attempted to join the Communist Party. Which was then, as it is now, the saddest single American organization outside of the DAR. I returned to Brooklyn College, there to pick my way through two and a half years of irrelevancies to earn a BA in psychology. Meanwhile, I discovered Greenwich Village, marijuana, and Marxism.

I fell in with a brilliant professor of economics who had just returned from Cuba and was aglow with tales of socialism triumphant. The pictures and stories of Fidel and his band rivaled anything America had to offer during the revolution of 1776, and contrasted with our line of folk heroes, which includes alcoholic presidents, despoilers of forests and wildlife, vicious generals, and the legendary list of gunfighters, bandits, and armies of men who committed genocide upon the Indian nation.

After Japan, where culture is an art and not a wild hope, the United States could be clearly seen for the brutal, exploitive, shallow, vulgar, and bellicose nation that it was. In a flash I saw that our entire nation was solidly built on the twin pillars of greed and violence. And it seemed that nothing short of a mighty and total upheaval could cure it. This was, of course, before I came to understand that the problem is not with any given society, but in the nature of mankind.

At the height of this fervor, I met Roger, whose love of truth blended imperceptibly into a grotesque personal neurosis, and who was finding his rhetoric in Marx, Lenin, Engels, Trotsky, Plekhanov, and Eisenstein. I moved in with him and his wife, Verna, into a Hassidic neighborhood in Brooklyn. And while the long-robed and bearded Jews, with their sweeping fur-lined hats stood like eighteenth-century Poles in the evening fog under the lamplights, the band of us declared our home to be the first Williamsburg Soviet, and we spent all our time in marathon discussions and study groups, producing pamphlets and slogans, and in general doing the classic leftist scenario. Concurrently, I was having a tender love affair with a *zaftig* solipsist from Bensonhurst, although I was consistently criticized for having truck with such a decadent female.

It was a strange brew and reached a high spot during an all-night party which mixed impassioned denunciations of capitalism with nude dancing on the roof. The Hassidim passed by, refusing to even notice us since we were goyim and therefore hardly better than thinly cultured savages. Their attitude was freakily fixed in my mind one night when I went in to buy some bread at a local bakery. The man ahead of me was Jewish, but clearly of the Reformed, or Amorphous, wing. He was treated with contempt by the stone-faced Hassid behind the counter. But when the storekeeper turned his eyes toward me, I experienced that uncanny sensation of being completely seen through. In his eyes, I didn't even exist.

Fairly soon, because of our constant involvement in marches, demonstrations, and courses at the Institute for Marxist Studies, we began to meet *real Communists*. Now, I had first gone to college during the days of McCarthy, and I knew of the concentration camp provisions of the Smith Act. Also, that was a time before the students had become the vanguard of the revolution, and HUAC was still droning through its Neanderthal hearings, counting each day a success if all the participants managed to keep awake during the entire proceedings. Also, through osmosis, I had been imbued with the rhetoric of the cold war, and despite myself, the notion of communist-inspired images of cloven-footed demons. In all, to my straight-thinking mentality, joining the Party was a fateful and decisive step. So I flirted with the idea a very long time. Ironically, since my father was a house painter, to the Party this gave him a "guild mentality" instead of a "proletarian outlook." And because I had been a Catholic (this was pre-Pope John) and, sin of all sins, a spy on the Chinese, they were equally hesitant to take me in.

I was to be given several tests of my sincerity and effectiveness. They began with selling the *Worker* in Greenpoint, a brooding black and Puerto Rican housing-project slum in Brooklyn. I peddled the paper to old women who thought I was from Jehovah's Witnesses, and housewives who were willing to pay fifteen cents just to get that white idiot away from the door, and once was met by a hulking dockworker who glowered at me from his door-jamb and said, "If you don't get that fucking Commie paper out of this building, I'm gonna crush your head in."

When I returned and told my co-workers of that last encounter, I was practically awarded the Socialist Medal of Labor. But while my almost-comrades were exulting over the number of papers sold, I was being privately appalled by the incredible seediness of the entire affair. They sang of raising the political consciousness of the masses, and their only contact with the masses took place with a newspaper or pamphlet or slogan, keeping a suspicious distance between the people and the Party.

Still, "they" were pleased with my work, superiors whose names were whispered only among those who had already joined. I began to be invited to social gatherings, where I met the old-timers, the heroes of the struggles of the thirties. And then I received word that I was to be given a high-level assignment. I worried for a week, wondering whether I would prove worthy. And then the orders came. I was to infiltrate the Brooklyn Heights Methodist Discussion Club, and inject Marxist thinking into their talks. If possible, I was to be elected to some office in the organization, preferably that of secretary, and wield structural as well as informational influence.

Visions of Stalin danced in my head. The secretary! I too had heard tales of how Uncle Joe never slept, of how a light always burned in his monklike cell in the Kremlin, as he pondered and wept over the fate of his people. While I went about my task, gaining influence through giving lectures and fucking the young Protestant ladies, it never occurred to me that my position was the most ludicrous posture a revolutionary might take. As continents went up in political flames, and massive economic war machines geared for the final battle in the history of man, I was bustling about, quite seriously, seizing control of the most inane, innocuous, and effete clique in a neighborhood composed of closet queens, déclassé executives, sex-starved secretaries, and Norman Mailer.

It was a tribute to my diligence and narrow-mindedness that within four months, I had become president of the organization. Success beyond my wildest dreams! The very next day I was told the names of the other members of the club who were also Communists, and I realized why I had won the election so easily. More than half of the eleven members of that desiccated WASP company were members of the Communist Party! In a sense, I had to admire their feeling for camouflage; this was the very last place J. Edgar Hoover would think to look.

Within a week, I received the word; I was to be accepted into the Party. I now had only to write a formal application, in which I denounced my parents' petit-bourgeois ways, my former Catholicism, my days working for the Air Force, and in general every anti-Marxist thought I had ever had in my life. Not having ever been in the Boy Scouts, I missed the irony of the gesture.

It was with moist eyes and heavily beating heart that I met the man who took my application, shook my hand, and uttered for the first time a word I had previously only aspired to. "Welcome, Comrade," he said.

Three months later he was found with excessive funds in his bank account, a wardrobe filled with custom-made clothing, and suspicious notebooks written in code. He was exposed, denounced, and expelled. And I watched with horror as the man who took that sheet of paper into his hands confessed that he was indeed on the payroll of the FBI.

I fled Brooklyn. I stayed away from everyone left of the Cardinal Spellman. I took refuge in corruption, and began paying attention to salary increases, decorating my pad, and seducing even more women. I was visited four times by FBI agents, and always there was a tall one and a short one, a heavy one and a reasonable one, and always with a barely hidden tape recorder. Our conversations were always congenial, and always ended with my refusing to give them names. In a sense, I felt a sense of shame in ratting on the gang. But also, since they obviously had agents in high places, it seemed stupid for them to ask information from me. I reasoned that they wanted my complicity more than my knowledge. The last I heard from them, the superintendent of one of my apartments let me know that the landlord had given the key to two thin, well-dressed men who entered my place and didn't leave it for two hours.

Subsequently, when I suddenly saw the Mickey Mouse nature of the entire scene and discarded politics as either a useful metaphor or a successful pragmatic, I have seen no trace of them. Yet, I rest secure in the knowledge that somewhere, right now, all the pertinent facts of my life have been programmed and stored on a punch card in one of the computers which form the bowels of our Central Intelligence Agency.

Some lessons have to be repeated often before they are learned, and I had suppressed all wisdom concerning groups that promise individual or collective salvation, on the evening I walked into the Scientology headquarters. I was still reeling from my bout with Mrs. R. and my first three acid trips. I was living with Aster, an Aquarius lady from Detroit, in a fourth floor walk-up on Greenwich Avenue, and earning my living turning out free-lance editorial work.

It had always been my nature to totally believe what any human being told me. I assumed honesty in others, and at the time I decided to "try" Scientology I was still entering into things with a blind passion. The advantage was that I penetrated to the heart of many matters in very short time, but the wear and tear on my system made it a Pyrrhic bargain. Aster had heard of Scientology from Prudence, the White Goddess of my twenty-fifth year, who got glowing reports from Cindy, who had been an Ayn Randite during my Marxist days. LSD was undermining what little conventional stability I had, and I had not as yet effected a new synthesis. Aster and I were locked in a sex-hate relationship, and when we weren't sharing perfect simultaneous orgasms, were shouting viciously at one another. And New York was continuing to wreak its ravages on my soul. In short, I was paranoid, exhausted, and confused. And in the middle of this wreckage, the message was delivered to me: SCIENTOLOGY SAVES!

I had translated the old Sufi saying, "If you can eat and pray with people, you can be at home anywhere in the world," to "If you can get into the same psychic space as other people, you can understand them totally." So I had no guards up as I entered the converted ballroom of the Martinique.

Dividers had been set up so that the place was partitioned into an entrance room, a library-bookshop, a huge study hall, rooms for secretaries, auditing chambers, and secret back rooms. My first impression was of Utopia. Everyone in the place was beautiful, moving about quietly, efficiently, with order. Almost everyone smiled continuously, and those who didn't were the newcomers. From the big room there would be an occasional burst of applause and loud cheering, from which would emerge a beaming, ecstatic person, accompanied by his auditor.

As I stood there watching, the receptionist said to one of her passing compatriots, "I have a headache. Could you give me an assist?" The girl who had been asked put her two forefingers at each temple of the receptionist's head and went into silent concentration for a minute. The girl sitting behind the desk worked along with her, closing her eyes and seeming to focus on some inner mood. Then the fingers were removed, and the two of them smiled at one another.

But there was something about the exchange that struck me as artificial. I got a flash on their inner experience, based on perception of facial tensions and subtle body attitudes, and realized that the headache hadn't gone away. And that the girl giving the assist was merely going through a ritual, without any inner substance. But when she finished, she looked down and said, "Aren't you happy that it's all gone?" and they intensified their smiles. In the eyes of the girl at the desk there showed a split second of confusion before she molded herself into an exact replica of the face smiling into her own. It was pure mind-fuck, invasion of the body snatchers.

But the whole thing was so fleeting, so subtly ambiguous, that I dismissed it, and with that the room came back into mundane focus. I looked around and admired the organization of the place, and after a moment realized that this was the single most organized place I had ever been in. Everything was programmed. The people shuttled back and forth like ants in a colony. They were always carrying papers and forms, and I soon learned that practically every conceivable office transaction possible had been catalogued and given an abbreviation. It was the perfect bureaucracy, run the way one imagines the managers at IBM wish IBM could be run. These were the machine people.

I walked up to the desk and the first thing the girl with the headache said was, "Would you please sign this?" It was astonishing that they were able to get a signature for a sale even before the pitch was made. I hesitated and was greeted with an insistent stare. It seemed I had to sign. This incident was to return to memory much later when a friend noted that Scientology sells enlightenment for about $3,000, or the same price as a medium-class Buick, showing a brilliant insight into the collective bargaining unconscious of America.

Within fifteen minutes, I had signed some ten sheets of paper, including one which promised me to an introductory course and a preliminary auditing session. The speed with which I was whisked past any reservations I might have had took my breath away. It was psychic Camp. The thing was in such blatantly bad taste that one had to admire the sheer audacity of it to exist. It was with fatal self-indulgent humor that I sat through a five-minute home movie of L. Ron Hubbard, listening to the banal being reduced to the trite. My critical faculty went to sleep and I entered into the metatheater of the moment. The fantasy machine went into full swing, and with a sort of giddy recklessness I began to indulge in sublimated paranoid fantasies of rising very rapidly to the top of this very slick, very powerful organization. The fantasies were duly fed by the slogans I heard all about me, such as, "The highest goal is power," and "The higher the responsibility, the higher the rewards." It was like the *Reader's Digest* and the Mafia rolled into one.

The fascist in me raised his head and sniffed about like some loathsome monster. I saw myself as the Pope of Scientology, fulfilling the oracle of a mad nun who taught me through the seventh and eighth grades, and whispered in my ear every afternoon, "God has destined you for great things." The world would at last be mine!

So I entered the game with sincerity and gusto, buying twenty dollars worth of books and diving headfirst into the manifest dream world of Mr. Hubbard, the classic American production which seems like an Orwellian nightmare choreographed by Walt Disney. I went home that night hypnotized into elation, and spent the next day immersed in the writings of El Ron, as he is chummily known by his minions. His work is an odd mixture of brilliant psychological insight, an eclectic synthesis of the high spots in all the world's knowledge, and a penchant for such gross oversimplification as to stagger the mind. I immediately wanted to meet the man. I felt that we could communicate very clearly very quickly. It was obvious to me that as with all organizations, Scientology was composed of a very few geniuses who put the thing together, and the hordes who blindly followed its dictates. I felt in the privileged position of knowing both that Scientology is a sham, and that in a very real sense, it does work.

The next afternoon, I took my first class in the large room that had been set up for some three hundred people. The two major groups were split up between listening to lectures and sitting, two by two, in completely frozen attitudes, staring into one another's eyes. I dutifully went through the preliminary indoctrination, and while I was disparaging the squareness of the teacher, was admiring his absolute ease in managing the situation. He said that he had been an accountant, had taken up Scientology as a part-time study, and soon converted to full-time staff member. Along with all the other low-level worker ants in the place, he worked some thirteen hours a day, seven days a week, teaching, studying, and recruiting. His eyes burned with an unholy fervor.

After a brief talk, during which he told us to leave our MEST— that is, our matter-energy-space-time—at the door, he set us to eyeballing one another. The scenario was to sit without expression while your partner attempts to make you laugh or blink or show any reaction whatsoever. The top grades in the organization have to be able to do it for two hours, showing no response while someone else attempts to push all one's "buttons," or weak spots in the personality. The point, I assume, is for a person to gain a sense of center from which to observe and operate, but since the process is managed through external conditioning with no concomitant sense of internal awareness, the result is the automaton quality by which one can spot Scientologists.

My partner was a burned-out product of Reichian therapy, and had been mangled by one of those horror-movie therapists of that particular school, where the second- and third-generation doctors had picked up all of Reich's sternness and implacability, without any of his warmth or genius. He was like one of hundreds of thousands of New Yorkers who float from scene to scene, seeking some escape from their inner emptiness. I was to be his button pusher the first time around, and while he sat still, I made disparaging remarks, tried to evoke anger, and in general acted like a prick. He kept flubbing, and each time he moved I had to say, "Flunk! You moved." I hadn't yet read *Giles Goat Boy* so I missed some of the richness of the moment. But he startled me out of my role when he leaned forward and whispered. "These people all have the emotional plague." It was like receiving a subversive message in a prison camp, and I looked up, startled.

The teacher caught my eye; something in the scene must have triggered his danger instinct, for he quickly came over to us. The student began to fight with him, telling him that this was an inhuman activity. They got into an argument and the teacher almost lost his cool. But then he drew a pad out of his pocket, scribbled something down, and thrust it at my partner. "I declare you to be in a state of nonexistence," he said. "Go to the registrar to be rerouted."

It got very curious, but I watched him leave with the *sang froid* of a desert rat who must leave his companion on the burning sands. War was not easy, and Scientology was waging an all-out struggle for ultimate peace and order. No Reichian agents could be allowed to infiltrate.

For my next partner I got someone who had been in the scene for over a year. He began by saying that he had had over eighty acid trips, and could tell me from deep knowledge that Scientology was the highest trip possible. This was still at a time when I naïvely believed that anyone who had taken acid was automatically made a more decent and honest human being by it, and his words helped me to dispel the doubts that had arisen when my first partner was banished to the void. He was very quick, and had me twitching and giggling all over the place. I got the flunk grade a few dozen times before the session ended. The one aspect of the experience which made the most impression was that he was able to put my mind through hoops, and although it was his turf, I had to respect whatever it was that had given him that ability. Scientology began to intrigue me in more complex ways.

The third day, I met Lana. Lana! Tall, fair, Scandinavian mouth like one of the blow queens used for Norwegian cigar commercials. Her breasts rose like hot loaves out of her low-cut bra. She was introduced to me, smiled deep into my libido, took me by the hand, and led me to a private room upstairs for my first auditing session. She explained the rules of the game very quickly, and soon we were sitting facing one another, her with a black pad and a black box, me holding two tin cans attached to a meter which measures electrical conductivity, a primitive form of "lie detector." She was going to repeat certain phrases, and she would write down my responses, all the while noting the movement of the needle on the meter.

The phrases were noncommittal, having to do with childhood memories, and I realized that I was being given the dianetic processing, whereby one relives the experiences of early traumas again and again until they are erased, and one becomes "clear," the Scientological equivalent of enlightenment. It has always amused me that Hubbard took his central metaphor from adding machines. The mixture of the vulgar and the sublime, was, as always, grotesquely enchanting.

As the session progressed, the process took hold. I went into immediate psychoanalytic overdrive. I started hyperventilating. The associations came hot and heavy. Lana looked at me with warm, devoted eyes; she was cheering me on. I began to spill out my soul, not caring any longer about the context or the ideology, but simply swimming with the wondrous relief which comes when the dam of repression bursts and the heart can sing out its total joy and pain. I was completely infatuated with the moment, and at the height of my confessions, the doubt struck. I looked up at her and knew that I couldn't withhold the slightest thing. She won from me the instant idiot loyalty that my poor Gurdjieff guru had tried to beat out of me. Once again, cunt proved superior to cunning.

My lips trembled. I spoke. "Lana," I said, "I have been in so many organizations, and always I have been disappointed. I hope Scientology won't let me down." She looked back, breathing hard. "In Scientology," she said, "you can have anything you want." The sexual tension reached the bursting point. "Anything?" I asked, peering between her swelling breasts. She returned my gaze, acknowledged. "Anything," she sighed.

My last reserve was gone. I brought forth my deepest sin. "Lana," I said, "in some ways Scientology seems to be a kind of fascism of the mind." Immediately, she froze. "Who told you that?" she said. The bond between us was broken and I was suddenly out in the cold, cast out of what I had hoped might at last be a family for me. I cast about in my mind for a scapegoat. I remembered one night, sitting stoned with Francis amid his paintings of coagulated inspiration and the dada artifacts of his ironic mind; we had been discussing Heraclitus in relation to

Long Island. He had suddenly flourished a Scientology poster and said, "Look, the thought patrol."

The words dribbled out of my mouth. "My friend...my friend...Francis...he said it..." I was horrified. I had betrayed one of my closest friends and to a plastic Mata Hari. She immediately closed her pad and said, "Wait here, I have to find out about this." I sat for fifteen minutes like a character in a Koestler novel, pondering the ambivalences of the cold war. She returned and sat facing me; she was conciliatory and warm. "It's quite simple," she said. "You'll just have to disconnect your friend."

Disconnect was the term used for severing all social, emotional, and honorable relations with anyone, including one's mother, who disparaged the organization. "Tell him you won't see him anymore," she said.

I went to Francis' loft with a heavy heart that night. This was my friend of many years. We had gone through all the scenes together, both understanding our mutual roles as mere costumes we wore as we went through the round of life, sharing the same space and time. We both realized that the fact that out of all the aeons of time, destiny had chosen us to know one another, was the single greatest miracle one might imagine, and all the details paled into insignificance beside that. We had sat for hundreds of hours, quietly smoking hash, reliving in our own form the partnerships of the ages, from Socrates and Plato to Lenin and Trotsky, with him always taking the path closer to the edge. While I was a Communist, he was editing a magazine called *Treason,* the editorial policy of which accepted any article on the single qualification that it would carry the death penalty if printed in time of war. When I was a hedonist, he was a solipsist. He had a permanent chair of philosophy on the astral plane, and was the founder of the East Village Wittgenstein Fan Club, of which he was one of three members. And now, I had to climb those familiar decaying stairs off the corner of Sixth Street and Avenue A and dispatch him, cleanly and with regret, but unequivocally.

We sat and smoked some grass, listened to Mozart, played a game of chess. Midway through the middle game, I looked up. "Francis, I must tell you something," I said.

"I see you coming," he said.

"I've become a Scientologist," I said.

He puffed on the pipe a moment, gave me a quick look, and

said, "Vassi, that's vulgar." Then he paused and added, "But if you have to take the trip, you have my blessings."

"It's worse than that," I said. "I had to turn you in."

His eyebrows shot up, an extreme change of expression for Francis. "Turn me in?" he said. "Turn me in for what?"

"I told them that you said they're fascists."

"Oh," he said, "that's quite true."

"And I have to disconnect you," I added.

He puffed some more hash. "Well, if that's part of the trip, sure, I can understand that."

"I hope this doesn't affect our friendship," I said.

He smiled. "No, not at all. In fact, I'm rather enjoying the irony of it." And with that we settled down to a quiet evening of serious smoking.

On the fourth day, I confronted Lana with a clear conscience. "I disconnected my friend," I announced.

"Oh, how wonderful," she bubbled. Then paused, and said, "How do you feel about it?"

"Oh, it's all right," I said. "We're still friends."

Somehow, the nuance of the transaction escaped her. She stood up once more, but with none of the gentleness which had marked yesterday's exit. As cummings would say, straightway she got grave. Once again she disappeared down the rabbit hole and this time came back with an order. "You are to accompany me to the Ethics Officer," she said.

The Ethics Officer! My blood ran cold. And with good reason when I saw the man who served as the Scientological Gestapo. He was short, thin, and fish-eyed. He was totally devoid of expression or inflection to his voice. He was implacable. "You are playing games," he said. I began to object but realized that from his point of view, I was. "You must disconnect your friend... *Totally*," he said. I looked at him and for the first time began to get an appreciation of the actuality of the situation. They were doing a tin-soldier version of fascism, but the stakes were real. "I can't do that,' I said.

For an answer, he reached into a drawer and took out a mimeographed sheet of paper. "You are familiar with the Scale of Being," he said. I nodded. It was a list showing some dozen states of existence, ranging from *enemy* at the bottom to *clear* at the top. "You are a suppressive person," he said. I blinked. That was one notch above enemy. My Reichian friend was lucky; he was only nonexistent, which was the middle point.

He handed me the sheet of paper which had SUPPRESSIVE PERSON printed across the top. It was an exercise in surrealism, and sounded like a list of admonitions to be given to a kindergarten students. The only unfunny thing about it was that these people were serious, and their activity was intended to have an actual effect on daily life. I became a bit frightened. The similarity to Nazism was becoming more than metaphoric. "Take this home and read it," he said, and dismissed me.

The paper was a guide as to what constituted a suppressive person, and what such a person had to do to remove himself from that category. I spent the entire night thinking about it, and the next morning walked into headquarters with shaking hands. The situation wasn't helping my clinical paranoia any. At the hotel I got a clear vision of what was happening: a mass of confused frightened people were milling around the evangelistic teachings of the world's most recent salvation sweepstakes. Scientology was a racket which played with politics and education and religion and the workings of people's minds with absolute cynicism and control. It was the perfect symptom of a decaying nation. I freaked.

I told the receptionist my name, and once again had to sign the registration book, and told her I had an appointment in the Ethics Office. She looked at me as though I were a leper and motioned me to sit down. Next to me was a thin, jumpy girl who had been waiting for the Ethics Officer for two hours, and was really pissed off at being made to wait. But like a nun to the Pope, she couldn't admit that he was simply a little bastard who ought to be kicked in the ass and told to grow up. We talked a bit and she allowed as how she was tired of waiting, but added, "Yet, I understand. They work so hard and have so much responsibility that we can't expect them to put everything aside to see us any old time."

For one of the few times in my life, I grew intensely angry.

By the time he was ready to see me, I was furious. I strode into the office. He stared up, unruffled. "Did you read it?" he asked. "Yes," I answered. "Well...?" he said. I took a breath. "Rarely in my life have I seen such a blend of inanity and viciousness as is exhibited here. I understand the philosophic premises and psychological underpinnings of your scene, but in purely human terms, you are all depraved."

He was about as impressed as the Spanish fascists were with

Unamono's denunciation. He didn't bat an eyelash. He reached down and grabbed another sheet of mimeographed paper. On the top of this one was a single word.

It said: ENEMY.

"You are now in a condition of enemy," he said.

"How did that happen?" I exploded. "I was just a suppressive person."

"Please read the conditions," he said, and handed me a book. It was the Scientology Ethics Handbook. As an enemy, I was informed, I could be beaten up, have my apartment ransacked, and my business destroyed by Scientologists. I took this as serious enough, but learned that I was lucky not to be any higher in the organization. For if I were in an advanced org, i.e., organization, and I became an enemy, I would be confined to quarters, forced to wear a gray armband, and constrained to perform acts above and beyond the call of duty to be reinstated, plus getting the individual consent of every person in the org to let me back in. By this time, I was sweating visibly. I had visions of assassinations.

"What do I have to do to stop being an enemy?" I croaked.

His eyes directed me to the sheet. It had one sentence. It read: FIND OUT WHO YOU ARE.

I couldn't believe my eyes. Whoever had put this thing together had constructed the nightmare down to its final imbecile conclusion, and the whole scene was held together by an impeccable inner logic. I looked up at the fish. "I have spent my entire life, and will spend the rest of my life, doing little more than asking myself that single question, and you dare to present it to me in this debased and mindless form. Fuck you!"

He wasn't impressed. He took a folder off the desk and put it into a file drawer with a large lock on it. "What's that?" I said. "Your file," he answered. I gazed at the file cabinet, horrified. In that file was everything I had said to Lana, the countless papers I had signed, a documented transcript of all my political crimes. The FBI had my life story in their files, but the Scientologists were cataloging my soul.

My mind raced ahead. What if they did become the political influence they were trying to be? What if they assumed real power? I screamed inside.

"You may go," he said.

I was a broken man. "Is there any way for me to stop being an enemy?" I asked. "Not unless you meet the condition," he said. "Or...every so often L. Ron Hubbard issues a general amnesty. The last one was two years ago." He pointed to a telegram tacked to the wall above my head. Sure enough, the man had ordered that all political crimes be forgiven and all files be destroyed.

"As of now," he said, "you may not enter any Scientology office, and if you do come back, you may not progress beyond Level Four.

At that, he motioned to another man in the room, and the two of them escorted me to the door.

For the following month, I saw Scientologists everywhere. I suspected cabdrivers, people walking next to me on the street, delivery men. I was certain that I would come home one night to find the Ethics Officer calmly waiting in the kitchen, smoking Balkan cigarettes, pointing a small-bore pistol with a silencer on it at my chest, with Aster lying naked in the bedroom, having achieved her revenge by betraying me to the foe.

There was nothing for it. I had to leave. My free-lance work offered no satisfaction, the air in the city was unbreathable, everything I touched crumbled, and anything I had thought to be a stable influence in my life was proving to be yet another menacing illusion. I arranged to sell my pad and furniture and books, and reduced all my possessions to what would fit into the back of a station wagon. I decided to go west!

I gave a farewell party to which I invited everyone I knew, some hundred and fifty people who had been and were lovers, friends, close acquaintances. It was like a cheerful wake. Although most of the people didn't know one another, since all my scenes were scattered, everyone was able to communicate using me as a focus. And through a fog of low, warm conversation, I drifted around, saying my farewells to each of the people there, giving them what seemed like my final words.

Since then, I have had almost nothing to do with Scientology, except for meeting people who were in various states of rapture or disillusionment with the organization. There has been some public recognition of Scientology in the popular press. England has declared them a menace, although they flourish in South Africa. William Burroughs brought his junk-addled mind to bear on the problem, and after being processed emerged with an odd attitude of complacent criticism.

Meanwhile, the Sea Org has some seven yachts, roaming the

seas of the world, calling unobtrusively at all the ports of all the nations, gathering data. And late at night, the dreams are spun, of how there will be a government of the world centered in North Africa, where all the countries will send their kings and presidents. And this world union will have its own army, the only army, while each nation will be allowed its own internal policing. And behind this neo-Pharaonic throne, like the Jesuits in the Vatican, the Scientologists will advise on how the human race should be run.

Aster and I left on a hot July afternoon, saying good-bye to my mother under the El on Roosevelt Avenue in Queens, as she went off to her job supervising forty Cuban refugee women who strung beads for a costume jeweler at a dollar an hour in one of our latter-day sweatshops. It took five days and two thousand miles for me to shed the immediate buzz of panic which had begun to drive me mad in New York. And as the vastness of America unrolled before my eyes, I began to breathe again.

But when I got to San Francisco, other modes of insanity were lying in wait, ready to ensnare my mind.

3.

I found a place in San Francisco's Bernal Heights, a hippie hobbitland at the end of the Mission District. It was an old Italian neighborhood where goats had once grazed on the hill which now served as the base for a giant Army radar screen. It was now peopled by a goodly number of *heads* who had much of the gentle anonymity of the early Haight love children. Aster and I came to an abrupt parting of the ways since the excitement of travel had somewhat supplanted the intensity of our sexual trip, and we were left with only the hate portion of the relationship. She split for a farm in Oregon and within a few weeks I found myself the sole inhabitant of a damp apartment that overlooked a dead-end street in the front, and opened on to a garden in the back.

Next door were Fred and Melissa who had been living together for two years, erupting every two months in another "final" separation which lasted for a week or so. Pat lived upstairs, a wise old/young lady of twenty-six years who read Doris Lessing and listened to Satie as she smoked each day away in vaguely pointed yearnings. Later, for a while, Leah was to be with me, my bisexual sister of a hundred encounters, with abyss-suggesting brown Taurus eyes and entrancingly small breasts. Across the way were Harry and Mary, a psychedelic version of the nice American couple. He played guitar and fixed motorcycles, while she tried to keep the house together and make babies. Above them were Paul and Cheryl who were later to become Christians.

Although I had about two thousand dollars and a car, easily enough to live on for six months on the Coast, I still had my New York habits, and was soon busy looking for something to "do." My best gig was, ironically enough, teaching classes in relaxation, which involved getting people just to lie down and breathe, until they entered a state of light hypnotism, at which time I would take them on mind trips. I had learned the gimmick some years earlier while working with a fearless and feckless therapist who kept rediscovering the psychological wheel. Every month she would come roaring in with a new theory, only to have it pointed out to her that Freud or Aristotle or Buddha or somebody had written it all down years before. I was her patient for a year, her partner for six months, and her therapist for six months after that. It was a strange relationship, but one which taught me more than a little about how simple it is to mold people in any direction whatsoever. During that time we stumbled onto Reichian breathing, thought transfer, body language, and the whole panoply of jargonized insights which has since made Esalen such a pile of loot.

I now began tracking down encounter group leaders through the *Barb,* and finally found myself at San Francisco State College, where the Experimental College on campus was in the midst of transforming the structure of education.

My introduction to the scene was through Loren Jones. Loren is a rare combination of scholar and revolutionary. He had been initiated by one of the secret esoteric orders, and could make a candle flame do tricks at ten paces. He was short, due to a spine defect which kept him in continual pain, and wore a noble beard. In all, a kind of hippie Toulouse-Lautrec.

The Experimental College was one of a group of student organizations, along with the Black Student Union and the Third World Liberation Front, which was in the process of radicalizing the almost thirty thousand students on campus. In addition, there were the usual splinter groups of political crazies, SDS, PL, and ad hoc freak brigades who wanted everything from instant assassination of Reagan to an end of Western civilization.

The EC was, unquestionably, the most successful and least

overtly threatening of all the groups. It was looked upon benignly by the administration because its courses consisted largely of
things like astrology, dance, poetry, and the other unmartial arts.
When I arrived in September, they were about to hold an open
registration, to run for an entire day. The approach was simplicity itself. Anyone who wanted to teach wrote up his course description in a catalogue. On registration day, each would-be teacher
would stand under a sign listing his course, and students would
have a chance to dig on the person teaching as well as the formal
catalogue blurb. The class size was limited by the appeal of the
teacher. The college allowed no credits for any courses taken at
the EC, but this didn't stop students from signing up for as many
as six courses, while letting their official schoolwork drop.

The reason was clear. Most of the people at the EC were
young, or knew what the young mind is about. The course descrip-
tions covered a general area, but almost every course at the EC
had a single subject matter: life. How to live well, fully. The arid-
ity of the academic curriculum stood out in sharp contrast to the
joyously pragmatic attitude of the counter-college. And the beauty of the entire scene was that the administration was so busy
looking in the closets of the overtly political organizations that
they missed the fact that the real revolution was taking place in
that hotbed of freaks in the gaudily painted barracks at the center of campus. Because the EC was allowing the students to dance
and laugh and exult, to let their minds roam freely, to take pride
in their sex and demand honor in their relations with their fellow
men. And this is what the right- and left-wing fascists cannot
stand: the sheer exuberance of living. It is not a political question;
it is a question of being.

That year, the registration was to take in over three thousand
students, and this was only in its second year of functioning.
Registration day was like a flea market of the mind, with every frus-
trated teacher, homegrown guru, and visionary in the Bay Area
hawking his psychic wares to the young people coming through.
It was held in the Gallery Lounge, a great flat building which
someone had the sense to leave completely empty. Of course,
everyone was stoned, on grass, on good vibrations, and the wild
music of the young Hassidim from the House of Love and Prayer.
It was a day of Renaissance, a birthday party for the new culture.

The EC itself was autocratically run, by the EC "staff." At

their head was Evan Standard, a twenty-six-year-old leonine and pockmarked saint. He was gaunt, with teeth missing, and a shock of hair and beard that totally covered his face and shoulders. As with most of the heavies there, he was thoroughly well-read in all matters of the metaphysical and occult, mostly through an Oriental bias. His major mode of expression was the guffaw.

Loren Jones was his right-hand man. During meetings Evan would sit, his six-inch aura dominating the room, with Loren next to him, cooling off the vibes. The rest of the staff were second-stringers, good people but not in the same class as the boss. Later, when I had precipitated a crisis by attempting to force my admission to the staff, Evan blocked my entry and disillusioned the others, who were under the impression that the staff was a democratic group. At the meeting, Loren announced to the group, "Evan *is* the EC. And I am here to protect him. That's the way it is, and nobody here have any notions to the contrary." I had succeeded in blowing the lid off the scene, and for my pains suffered ostracism from the overlord and his underlings.

It is odd that the single most radical force on the campus should have been run dictatorially, and that period of my life once and for all dispelled the idea in my mind that there is something inherently better about democracy as a social form. I suspect that the health of a state depends on the quality of the people, and it doesn't matter what particular form they choose to express their sanity or their madness.

By registration day, I had written up a blurb for a workshop in "Relaxation, Awareness, and Breathing." At the time, I was floating in a more or less continual euphoria. The sheer joy of San Francisco, the golden rich September days, the freedom from all the habits of my New York life, came together to keep me permanently high. The campus was such a continual feast day that soon I had shed all the gray eastern film, and had begun going barefoot, wearing a leopardskin cloak, carrying a wooden staff, and playing a harmonica instead of talking. It was a perfect time. I could do nothing wrong. If I danced in the street, I would have an appreciative audience. If I wanted a particular girl, I had only to smile at her.

I was getting very deeply into the power of dance and mime, learning that in any given communication, if one responds to breathing patterns, muscle tensions, and eye contact, and if one is sensitive to the nonverbal vibrations in any given group, then one is like the man with one eye in the land of the blind. I found that charisma was nothing more than letting this multileveled awareness, and its concomitant energy, glow. In short, I was becoming a strangely influential force, and the fear of the EC rulers had a basis in fact.

All around the Gallery Lounge we stood and sat. All the current legends were there, and as the morning progressed, and the crowds grew, and music swelled, and the grass circulated, the entire place began to lift off the ground. The vibes were so high that just to walk through the door was like smoking a joint of good-grade dope.

Michael Parker had the booth next to mine, and just to be in Michael's presence is the equivalent of a lick of acid, so by midafternoon I was infatuated with enlightenment. The energy poured out of me like sweat. When I went to the john, my eyes in the mirror were like strobe kaleidoscopes. The Spirit was in me, and the people saw. I started dancing, and soon, scores of students were flocking to the booth, wanting to sign up, not even knowing what it was I was teaching, not caring. It was the classic guru scene; one judges the master not by what he says, but by the force of life which flows through him.

By day's end, I had over two hundred people signed up for a workshop which was designed for no more than twelve. The other high tally was for Michael's Monday Night Class, and he drew almost three hundred. Michael continued his class even after the EC closed down, and eventually went on to become perhaps the foremost American-born spiritual teacher, with over fifteen hundred people coming every Monday night to hear his rap, and share in the circle of beauty and truth he and his family have created.

My first class was for a Wednesday night, and all that week, I prepared. I drew up a list of graduated exercises, beginning with deep physical relaxation, and going into mutual support workouts, and ending with group movement and chanting. The point was to get everyone into the same psychic space by relaxing the normal tensions of uptight daily life. There was a danger of creating a cheap instant-intimacy, such as the kind that Esalen thrives on, but I was guarding against that. It was possible to keep critical intelligence even in the midst of the most turgid touchie-feelies.

That Wednesday I held silence until evening, eating lightly, spending a good deal of time sitting quietly. I hitched to the campus, finding that a freer way of travel than driving, and loosened up with a light rap with the cats who were driving. On campus, I went to the Lounge, and spent an hour moving chairs and picking trash up off the floor. This was the necessary self-humbling that the religious cookbooks recommend for any holy venture.

I went out onto the grounds and sat under a tree, smoking three joints, and watching the evening star emerge from the growing dusk. I made peace with the universe, switched my consciousness onto No-Mind, and prepared to begin an adventure the parameters of which were totally unknown to me. At least, consciously. As always, the twin threads of sexuality and mysticism wove their fantastic pattern through all my actions, but the final result of that mix wasn't to be seen until four weeks later.

A hundred and ten people showed up. All young, all beautiful, all stoned. When the class began, I sat crosslegged on the floor, and watched all those eyes looking at me, waiting, expecting. All of my preparation steadied me, and I gazed slowly over the crowd which I had to transform into a single organism before three hours. Countless thoughts tumbled through my mind, so quickly and profusely that I couldn't even check them as they passed. I merely watched and let them register.

"What do they want?" I wondered. "Here are a bunch of kids who are healthy, pretty, and living in the most beautiful city of the richest nation on earth. They have access to some of the earth's most wondrous offerings. Their government is becoming militarily fascistic and their heads are being wooed by psychedelics. Their parents and teachers are wooden automatons for the most part. Why aren't they somewhere else, fucking or turning on or blowing up banks? What do they hope to get here, in this public place, from this stranger from New York?"

I checked my catalogue of basics: food, shelter, clothing, recognition, meditation, orgasms, truth, and love. The first three were out of my domain. So I went to the other five. Each of these people was starved for recognition; not the surface hello we give to one another. But every one of them wanted that deep inner part, that part that is most central, to be seen and known as valuable and beautiful. As far as meditation, it was clear that not a one of them had any notion what that meant. Those who were even at all familiar with the word had probably been introduced through one of the Maharishi-type charlatans who infest the nation with their lotus poses and self-induced visions. Orgasm was always a problem; men could ejaculate and women could clitorally twitch, but few could sail into the totally convulsive realm of pure vegetative release. Truth, of course, being practically nonexistent among the human race, was to be another necessary element, but the transmission of truth can never be articulated in any symbology whatsoever. And as for love, I put that on the shelf of hopefulness. The best thing to do was prime the subconscious with an awareness of the elements and then not consider them again.

The workshop was successful but unspectacular. I ran through several of the standard routines, including facial relaxation and eye contact, mutual massage and suggestion of imagery. That night I ended with an exercise I had originated, called "the Puppet." After having everyone go into very deep physical relaxation lying in the corpse pose, I had them imagine a guillotine above them, with the blade dropping down at intervals to chop off, one by one, each of the limbs and head. The sense of imagining one's body being cut to pieces allows a muscular relaxation not otherwise attained. At least, in most cases. Several of the people that night, when I said, "Now let the blade drop down and slice off your head," sat bolt upright, blinking in sheer terror. But, to paraphrase Lenin, "You can't make a revolution without blowing a few minds."

Afterward, I put on a recording of Ravi Shankar's, and led the group in a period of spontaneous movement, telling them to imagine that they were puppets, and that each of their severed parts was attached by strings to the fingers of a great puppet master. Using this artifice allowed them to let their bodies move without the usual tension clichés, and the total effect of over a hundred people moving easily and sensually was glorious. We ended by chanting Om, and when the class was over, the strangers had shared a moment of pleasant ease. I left very quickly, before anyone could talk to me; the night had exhausted me and I just needed to crash. What I didn't know was that my honest performance and sudden departure planted the seeds of a myth. The people began to whisper that a true holy man had come among them.

Meanwhile, the guru was having his problems. I had just begun a ménage with Rita and Leah. It was a blind attempt at union which swung between ecstasy and despair, during the course of which I learned how two women can make love, and have since been forever humbled in my own sexuality. We were swept up in the beauty of what happens when three people can, even for a brief time, become one organism on at least two levels of consciousness. But we also suffered the pain and paranoia which follows the tearing of the fabric, when all the delicacy of give-to-get builds higher and finer until the slim foundation of time-shared can't sustain the great elaborations of the erotic superstructure. We were at a point where I was finding out the difference between male chauvinism and manhood, and the women were struggling between the desire for wider communion and the biological instinct of possessiveness of the mate.

That week, my preparation for the class navigated the tricky rhythms of our troika. By the time Wednesday came, my subconscious was totally enmeshed in questions of human sexual relationship. I arrived only two hours early this time, cleaned up the Lounge in a hurry, and on my way back from smoking a joint sent up a prayer to Venus, which had just begun to glow. It was getting darker earlier as the year dipped toward winter.

Once again I put the crew through their paces. This time there were almost a hundred and fifty of them. When I started my opening rap, I found myself talking about sensuality. I spun an elaborate schema of the way in which sexuality tends to burn out the more delicate needs of touch and glance and breath, and ended by noting that many people wind up fucking someone just because they need to be held. The admiration from the psychically pubescent women in the class was palpable.

But I was feeling expansive and depleted from my efforts of the week. It suddenly came upon me that tonight I should teach the men how to make love to the women, how to be gentle and responsive. So, after the softening-up relaxation period, I broke the class down into groups of four, and led them into a mutual feeling session, in which three people massage the fourth, until all have been both active and passive. I took great pains to outline what to look for, what kinaesthetic clues lurked inside the body, and what could be learned from observing another's breathing and skin tone and subtle motions. Halfway through the exercise, the air started getting steamy. Everywhere I looked half-erect cocks bulged through jeans, female crotches yawned over the entire floor, and succulent buttocks contracted and expanded as unimaginable eddies of exquisite sensation ran through dozens of nearly virginal thighs.

By the end of that round, I was slightly out of control. I took an unexpected turn, and had them all lie down again, and once again took them on an inner voyage, feeling their bodies with their bodies, or letting the bodies be aware of themselves. But this time I lingered over the genitals, spinning out fantasies about what the inside of a cunt feels like, of what happens inside a penis when it expands. Aroused, half-hypnotized, willing, they let themselves be swayed, and soon sighs of rapture and moans of pleasure began to erupt. They were beginning to let it all hang out.

The music I used that night was from the Stones, which perfectly took the amorphous sexual flow and coagulated it into a driving hard rhythm. At the end of the first side of the album, everyone had blood in their eyes. I took the vibes down again, and ended with a large circle, with everyone's arms around everyone else's shoulders. Of course, with all that kundalini running free, the circle became electric, and soon, eyes closed, they were swaying in the single most beautiful jellyfish I had ever seen. I asked them to let sounds out, and within a minute the room was filled with all those different voices, each in a different pitch, with the whole blending into a giant sound of praise. My eyes began tearing, and I couldn't absorb any more, so before they finished, I quietly left.

I learned later that they stayed for a half hour after the class, not wanting to leave one another's physical presence, and talking about the mysterious man who comes to perform miracles and then leaves before anyone can speak to him.

During the next week, the thing with Leah and Rita fell totally apart. We reached the point where we were criticizing one another's method of washing dishes. The viciousness was barely ameliorated by its pettiness. We were all heartbroken, because we all loved the hurting moments when we sat at the kitchen table, holding hands before dinner, listening to the silence of the house. But the scene was beyond our ability to manage, and we knew it, and now had to do the deadly business of getting to hate one another before we could garner the energy to split.

I took refuge, as I often did in those days, in *The Tibetan Book of the Great Liberation*. Between the heavy blows dealt my mind by that book, and the emotional upheaval I was experiencing, and the growing unreality of my scene at the college, I freaked. It suddenly occurred to me that I was gathering hubris at a rapid rate. The underbelly of megalomania showed its greenish light, and all of a sudden I saw myself as a charlatan, a breaker of hearts, and agreed with Evan that I was a black magician.

My mind turned around. I remembered that I had forgotten God, and had fallen into the modern heresy of thinking that man was the supreme entity in the universe, that I had forgotten my own limitations. I decided that I was leading the people astray, and during the next class, would call for a spiritual regeneration. That this fell in with the image they were forming of me as a spiritual leader was the type of coincidence that would have delighted Jung.

I got to the campus very early the next morning. To my surprise, strangers kept approaching me, asking me if they might join the class. One girl came up to me, and after some preliminary small talk, suddenly grabbed my hand and said urgently, "I can't come. Please help me. I know you can." I gave her my phone number and told her to call me in a few days. The scene was too much out of Feiffer to be erotic. Members of my class, as they recognized me sitting on the grass, would come up and sit silently in front of me for long periods of time and then, reverentially, get up and leave without saying a word. Without doing a single thing butt following the inner logic of my madness to its most baroque extension, I was becoming a guru to an entire generation.

The third week's class was a masterpiece of metatheater. I *very* humbly cleaned up the Lounge this time, picking up every cigarette butt by hand. I found that four or five women were helping me, and I realized that my first group of inner disciples was forming. Then I sat on a piano bench in full lotus, and waited for the throngs to arrive. They came slowly and made a giant crowd at my feet. One thin blond girl came up and laid a bouquet of flowers before me. Here and there, joss sticks were lit.

And, in a phosphorescent flash before my third eye, the solution hit. To blend the erotic and the godly, the path was through Tantra.

My talk that night was all about the superhedonistic yoga of quintessential fucking, that marvelous ritual whereby color and scent and fabric and food and long, careful preparation go into making that consummate human action. I spoke of the way in which the male sits rigid and knowing, moving the kundalini up from the base of his spine to the thousand-petaled lotus above his head, while the female works in the ecstatic movements of Sirasvati until, at one grand moment, the male explodes in cosmic consciousness and full physical orgasm, and the female rides the tumultuous waves of universal orgasm, that of the Great Mother giving birth to existence itself.

Everyone got stoned on the image.

The class that night was all breathing, very slow movement, and exercises in penetrating perception. I did a very long facial relaxation, and then had everyone let themselves be seen in their full inner nakedness, while they gazed on all the others in that state. At the very end, I allowed the gentlest of touching to take place. It all went so beautifully that I forgot to check my meters, to see what kinds and levels of energy were building beneath the surface of appearances.

I asked them all to form a large circle, and begin closing in on the center, my idea being to bring together on the physical plane the communion that was taking place spiritually. But no sooner did that troupe of bodies pass a certain critical mass than the tension snapped, and in a flash the Gallery Lounge was a pile of writhing, meshing, groping bodies. I was horrified, much as the old Tibetan monk leading a group of novices in Tantric practices, and leaving the room for a minute to come back to find his charges fucking merrily on the floor.

It grew orgiastic. Hands grabbed cunts, mouths went to nipples, asses flashed and rolled. I stepped to the edge. "Stop," I cried. "Stop." As an answer, three pairs of arms reached up and grabbed me, and before I could react, I was pulled into the sea of flesh.

It was a most peculiar experience, for on the one hand I was sinking under the sheer sensuality of the scene, and at the same time I was trying to maintain my spiritual stance. It took me minutes to crawl out, and I fled from the scene, shaken. They went on like that for almost an hour, and many of them went off by twos and threes and fours to the beach and various apartments.

During the following week, I struggled for the proper way to continue the class, but during that time, I was converted to Christianity.

It happened one night when I dropped by to visit Paul and Cheryl. When I had first met them, Paul was one of the single most generous and warm-hearted people I had ever known. He was forever giving people presents of sculpture he had made, and was always willing to help someone in difficulty or to extend hospitality, but Cheryl continually talked about leaving him when he wasn't around to hear her. "Paul is so sweet," she would say, "but he doesn't, you know, *understand*." In her frustration, she rushed them through the several thousand dollars they had received in wedding presents, and ended by leaving the keys in their new MG one afternoon, and having it stolen.

Finally, she did leave him, and went to stay at her cousin's house, which was a Christian community north of the city. She returned two weeks later, burning with an inner light, and I agreed to go with her to meet the people who had brought about the change in her. Paul had immediately bought the trip; more, I suspect, to save his marriage than out of any deep conviction, although the Christian rhetoric fit in perfectly with the selfless life he was already living.

At the commune there were the usual percentages of fanatics, lunatics, and sincerely intelligent people. The house was led by Steven, whose notion of Christianity was simply to "be all things to all men." But it also included Walter who kept laying down, in Steven's words, "that godawful pentecostal rap." Walter was Cheryl's cousin's fiancé.

Of course, they tried to convert me. Time and again I patiently explained to Paul that while I empathized with his truth, I could only see it as a solution congenial to him, not to me. With untiring goodwill, he continued to try to bring my soul to Jesus. I did the Bible thumper's equivalent of selling the *Worker*, accompanying them to the Haight, to bring light into the hearts of the erring hippies. It was quite tricky, attempting to keep Paul's friendship while fending off his attempts to drag me into his metaphor. Accompanying him on his conversion crusades was a way of keeping all bases covered.

One night, after a day on the salvation trail, and after a beautiful dinner at their home, I went out to look at the stars and smoke some grass. A feeling of bliss and love for all mankind filled my heart, so peaceful was the evening. I went back to Paul's to share my feeling with them, and tried to convey it in words I thought they could appreciate. "I feel that God is within me tonight," I said to them.

They immediately leapt to. Now was the time, urged Paul, now was the moment when I should accept Jesus into my heart. I began to remonstrate, but some yielding took place inside me and I said instead, "All right, Paul, if you can convince me, I'll become a Christian."

We sat down facing one another and a lovely brotherliness shone in his face. At that moment, I really loved him.

"What times cause you the most pain?" he began.

I paused for a moment.

"Isn't it when you are most confused?" he continued.

I thought a bit. Yes, when things were clear, they were tolerable. It was only when I no longer knew who I was or what was happening that I became unhappy. I agreed with him, my estimate of his perspicacity going up somewhat.

He leaned forward. "Now," he said, "confusion is the weapon of the Devil. It's the Devil who makes your mind all muddy."

I considered that. Yes, it certainly felt that way sometimes, as though some evil force were entering me and driving out all the joy and intelligence. I was willing to accept the Devil metaphor, but when I told him that, it sounded as though I were recognizing an actual demonic entity, not merely a symbol.

"The Devil begins by injecting doubt into your heart. He makes you believe that God doesn't exist, that life is a pathway to sin, and that only your greed and pride should be served."

A light bulb went on over my head. It was beginning to make sense! "Go on," I said.

"It is doubt which confounds you," he said.

"Yes, I can see that," I said. "But what do I do about doubt? How can I handle it?"

He looked straight at me. "Jesus said, 'Cast out doubt.'"

I looked up, a slow smile forming on my lips. "Of course," I said. The logic was unassailable. "How do you cast out doubt?" I asked.

"That's the easiest thing in the world," said Paul. "Just believe."

"Believe?" I said. "Believe in what?"

And with a voice like thunder he laid it on me. "BELIEVE IN JESUS AND YOU SHALL BE SAVED!"

It was as though lightning struck my brain. I saw how, in a single gesture, I could solve all the problems of my entire life, simply by putting all of my confusions in the hands of Jesus. It made no difference what my intellect thought of the matter, my emotion reigned supreme. I jumped up from my chair, grace pouring down on me from Heaven.

"I believe!" I shouted.

"Say, 'I believe in Jesus,'" said Paul.

I lifted my hand in the air, very giddy by now, and sang out,

"I BELIEVE IN JESUS!"

"HALLELUJAH!" shouted Paul.

"PRAISE BE!" Cheryl said.

And all three of us stood there jiggling and beaming, oozing energy out of our pores and into the rocketing space of their small living room. I fell back down into the chair, elated and stunned.

A vibrating white glow seemed to light on all the objects in the room, and I became aware of the sheer presence of everything. "God is here," said Paul, so simply, so matter-of-factly, that I bowed my head before the reality of that.

"I'll have to give up my sophistication," I thought.

"Your sophistication isn't worth anything anyway," Cheryl said, and I looked up at her, amazed.

"Perhaps I'll be the first saint of the Aquarian Age," I thought as my fantasy machine began leeching off all the liberated energy in my system. I realized that I was playing with potentially dangerous, very powerful psychic dynamics, I had seen these two people undergo radical changes overnight. The scene had me very high.

But, of course, Satan was waiting in the wings.

I developed a crush on Laura, Cheryl's friend. Her fiancé, Walter, was an ex-con, ex-Marine, ex-speed freak, who was willing to kill for Jesus. His main rap was fire and brimstone and war on atheistic communism. And he was very suspicious of me, although he was willing to accept my conversion at face value.

One afternoon, I went to Paul's and found Laura there alone. She gave me some coffee, and for a while we made some holy small talk and laced our sentences with "Praise be," and then just once, in the midst of the scene, looked straight into one another's eyes. And that did it. Pure lust smoldered. Instant flashes of fornication exploded all around us. All the hidden excitement of forbidden sex inflamed our limbs. I had grown so blasé in the air of sexual permissiveness which I breathed in the circles I traveled, that I had forgotten how delicious it could be to break a commandment. It also gave me an insight into the words a veteran Christian had once told me: "You don't know what fucking is until you and your wife fuck in Jesus' name." I experienced the truth of it a while later when Leah also stumbled into Paul and Cheryl's one afternoon and also converted for a day. That night, while coming, she spread her arms wide and shouted, "Oh fuck me,

Jesus!" And with Jesus backing me up, so to speak, I sailed into an orgasm that I had never attained on the purely material plane.

Laura and I stared at one another; we were trembling. She reached out and took my hands. "Let us pray," she said, and sank to her knees. I knelt down with her. We came close, our hands holding, our chests almost touching. Sublimation had never scaled higher peaks. "Oh Lord..." she began, and our mouths moved ever so slightly toward each other when, suddenly, loud footsteps clunked on the wooden stairs outside.

She turned sheet-white. "It's Walter," she said.

Now, theoretically, we weren't doing anything wrong. In fact, her fiancé should have been pleased to find his old lady leading a recent convert in prayer. But sex hung heavy enough in the air to be smelled by anyone who walked in. She jumped up. I jumped up. We stood there in confusion (the Devil again!) and looked classically guilty as he came in the door. He took one look, and he KNEW.

Laura ran out of the room. Walter dropped the groceries he was carrying and advanced on me with clenched fists. Mutilation was close when, with a brilliant inspiration, I snatched up a Bible, brandished it before me, and yelled, "In Jesus' name, I ask you to consider."

The conflicting emotions of murderous rage and ideological commitment stormed inside him. But that stopped him long enough for me to regain my balance, and I said, very quickly and forcibly, "We were praying, Brother Walter. You startled us." He gave me a wary glance and went into the other room. In a few moments I heard shouting and thumping and a woman's crying. After a while, he came back in. He was sober and deadly.

"Laura told me what happened," he said, and from the way he said it I knew the game was up. "In a Christian marriage," he continued, "the woman is beholding to the man, and the man is beholding to God. I can't allow anyone to come in the way. So you leave, and never come back, and pray to Jesus to save your rotten soul."

It was with this baggage that I entered my fourth class at the Gallery Lounge. I gave a stern lecture to the now more than two hundred eager faces waiting for bigger and better orgies. I spoke to them of the need for sobriety, and warned that, from now on, there would be no such shenanigans as took place the week before. I canceled the class for the night and told them that only those who were serious about using the body as a vehicle to reach the Holy Spirit should come back.

There was much shuffling, but I ended the talk by standing up and walking out. Several people stopped me. Among them was a young sophomore who assured me that I was the holiest man he had ever known. While another young man, who couldn't have been more than sixteen, and who was very hip in the ways of being stoned, just looked at me a long while, and then shook his head and said, "Far out."

During the following week, I woke up from the spell, and relegated my conversion to the long list of experiences which make up the mosaic of life. I was at a loss as to what to do for my next class, but never had to make that decision, for the students called for a general strike against the college.

Reagan, having become hip to the influence of student groups on campus, was maneuvering for a cutback of funds from all left-wing student organizations. The political crazies panicked, and at a meeting of the EC the next day, I was informed of the decision to strike. The Experimental College had come to an internal decision to vote against the strike, arguing that to strike would be to call in the police, and to call in the police would be to squash all freedom on campus. but the prevailing opinion of the other groups was against them, so they went along with the majority. And so, the strike that was to enter history began.

At a general meeting of all the student organizations, the Panthers dropped by. Since they had no immediate involvement at the school, they decided not to intervene, but were explicit about their advice, which was addressed mainly to Progressive Labor. "If anybody starts any violence, they gonna answer to us, and we gonna kick ass." PL got surly, but in the face of overpowering brawn, they acquiesced, and the strike was peaceful for a while, until the momentum of events swept everyone away.

I remembered when I first came into contact with Progressive Labor. Milt Rosen had just been expelled from the Party and was starting his Maoist wing. The people he gathered around him were all young pros, capable of creating a disturbance and hypnotizing a meeting. But there was something seedy about the lot of them. As Alan Krebs once observed, "Marginal institutions attract marginal people." I sat in on a few of the early meetings Milt had, and found them even more tedious and regimented than those of the Party. There was an incredibly fanatic need to translate every facet of human experience into the collected works of Mao Tse-tung. Possibly no greater tunnel vision has existed since the days of the Inquisition.

One day, on campus, I had passed one of the many tables that different groups placed in front of the student cafeteria. I saw the PL banner, and a twinge of nostalgia gripped me. There was the usual stringy girl behind the table, with the same expression of beady intensity that marks a PL–er more clearly than any membership form. I smiled at her, and she greeted me with disdain, since I was quite stoned and dressed in an Indian robe. Nothing daunted, I started a conversation.

"PL," I said, "I remember when Milt Rosen started PL."

Her eyes lit up. "You *know* Milt Rosen?" she gasped.

"Knew him," I said. "I'm not in touch anymore."

Her attitude softened. "Yes," I said, "I was there when he was expelled from the Party."

"He quit!" she shot back.

I answered with a wave of my hand. "What are you people into now?" I asked.

She grew chatty. "Well, we're mostly in the factories now, working with the consciousness of the workers." Now, if there is any group more stolidly reactionary than the American working class, it must be the young Turks of PL. I was amused.

She looked at me suspiciously. "What are you doing now?" she said.

"Oh, I'm teaching relaxation." I said.

She leapt up from the chair and almost spat at me. "Relaxation," she said scornfully. "What's that going to do for the working class?"

"Oh, I don't know," I said. "Relax them, I guess. Make them less unimaginative."

If she had had a gun she would have shot me, but that was not to be. The revenge of Progressive Labor was to come in adding poisoned fuel to the flames of the strike. SDS, of course, added its strident voice, calling for lists of non-negotiable demands. And the Black Student Union, with their Urban League mentality, got all liquored up at the prospect of being *real* militants. Great secret caucuses were held. Guns were strapped on. Plans were made to enlist the aid of all the student bodies of California, to close down the entire so-called educational system. I stepped out of my guru role for a minute, put on my political glasses,

and offered an opinion that one should not call for violent revolution unless one were militarily stronger than the opponent, or
unless one had the support of large masses of the people. But
my voice was lost in the din.

It was laughable, in a tragic way, for the American ruling class,
that odd amalgam of bankers, generals, top politicos, industrialists,
oil barons, and heads of advertising agencies, has grown as stupid
as dinosaurs in the ways of the world. They understand the fact of
power, but have grown so lazy in their wealth that they have forgotten about the bases of power, and the ways in which they can
be changed and lost. In short, they can't recognize an enemy until
the enemy hoists a great big sign of itself saying, "I am the enemy."

Which is precisely what the strike accomplished.

It was the day before my thirty-first birthday, with Scorpio at
the height of its influence, that the demonic forces were unleashed.

Overnight, the campus became a tense, ugly place. The radicals chanted, held mass rallies, presented demands, broke windows,
and in general acted like a second-rate newsreel. There was the
predictable litany of pompous speeches, much venting of justified
rage, and the arrival of the police.

At the end of the first day, the spectacle had reached the point
where the local SDS firebrand was shouting invectives at the
administration building, while the college president, flanked by
gray-faced attendants, stared at the students in stunned, stupid confusion. The twentieth century had just burst upon the poor man's
consciousness, and he was at a total loss as to how to relate to it.

The next day, I bought five hundred tabs of acid and flew
back to New York, where I spent a paranoid ten days unsuccess-
fully trying to sell it to a city that was reeling from rumors of
the Mafia's putting strychnine in the LSD. "But this is pure," I
pleaded. "Right from the Coast." The entire time was cold and
bone-chilling, the telephone system suffering the first of its later-
to-be-chronic breakdowns, the garbage men going out on strike,
and the airlines grounding flights left and right. I finally got
back, eight hundred dollars poorer, with a traveling lady of three
days acquaintance who was drifting around the world at the time.
But, by then, Hayakawa had arrived.

I caught his act a few times, and got bored. It saddened me that
the hero of my youth, the man who first turned me on to language
as a phenomenon, had become such an addled old romantic that
he could, with clear conscience, make himself entirely misun-

derstood by the student body. After so many years as a popular-
izer of other people's thinking, he was finding his moment of
original glory. It was a poor show for a semanticist.

The college finally returned to placidity, after most of the hip
teachers and radical students had left or been fired. And the
Experimental College became a memory in the hearts of those
who, for one brief moment, saw a possible way out of the nut-
cracker which is crushing the skull of America. The tragedy is
not that one or another political force had won, but that something beautiful and life-affirming was squashed in the nation's
forced march toward chaos and brutality.

Yet, in retrospect, I realize that the EC was only a dream. The
sins of this nation have gone too long unpunished. And since we
are the strongest military power in the world, retribution cannot
come from outside. We are condemned by destiny to be our own
torturers, judges, and executioners. We are doomed, like so many
civilizations before us, to commit a ghastly suicide. And the only
pity is that we may take the rest of life on earth with us.

But none of these considerations was active at the time, for I
had begun to hear the siren call of Haight-Ashbury. I still had
more than four hundred hits of acid left. I sold my car. And visited the Lexington and Concord of the Psychedelic Revolution.

4.

The most pungent memory of those days was Olompali, a sprawling estate in Novato, northeast of San Francisco. It had a main house, and several cottages and stables, horses, dogs, and some forty families living there. The rent was paid by the son of a business magnate who had left over a million dollars for the supposed continuance of the family empire. But the son took the bread, dropped out, and began the support of a small portion of the Coast's indigent people. Before long, Rancho Olompali had joined Morningstar and Frontiers of Science as one of the quasi-permanent scenes of the time.

At this time, my experience with communes was limited to the one that I had visited in Oregon. That was a forty-acre farm which had a dropout mathematician as its head. He did freelance computer programming to support the place, and ran the farm on pure communist principles. Everything was held in common, including clothing and sexual partners. It was a sort of intellectual Tobacco Road, since most of the people there were from the cities and had fairly good educational backgrounds but had decided to drop all the civilization games. Their major activities were farming, cooking, and fucking. Everyone had his or her own room, or nest, and there was a large common bedroom for group sex in the main house. They were people totally without ambition and lived for no other reason except the living. After two years, they had transmogrified into a large, amorphous family. Interestingly, most of them were from Minnesota, and were in contact with the great Minnesota dope circle that operated up and down the Coast. At the commune, grass came in kilos and acid came in numbers.

Olompali was quite different, since it was close to San Francisco and was plugged in to the urban scene very heavily. The mise-en-scène the day Leah and I visited was extraordinary; they were having a party. Hundreds of acres of rolling hills, horses cantering by, a huge, sparkling swimming pool, and almost five hundred men, women, and children. The dress ranged from nudity to Renaissance gear. The entire mood was one of freedom. Here were a horde of strangers, suddenly thrown into an intimate and random situation, with the result being a peaceful and loving communion. Some years later, Woodstock was to attain national prominence for the same scene, only over three days and with half a million people. But the seeds had been planted long before in places like Olompali up and down the West Coast.

There was some desultory music-making and dancing, until, around two o'clock, a middle-aged man with a shaved head walked out to the table near the pool and plunked down two plastic bags. It was four pounds of pure THC. He looked around at the assemblage and with a small smile said, "Cocktails."

By twos and threes we worked our way to the source. I had never had the stuff before, so I didn't know how to judge amount. As usual, I was ready to err in the direction of too much. I took four hits, two in each nostril, and then waited for some fifteen minutes. I felt a slow rise, and had four more hits. I was chatting with a bearded blond boy who suddenly began to look like an ancient Greek, when my body dissolved into a mass of watery pinpricks. I got hung up on the fear flash which often accompanies such sudden changes in the state of the sensorium, and immediately walked off by myself to wait until the mood passed. I walked halfway to the large house when I turned, saw Leah, now also quite stoned, looking at me with knowing affection, and then, without warning, we were both racing for the pool, only to dive wildly in, laughing and quite prepared to drown.

We didn't leave the water for four hours. During that time all the possible sea changes took place. We became fish, we became seals, became coral reefs. At one point, Leah did a bit of womb therapy on me, allowing me to float in her arms in the water until every last bit of tension had washed out of my body and I had regressed to the consciousness of an embryo.

Midway through the madness, a naked young man with a Roman helmet on surfaced near me. He blew the water away from his face, turned to me and shouted, "To all good things of the earth you are invited; the price of admission is sin." And then dove under the water and swam away, helmet and all.

Our paths kept crossing, as well as those of several others. Leah and I found ourselves part of a group. Before we fully realized it, we had become a troupe, doing psychedelic guerilla theater in an arena which was already in the upper realms of living theater. With the heat and the dope and fantastic vibrations and naked bodies and period costumes, all sense of the twentieth century had disappeared. We were in a timeless state. And while this is common enough when one gets stoned, it rarely happens with so many people in such perfect communion.

We came to name our group, "the Verbals—a Mime Troupe," and began with some of the usual games. We did a finger lift, laying Leah down and lifting her with our forefingers, just five of us using one finger apiece. We built a human monkey cage, and did parodies of every movie ever made ("You there, down in the life raft."). Terms like "reality" and "fantasy" became utterly meaningless, for we were in the realm of pure play.

When the sun began to go down, many of the people began to get worried. We all flashed the existential dilemma of our reliance on the sun, that source of all life which is so obvious we come, stupidly, to take it for granted and forget, each day, to reel in the wonder of its existence. "What if it doesn't come up tomorrow?" someone asked. Our troupe went from person to person, trying to find a volunteer to take care of the sun's rising in the morning. Finally, we found someone ready for the responsibility. We put him in our astral elevator and went up to the sixth dimension, and left him off, where he promised faithfully to insure that we would indeed have a dawn the following day.

And now a strange thing happened. The guests began to leave and each of the families came down by the pool, and stood in knots on the grass, watching us. The Verbals took stock. We were not only strangers to them, but we did not know one another. A moment of decision came down, and all at once, we began, raggedly at first, a long ululating howl, aimed directly at the moon, and in a moment, we were sending up the most beautiful wavering cries of passion and longing that had been heard in those hills since the wolves had been driven out. Soon, the other families joined in, and before long, the entire night sky resounded with the untrammeled vibrato of human voices in their full power and expression. I remember thinking that if any of the straight people from the outside world had come in at that moment, they would have thought us insane, and the next day would have filled the gray morning of millions of office slaves with the newspaper pictures of bearded and naked loonies howling at the stars. How far civilization has brought man down, to the status of a frightened cloth robot who cannot understand the joy of sheer exuberance.

The cries died down, the families began making for their rooms, and we knew that we were in. The man with the shaved head came up and invited us to his room. And then the trip began to get really strange. I had finished reading *The Magus* not too long before, and suddenly I saw our mysterious host as Conchis, and me as the fuddled Englishman. We entered the main house, and went up the baroque stairway. The scene became Fellini, and as we wound our way upstairs, we started to chant Gregorian hymns.

His room was done in rich rock style. Silk banners and grotesque posters and cunningly arranged lights. Half the room was a bed that stretched twenty by twenty feet. We settled down and our host began to roll hash joints as big as a ring finger. Opium appeared. Trays and tumblers of cocaine. Harry began doing imitations of hash peddlers in Morocco and then sang "Codeine."

It is impossible to describe just how high we got. Our mysterious benefactor kept nodding and saying, "You people are fantastic. I would like to back you as a group." And then smiling wickedly and adding, "What else can you do?"

Of course! I immediately flashed that he wanted us to perform an orgy for him. I went up to him, took him aside, and said, "Is it you, Mr. Conchis?" His eyes gleamed. "Don't tell the others," he said.

By this time I had relegated critical judgment to the level of obstruction. Everything was happening too high too fast for me even to begin to stop for questions. The only confusion came in, as always, when it became clear to me that the others were getting an entirely different reading from the scene. I realized that this reality, as all realities, was totally open-ended and could develop in any direction whatsoever. I thought I knew what the director had in mind, and even had his mysterious wink to use as evidence. But the others were drifting off into unknown realms. Paranoia set in.

I began to get nervous. I started opening and closing windows. I searched for clues to verify my existence. None was forthcoming. Each of us had consumed about half a pound of dope apiece, just in weight alone, not counting quality and kind. And the lines of communication had not been checked at each point along the way. Everything was going so well that I assumed that everyone was on the same trip. And now, as I felt forced to some kind of decision, there was no one to talk to. The formerly friendly faces of the others began to look sinister, and the random events of the day seemed, in retrospect, to be part of an enmeshing pattern. It reached a point of gibbering panic when, like an angel of mercy, Leah came up to me.

"Let's split," she said. "I can't take these vibes any longer." Gratefully, I led her out to the car.

The car! I realized that I had to drive over forty miles back to San Francisco, and I didn't even know what my name was. Extreme circumstances make for heros and fools, and a bit of both. I started back. One of the discoveries I made during that trip of two eternities was the probable reason why accidents happen so readily on highways. My body had been extremely sensitized by the drugs, and I got into the rhythm of the tires on the road. In that direction, it was all soft, all air and rubber, so much so that I forgot the steel and glass component of the car. At one point, I was dreaming along, anesthetized by the soft swaying the machine, when I became suddenly aware that I was in an iron juggernaut, hurtling down a black ribbon of highway, with other monster machines whizzing by within inches of me. I freaked, but there was noting to do except trust my instincts and keep going forward.

I found the perfect speed to be 37.5 miles an hour. Faster than that, and the road blurred; slower, and the wheel wavered. I came upon stoplights like a diver coming upon a sunken galleon, foggily, as from a great distance. Interestingly, although my mind was lost in some lotus land of indescribable fantasy, my physical reflexes remained perfect, and I brought the car to rest in front of my house with the delicacy of a ship landing on the moon.

For weeks afterward I floated on the high I received that day, digesting it, reliving it, weeping at the sheer beauty of it, tortured because I knew such a time could never be repeated, could never be accurately described. It was one of those moments that make one realize the poignancy of the haiku which goes, "'How exquisite,' I say, but with each thing I see, spring passes."

Yet, that was not the heaviest of things which happened during the Haight sojourn. I had yet to come into contact with Frontiers of Science.

Since I was used to the New York brand of scene, with its rapid-fire punch and localized geography, it took some time before I could see the pattern of places and events which Rod Confers had put together. He was a physicist who claimed to have been taken up by a flying saucer one night and given a mission to turn on the world. It was part of the sublime naïveté of the man that when he told the story, it was impossible not to believe him. He held Wednesday and Thursday night gatherings, usually in the Grace Memorial Church and at the College of Marin. His basic trip was the formation of a kind of humanistic religion based on scientific principles, and he rented a huge run-down country club a few hundred miles north of San Francisco, where he began to put together one of the most outlandish communes on the Coast.

In the beginning, he attracted only true believers. These were people who fell into his scene the way I had dropped into Scientology. The essential difference was that Rod had no power trip going, nor any plans for world domination. Also, no money lined his pockets. In the beginning, one heard him talk, was moved, and simply turned over all one's belonging to the Foundation. They took money, clothes, car, etc., and in return you were given a room, fed, and allowed to become one of the family.

The notion of "family" is a very important one on the Coast. One belongs or one doesn't, and as in any family, there are no identification cards or passwords. You are known simply by your own face. This is why, when people went up to Harbinger Springs—the name of the place where Frontiers had its home—and asked if they could join, they were given a very elaborate runaround. If one felt he were part of the family, he just stayed, and then let the others decide on whether he could remain or not.

As with so much else in California, a tacit agreement went a long way, and anyone who tried to be too explicit about things was vastly suspect.

The scene at Harbinger rapidly became one of dope and spirituality. The notion was that if a group of people could get it together and raise huge positive vibes, they would form a center from which salvation would flow. They did some dabbling in orgone meters, and were quite orthodox about diet. They also had some of the most beautiful hot spring baths in the area, and on any given afternoon there would be a small group of people sitting in the healing waters, gently stoned and smiling at one another.

Before long, they began to attract the attention of the straight world. They started to interest IBM executives and mathematicians and scientists from all parts of the country. The appeal was easy to understand. These were brilliant and sensitive men who had all their lives been channeled into the one arena society opened to them, and while they found its money and prestige and opportunity to use their brains attractive, they hated the regimentation, the deadly dullness of conformity and superficiality. Many of them also loathed the military meatheads who were turning their efforts into more vicious weapons of genocide.

Now, at Harbinger, they could move in a company of peers, for along with Confers there were gathered some of the finest acid minds of the day. The thing with LSD—which Confers himself never took, oddly enough—is that it illumines all the natural propensities and conditioning of the individual. The problem is that it has been taken mostly by people with little sense of culture or education, and has thereby bred an entire generation of idiots savants. One meets them constantly in California, smiling, wise, somber men whose eyes reflect the profundity of the sages, and yet who can barely string together two sentences in any kind of articulate discourse. At Frontiers, there were people who had a high degree of native intelligence, who were well educated, and who had mastered the vicissitudes of acid. In addition, there was the countryside, hundreds of luscious and often nude women, healthy babies, and pulse-pounding music.

Within a short while, Frontiers had become the psychedelic country club of the nation's hip intelligentsia. If it had continued to succeed, it might have turned on an army of men who live at the heart of machine-America, inside the veins and arteries of its computers. But the government could not allow such diabolic rites in the woods to exist for long. At first, the local cops began harassment. They found health violations, and when these were taken care of, they began "looking for runaways." One memorable night, six stalwarts from the local constabulary, pudgy and apple-cheeked innocents from the boondocks of northern California, pulled a surprise raid. Except it was they who suffered the greater surprise. They found six or seven hundred naked freaks, dancing and swilling acid punch, setting up a soaring cry which set the leaves on the trees to spinning. They rushed into the dining hall where the bulk of the party was going on, and froze to the spot. To a man, they blushed. They stated their official business, which was looking for underage runaways, and then quickly left, but not before four of them had been approached by a number of people and asked to come back when they were off-duty. The next step was to humanize the police.

Yet, from that day on, the group's days were numbered. For in addition to outside pressure, they suffered from internal disunion. Less and less emphasis was put on work; more and more the place became a great sloppy crash pad in the woods. Money ran out, and hidden jealousies and suspicions sprang to the fore. Every two weeks saw a new regimen posted on one of the bulletin boards, and as any veteran of communes knows, once the rules have to be promulgated in print, the organization has become as rigid as the society which had been fled from.

My finest memory of Frontiers comes, however, from one of the way stations that had begun to spring up around the organization. Since the Springs could accommodate only so many people, those who were quasi members had begun to set up a series of houses going from Vancouver to Big Sur. They had no official status, but once one cracked the Frontiers circuit, it was possible to live for months without money, simply traveling from house to house in the company of hundreds of other members of this subculture of a subculture. Again, to become part of the family involved learning a set of extremely subtle responses and mannerisms, none of which could be described by anything short of a kineticist and video camera. Since I am a chameleon on the level of personality, it took no great trouble to blend in with the mix, and one weekend I found myself with almost eighty others in a haunted chalet at Clear Lake, near Ukiah (which, as someone pointed out, is "haiku" spelled backwards).

The people there were mostly between the ages of sixteen and twenty-five, and were typical of the young acid graduates who lack the critical intelligence to view themselves as products of history as well as of eternity. These are the kids who speak with a vague optimism about the Aquarian Age, and in the face of the most mammoth evils maintain a faith in the salvageability of man that is simultaneously inspiring and appalling. They remind one of the ancient Chinese maxim which runs, "When the people begin to use auguries and superstitions to solve the problems of daily living, one may know that the state is in decay."

Any attempt at perspective was taken by them as bad vibes, or paranoia. They had not yet reached the stage of understanding that the existence of real enemies is one of the ground rules of life, for all species. They were still at that vulgar level of misunderstanding which equates the Buddhist Nirvana with the Christian notions of Paradise.

The three days there were typical. Dozens of people came and went. Sacks of grain appeared mysteriously. No one had any money, no one had any plans, no one knew who lived there or how the rent was paid. Somehow, the house existed as an energy center and served as a focal point for a continual grouping and regrouping of these many ministers of some obscure god. They were as lovable as they were infuriating.

There was trouble with the town. The people there, like most people in small towns, were willing to be tolerant of anyone who didn't blatantly upset the social ecology. If fifty freaks had moved into the old chalet, and held obscene orgies and cabalistic rites, no one would have objected so long as, during the daytime, they dressed and acted in a conventional fashion. One could understand their viewpoint; they were living way out of the city in order to escape the insanity of the city, and while they were closed to a good many things, and steeped in ignorance and prejudice, they could be friendly if one didn't invade their homes with frightening displays of weirdness. But the young people had no sense of propriety. As far as they were concerned, the earth was theirs, totally, and they would allow others to live on it, as long as they didn't interfere with their own sprawling, chaotic ways. They insisted on wearing the wildest of hippie-type costumes, and driving through the streets in psychedelically painted trucks. They flaunted their beards and bra-less chicks and smoked dope outrageously. Of course, they were merely flaunting their deep insecurity, but the effect was to give the insecurity a basis in reality. The townspeople began the usual harassment, beginning with edicts from the health inspector.

They were to be evicted some two months after the weekend I spent there, but that weekend ought to have been enough to rip the minds of any one of the good burghers if they had seen the goings-on. A good six hours after dinner was spent with serious turning-on. Several pounds of grass was smoked. Slowly, those who weren't already coupled began to drift toward mates, and near midnight, we started moving toward the bedroom.

The bedroom was a single room, some sixty by sixty feet, totally covered with mattresses which had a single sheet over them. Some industrious chick had taken dozens of sheets, sewn them together, and made a covering for the state's largest single bed.

Now, everyone there had to some degree or another dipped his hand into some form of pseudo-meditation, group chanting, massage, and relaxation. So, almost like saying prayers before bedtime, we began a round of head and body games, under the rubric of some eclectic Oriental structure. Within a short time, hands were kneading backs, nostrils blew in and out with alternate breathing, headstands were performed, and a low level sighing permeated the air. The scene lasted for half an hour or so, and then the lights were snapped out, as some forty couples lay down to sleep.

We formed a circle with all our feet toward the center, so that our bodies stretched out like spokes on a wheel. Within seconds, the sense of sexuality grew very heavy. Forty cocks lay to the ready; forty cunts yearned in secret anticipation. All the dope and gymnastics had worked everyone up into a fine sweat, and most of the people here were sexual strangers to one another, adding an edge of anticipatory excitement to the brew. All of that, coupled with the insane sense of religious fervor which sparked our every rustle, made the place as combustible as a Freedom March through Georgia.

Total silence ensued. Everyone was awake. Everyone knew everyone was awake. And everyone knew that everyone knew. And was waiting. A very long five minutes passed, and suddenly, from a segment of the wheel on the rim opposite from me, a sleeping bag rustled! Our ears strained to the sound. Another rustle. Silence. And then, the unmistakable slithering of a hand against fabric. And shortly after, a clear female sigh.

The room collectively relaxed.

The rest was fairly standard, except for the time intervals. Everything happened more slowly as the couple worked their way upstream through the consciousness of everyone else in the place. As for the rest of us, we had to navigate the waters of their fucking through sound alone.

Finally, we heard him mount, and the moaning explosion of breath as he entered, and then the joyous crying out as he moved inside her. "Ohhhh," she said. "Ohhhh," he said. "Ohhhh," we all thought.

Of course, the domino effect took place. A few seconds later, a new moaning began. And then a third. And within five minutes, every single person in that room had thrown back his sleeping bag and was balling in full gusto. Cries rang out, and the air filled with the perfume of dozens of young snatches. It was the single most happy sexual time I had ever experienced, and more taboos came ringing down in an hour than Ellis was able to catalogue in a lifetime.

I found myself with a girl I knew slightly and a bullish young man who had attached himself to us. The three of us went at it, he with greater fervor than I since it was his first time with the woman. By the time everyone else had finished, he and she were still at it, and he bucked all his young strength into her as she let out the first uncensored yells of the night. Whereas everyone else had maintained a certain vocal discretion, Judy just lay back and wailed. At the height of her orgasm, someone switched the lights back on, and everyone else sat up, blinking, to see who was making all the noise. The two of them sat up after a moment and received the applause and cheers of their brothers and sisters with innocent smiles of joy.

We all smoked some more dope, the lights went out again, and one by one we fell asleep, to the sounds of stray couples who were having a second go at it. The next day we woke to a breakfast of fresh fruit and groats, and headed back to San Francisco.

During that time, I lived mostly in a commune on Waller Street. It was supported by Gerard, a dropout landlord who, one day, had sold all his houses in Philadelphia and decided to be a hippie, and then diligently set about learning how. I had met him in one of my classes at the Experimental College, and one afternoon, as I was waiting for a bus to take me to North Beach, he called to me from the second story of one of those Victorian houses which people the Haight like so many great Japanese wrestlers.

I went up, and found a family in the making. Gerard was there, a kind of benignly confused paterfamilias, paying the rent and buying some of the food, and in general walking the thin line between financial commitment and just being one of the gang. Ernesto was there, one of the true legends of the Haight, a fifty-year-old Italian who had dropped out at the age of forty-seven and become an actual saint, white-haired, bearded, gentle, pained, going from commune to commune, teaching them how to put together compost heaps, how to love one another. For all the time I knew him, he never carried a penny in his pocket, nor owned anything but the clothes on his back, nor had a home of his own. But the Son of Man hath not where to lay his head, and so forth, and Ernesto was the closest thing to the reincarnation of Jesus that I had ever seen, but with a jovial Italian pessimism instead of poor Christ's Jewish *schmerz*.

Martin was there too, Ernesto's brother, a gentle dockworker who got high from running the length of Golden Gate Park every day. He lived in almost total silence and in complete simplicity, a younger version of the man his brother had become. Shirley lived there, in red-haired confusion. And Lucy Sunshine, who couldn't stop smiling, except to cry. And Gypsy, who couldn't make the break with his criminal past.

In all, some two hundred people must have passed through those rooms in the few months I lived there. When I moved in, a decision was being made to close the place off, to try to bring the people living there together into a family. But the same problem kept tearing us apart: how to strike a balance between the need for privacy and intimacy which keeps a family together, and the desire to allow any one of the family who needed to crash to come in for as long as he needed. In this case, the notion of "family" extended to the entire human race.

The day I went there, I had a pocketful of acid with me, and Gerard decided to have a party in honor of the occasion of our meeting one another again. There were over forty people at the house that day, and I immediately went into the kitchen, poured four large containers of orange juice into a bowl, and dropped fifty tabs into the mix. We sat around sipping the brew until, about an hour later, everyone lifted off.

What happened during the next twenty-four hours was both

the best and worst of acid. People standing for hours with their arms around one another's shoulders, forming human flowers, chanting, having psychic orgasms. People freaking out when they would suddenly pop to and find themselves under a pile of bodies or looking out a window to a totally unrecognizable street scene in an alien universe. Comic vignettes such as a sensitive young girl staring for over an hour at a tall black man sitting totally fogged in a corner. He was gazing with empty eyes at his lap. As she looked at him, tears came to her eyes. Probably she was hallucinating some hallowed figure onto the man and mistaking his stupor for satori. Finally, she crawled over, put her face in his lap, and gave him a long and exquisite blowjob. When she finished, she looked up into his face and said, "Thank you." And crawled away. I watched him for another ten minutes, during which time some very slow, very heavy changes went on in his face. The major question he seemed to be trying to decide was where in his obvious stream of hallucinations the scene with the chick would fit. I have often wondered whether he ever realized that what had happened was actual.

By the middle of the next afternoon, most of the people had left, with Gerard, Martin, Ernesto, and myself remaining as the males of the household, and Shirley, Sunshine, and Marilyn as the females.

Considering the fact that none of us had the slightest idea what we were doing, the commune held together very well for several months. It had a number of things going for it: the rent was paid, food was available, dope was plentiful, and there were always at least a few people with yang vibrations in the place. It became a center, and soon people from New Mexico and New York were coming through, crashing for a while on their way to other places. Everyone had a friend who had a friend who knew about the pad. We became terribly close, running as we were a cross between a psychedelic hotel and a church.

The pad was occasionally highlighted by someone of extraordinary capacities, such as Robert. He had been making the commune circuit, following the sun, for over ten years, and his ultimate ambition was to go to India to become a sun yogi where he would need to do nothing but sit and stare at the sun from morning to night, living on a bare handful of food each day. He was a master of asanas, although he never did a regular program of yoga. But every once in awhile he would stand on his head or break into the fantastically difficult scorpion pose, as easily as anyone else might walk across the room.

He taught us the snore pose. It is used to stay awake while driving at night. The point is that one can't sleep while someone is snoring, so if you do the snore pose yourself, you will keep yourself awake behind the wheel. He stayed for three weeks, during which time he hardly ever left his room. Mostly, he meditated, or read, or talked gently to whoever was there. Friends of his would come, including an old Okie couple right out of Steinbeck. The man was a toothless farmer who, when toking grass, would say, "O Lord, make me perfect, but not just yet."

On one of his rare walks Robert met a young blind man who worked in one of the health food stores run by the Tibetan Mountain Yogis. They were a group of hard-climbing, hard-fucking types who went up Mount Tamalpais every week, there to sit and chant mantras late into the evening. Their trip was to grow organic vegetables on their country place, and sell them in their two stores in the city. Their goal was to open a school in which, as it said in their pamphlet, "it would be understood that we, the monks, would have no knowledge of those very subjects our school would teach. We would rely on the technical expertise of others to provide detailed knowledge." They were a self-conscious hierarchy, and were sponsored by Lama Govinda, whose political nose had already smelled out the fact that the United States, and not Tibet, is the place to set up a spiritual autocracy. Their motto was, "The highest art is to live an ordinary life in an extraordinary manner."

Technically, they allowed no drugs, but there was hardly a soul in San Francisco who didn't do dope in one form or another. The blind cat had a freezer filled with peyote buttons which he used by boiling them into a soup and taking it via enemas, which allowed for rapid absorption and bypassed any risk of nausea. He came by with a few dozen buttons one day, and the bunch of us gobbled down the bitter fruit in between bites of banana. Robert began rapping about seeing the clear white light, and the blind cat kept hollering for him to shut up talking about *light*. We reached one of those points where everyone in the room was simultaneously sailing off into an unbearable awareness of the fact of our actually existing, there, in that time and place, when Robert remarked, "Oh, but it's so obvious, so obvious that we should all one day be sitting here, in this room, with these people, understanding all these things." My hair stood on end, and I stepped sideways into cosmic perception. One of the chicks was hit by the same revelation and began keening, "All hail to the Holy Truth, all hail to the Holy Truth."

With the scene at the pad, spending long, amorphous afternoons smoking grass, swimming in people who were always strangers and always immediately intimates, moving in an ambience of religious vibration and political confusion, I began once more to slowly go mad.

To step outside the house was itself a trip of great magnitude. All around the Haight were the dregs of the psychedelic revolution, those few honest souls who still had faith in the Hashbury as a community, those who were trying to remind the others not to get lost in the miasma of speed and violence which rose from the streets, and those who had nothing left of their humanity except their physical bodies. To walk into the street was to confront the Diggers in their Free Store, the Hare Krishna freaks overcompensating for their basic cosmic insecurity, Lad playing his Kerista flute in the park.

A few blocks away was Golden Gate Park itself, and hippie hill, where the golden exhibitionists did their thing on sunny afternoons. Nearby was the Donut Shop, where the amphetamine heads nodded out until four in the morning, and Stanley the Astrologer got stabbed by a motorcycle gang because he was walking with a black friend who got killed that same night. From time to time, some of the Berkeley people would come by, wanting to sop up some of our relative peace and at the same time putting us all down for being apolitical.

I started to retreat into myself. I picked up, by some bizarre stroke of fate, DeRopp's *Master Game,* the handbook of psychic fascism. And in the mornings, after breakfast at the Krishna Temple (which ended when they caught me wearing leather sandals), I would walk through the park, trying to "step into the silence."

As I lost my own center, I began to become tyrannical with others. At the commune, I started to insist that we cut down on the number of people who could crash there. The family split into opposing camps. And finally Ernesto left, looking at me sadly and saying, "Someday you'll learn that there's no way to keep *anybody* out. Everybody is part of our family."

I got onto a baroque Zen trip again, and took to wearing red robes and carrying a staff. I took the smallest room in the house, no larger than a pantry and having no windows, and fixed it up with madras cloths and pictures of Meher Baba. I went in heavy for incense and long hours of mysterious wall-gazing. I refused to laugh. I hid the rest of my acid. I stopped fucking. I felt an inner call to purify my people, to raise them above the level of mere getting stoned and thrashing about a crash pad.

"We must center ourselves, we must find our own soul, before we can help others," I taught. "There must be silence in the house at all times, and one must speak only when there is something immediately necessary to say. Meditation is foremost. There will be hatha yoga every day. We will eat only rice."

As usual in such circumstances, my program was met with the twin reactions of submission and hatred. Those who understood what I was trying to do responded to the honest attempt I was making to bring order out of confusion. For, with all the good times and parties, there was an underlying unhappiness from no one's having the slightest sense of who he or she was, and covering that ignorance with jargon and drugs and activity. The others saw me merely as a troublemaker, one to be overthrown as quickly as possible. On occasion, one of my friends would drop in, and the response would be a snicker, a realization that I was on another one of my trips, and nothing could be done with me for the duration of it.

But the fire was in me. I began to give classes again, only this time I didn't have the restrictions of working on a college campus. Once again I discovered the great inner poverty in people which allows them to place themselves in the hands of total strangers, bringing their confusions and problems to someone who may be in deeper personal trouble than they. It was on the basis of this facet of human nature that the therapists, and priests, and gurus plied their trade. It was only necessary to let it be known that I was available for consultation, and people responded, almost certainly to the image of the man I was pretending to be.

And because I had begun to believe in myself, I manifested an energy which translated into consistency, and in any given endeavor, consistency is the major rule for success. As I became successful, I became outrageous. I took greater risks, feeling that I couldn't fail. A girl came to me because she couldn't get her warlock boyfriend out of her consciousness. She claimed that he would invade her mind each night, even when she slept alone, and bedevil her with his evil words. And at the same time, she couldn't stop seeing him. What could she do?

"Take off your clothes," I commanded. She did as I ordered.

"Lie down," I said, "and spread your legs." She did.

I picked up my staff and placed the tip of it against her cunt. "When you realize that the only interesting thing about you lies between your legs, and stop this fantasy concerning the value of your mind, you'll have no further trouble with warlocks."

She leapt up in anger, mortified. She began to reproach me. "Put on your clothes and get out," I barked.

A week later, she returned. She wanted to thank me for the lesson, and told me that she was free of her boyfriend's influence. But by this time I had forgotten what it was I had told her, being eyeball deep in a dozen other involvements at the time. She was quite put out and, I'm told, later spent a good deal of time talking about how the guru was a fraud.

Another night I led a relaxation group, during which I offered to take one of the delicious young aspirants into the next room for a massage. She said, "Later." But when she came around later, I was already negotiating with another young thing for the same treatment. So I took both of them to my chamber. And there laid them down, face down, side by side, naked and expectant, and slowly, with a low droning voice, put them into a light hypnotic trance. From there on it was pure pornography, fucking first one and then the other, my red robes flapping behind me, my holy man's staff a symbolic phallus propped against the wall. Over my head was the sign I had made two days earlier when, after two weeks of celibate holymanship, I suddenly realized that all my energies were going into other people's balling. It read, "Stop teaching, start fucking."

The trip culminated the night of the nude encounter group. Once again I retreated into the mode that I knew best, understanding that no matter how hip or stoned anyone was, there was always a great pool of tension formed deep in the musculature and perceptual systems. And to unlock these orgone knots required little more than having people lie down, experience their bodies from the inside, release their breathing, and enter a yielding and passive state. Ethically, the leader in such a situation should then allow whatever develops to flower freely, and not attempt to structure it in any way whatsoever, but the scene was jumping with groovy possibilities, and I was quite willing to use my techniques for corrupt ends.

I was high on my own potency and on acid; I was high on the continual flow of energies coursing through the commune; I was high on the potential of the human species when it begins to really swing in a beautiful way. And I was high on the sight of a dozen naked women who looked to me as a guru and were ready to experience the ALL under my supervision.

There had always been an atavistic corner of my mind which harbored resentful fantasies of those men who have been able to command stables of women in sexual thrall, using them to make orgiastic murals the way an artist uses his paints. At a later time poor old Charlie Manson was to stare out demonically from the cover of the major magazines through having mounted the same kind of scene. Of course, the minute one human being uses another, in any form whatsoever, whether as a sex slave or as a corporate employee, he has committed murder. Since we all do this in one form or another, it seemed to me simply a matter of degree. If one were to be a sinner, he might as well go into it on a grand scale. Better a pirate than a petty thief.

That night I gave orders. No one was to remain in the house who was not participating in my class. Several left, and a dozen arrived. In all, seventeen people were ready to get experienced.

I began in chilling fashion, walking among them and glowering. Two or three who made foolish remarks or asked inane questions were rewarded by a blow from my staff. To my amazement, no one got up and wrapped the thing around my head. If one can play a role with enough self-assurance, there will always be enough of those who will take complementary submissive postures. I suppose that if I had had neither a sense of humor, nor an innate capacity for fucking up, I might have become a religious leader of some charisma. I have often wondered whether the main thing Jesus had going for him was a thorough commitment to his paranoia. Who else would speak of "loving your enemies"? Buddha never spoke of enemies. The notion that I was a species of Jesus has visited me more than once, and rarely have I been able to separate the delusions of grandeur from the realistic parallels. For Jesus was just a man; he knew no more about the nature of the universe than you or I. Even God may not answer the question, "Why is there anything at all?" He seemed to have one thing going for him: an ability to persevere throughout the most tortuous bendings which his febrile mind led him into.

I took down the hammock which hung over the entire living room, that cavernous space appointed with the barest essentials—a stereo, tie-dyes on the walls, a couple of roach clips. The assembly came to order. "We're going to do this workshop in the nude," I said, "so take off your clothes." The men were eager but embarrassed; the women were more ready but more reserved. Among them were several of my followers from the Experimental College, and I was ruthless in collecting the proper amount of spiritual tithe from them.

I began in the usual manner, with everyone lying down. The difference now was that we were in a totally private space, everyone had their quota of drugs going through their veins, and I had a wild hair up my ass. I did not know what I was doing; that is to say, although I maintained my technical cool, I had no notion as to my purposes for going through with the scene. At another time, this might have made me wary; but as it was, I took it for evidence that my mind was truly operating in an uncluttered space.

The relaxation and breathing portions went well, and soon there were a number of bodies in total repose. I mentally leaned back to admire the way the candlelight played shadows over thighs and breasts, the way the pubic hair frizzled into sensuous valleys between the opened legs. I went around and pulled arms, lifted legs, massaged necks. I may have been mad at the moment, but the insanity manifested itself in a cool, detached expertise. It was the Adolph Eichmann of Esalen doing his thing.

I don't know how the affair would have gone if I hadn't begun hallucinating. Perhaps it would have slid into a friendly orgy, with some gentle and harmless fucking, the teacher taking the ripest plums for his private preserve, and letting the others fend for themselves. But I was struck by a reincarnation flash. Suddenly, I realized that I had done something like this before. I closed my eyes and saw myself as an Aztec priest. Thousands of screaming worshippers were massed at the base of the pyramid; the jungle sun beat down from an open sky. I wore a plumed helmet and a great cape; and in my hand I held an obsidian blade.

The inaccuracy of detail paled before the romance of history. It is another aspect of acid culture that the most illiterate young people can have racial flashes, coming clear from the archetypal consciousness, which teach them more about the smell and feel of an era than the thousand dusty tomes pored over by the PhD candidates in their molelike effort to understand an era by amassing detail. If the young acid head would study history, or if the historians would drop acid, we might have some true scholarship taking place, but none of that is likely to happen in America.

I stood there amidst the bare bodies gleaming dully in the Haight-Ashbury night. I spoke. "Everyone, very slowly, begin to feel where the center of movement is in your body. Find that spot which calls itself to your attention and begin to move from there. Let the stretch be slow, total, and complete. And when that stretch is finished, rest...until you find another center to move from. Do this until you are moving freely, rolling and stretching, coming to your knees or feet. If you roll over or touch someone else, let that be part of the experience. Accept everything that happens to your body as you come to a sitting position."

And for ten minutes they did just that, going through all the predictable changes, the awakening of sensuality, the surprised delight that simple movement could be so rich, the flashes of rich sexuality, and the flow which comes from just being in a room with naked, beautiful, relaxed people. When they had all come to, I sat down among them. "I need a virgin," I said.

There was a quick shuttling of glances. Clearly, it was an absurd request.

"Well, are there any Virgos in the room?" I said. One girl lifted her hand. It was Adrienne, a student who seemed to hold me in some form of blind reverence. "Lie down here," I said, indicating the floor in front of me.

She lay down on her belly, her arms at her sides, her eyes closed in complete trust. Her face was full, her breathing relaxed, and her buttocks loomed like cotton candy cones. My throat became dry.

I looked at the others. "We are going to reenact an ancient sacrifice," I said. "Just relax, and get the sense of a very hot sun burning into your shoulders. See if you can feel the sweat trickling down your arms, and the way the light makes your eyes hurt. You are staring up at a very high altar where the priest of the tribe is going to sacrifice a young virgin for the health and prosperity of the people.

"Picture the girl, much like Adrienne here. She is lovely, heavy-limbed. She has never known the touch of a man's lips, the ecstasy of a caress. She has never had the moment of sheer bliss when two human beings interpenetrate and become one body, one consciousness. She has never known love.

"She is frightened and excited. She is going to experience brutal, painful, swift death, before she has even begun to taste the juices of life. Never will she have her center penetrated by the firmness of a man's passion. Never will she have a child sucking at her nipple. Soon, her wondering eyes will be closed forever as the black blade pierces her tender belly. And, as her soul flies to the gods above, the priest will tear out her heart and eat it, still beating and bleeding, before the hoarse cries of the multitude."

As I spoke, Adrienne's breathing became heavier. The others in the room came closer. There was not one of them whose blood lust had not been touched. All the savage instincts, bubbling so close to the surface, had been given permission to burst loose, and they leapt about in joyous dance. I had flashes of burning witches and Nazi storm troopers, I saw the sacking of libraries and the ravages of looting horsemen, I saw every viciousness and evil that man has ever committed in his blind rage. All the violence of the species burned in the room that night, and it was directed at the most innocent one among us, the virgin who had done no harm, and had no cause to experience this brutality.

Slowly, I turned her over so that her vulnerable front lay exposed. Her full breasts lay to each side of her torso, her chest rose and fell as her breath quickened. Her legs lay partially opened and her cunt lips twinkled from under the pubic hair. The tension had reached sublime heights.

I looked up into the imaginary Peruvian skies which had become so real. I said a silent prayer to the deities who hovered overhead, waiting for the soul of the girl, and then, with great theatrical slowness, I raised my right arm. I could feel, I had a sense-memory, of a heavy stone knife in my hand. The eyes of the others went half to the girl, half to my hand. I gritted my teeth, and with a savage cry, plunged the dagger deep into her bowels.

Cascading freakiness ensued.

Three of the women in the room cried out; one fainted. The men came halfway to their feet. Adrienne screamed, a long, piercing wail that curled the hairs on the back of my head. She folded in half, and for a split giddy moment of terror, I wondered if the power of suggestion from the entire group had somehow materialized a knife, and whether she now lay with a mortal wound in her belly.

Slowly, the spasm passed, and I saw with a great relief that her skin was intact. A general sigh of nervousness ran through the room, and then Adrienne rolled over, to lie once more on her stomach. My palms were wet and my context was blown. All I knew was that there was a delicious naked woman in front of me, so flipped-out she was ready to relive being a human sacrifice just to be able to dig on the passing scene. So I did what an acid-laden Aztec priest and Zen monk would have done. I lifted my robe, lowered myself on her quivering form, and fucked her with rapid, mounting pleasure.

This was the signal for the festivities to begin, and within minutes there was yet another tangle of bodies on yet another floor, and my career as orgymaster was beginning to assume a distinct direction.

After that night, the scene at the commune fell rapidly apart. And I didn't want to hang around to see the death throes. Half of the original core group had left, and I didn't have the energy to keep the vortex spinning, to integrate the new people coming through. Crashers appeared at an even greater rate.

Three days later, I lay in the hammock, watching the fog roll in off the Panhandle, and leafing through the *Barb*. One of the sex ads caught my eye: "Swingers Club—an exclusive meeting place for swinging couples," followed by an address and phone number. Without any conscious intent, I began making plans to move in the direction of North Beach, where the decadence had a more refined shape. That afternoon, after getting stoned with Tommy and reading *The Pit and the Pendulum* together, laughing uproariously at that tale of mounting horror, I left Waller Street and went to the freeway entrance to hitch downtown.

Tommy came with me, looking for a ride to Palo Alto. He was dressed in his usual Sherlock Holmes outfit, complete with checkered cape and hat. His general air of unreality, and the fact that he had no thumb on his right hand, made him a most peculiar hitchhiker indeed. "Tommy," I said, "you don't have any thumb on your hand; how can the people tell what direction you want to go in?" He thought a moment, and said, "It doesn't matter. Every direction leads someplace."

I left him standing there as I got a ride heading north, and had no knowledge that the gods of mirth were waiting in the wings and already snickering as I made my way to Broadway and the commercial wing of the sexual revolution.

5.

The club consisted of the two top floors of a three-story building. On the ground floor was a belly-dance bar, with girls imported from Eighth Avenue in New York, and deriving ultimately from Brooklyn. North Beach was, of course, the publicized home of the beatnik era, and the City Lights Bookshop still hung in as a relic from the old days, with Ginsberg or Ferlinghetti or Snyder occasionally showing their faces, looking like refugees from a psychedelic Mount Rushmore.

The area is now mostly topless-and-bottomless, interlaced with pornie movie theaters and topped with the transvestite revue at Finocchio's, where the tourists gawk in derision and hidden envy at their fellow human beings. The commercial-entertainment strip is surrounded by three utterly distinct areas. There is Chinatown, which provides, for all its bustling, an odd note of busy quietness as its members continue in their steadfast refusal to be assimilated. Thousands of newly arrived immigrants cough their lungs out in squalid rooms, while their more prosperous brothers operate the lacquered stores along the narrow streets. The young Chinese hoods, reacting against the hundred years during which their people have been the niggers of the West Coast, are letting their hair grow, and travel in small packs at night, snarling at the fat white faces along the strip. Next door lies the Italian section, with its usual complement of pizza places, espresso joints, and funeral parlors. And overshadowing all is the new Bank of America building, San Francisco's first true skyscraper, defying the San Andreas fault, and announcing the power of American imperialism to Asia.

The swingers' club was the mongoloid brain child of an ex-used car salesman, ex-masseur, ex-bouncer named Jim, who summed up within himself all that was wrong with the business mind of Western man. As usual, when meeting such people, my admiration for his ability to manifest all the ills of civilization within a single distorted personality far outweighed the trauma of spending time with him. Jim had a mind which was incapable of perceiving anything except in terms of its possible income. He spoke with clenched jaws, and with a fervor ordinarily found only in maniacal gospel preachers and politicians on the make. The one thing which saved him from being a total monster was his mammoth ineptitude, a pervasive inability to bring any project to a successful conclusion. Like other anal retentives, the energy he used to conceive his ideas obscured any grasp of larger issues, and he spent untold hours with pencil and paper, figuring out the smallest details of complicated schemes whose salient feature was their total unrelatedness to reality.

The idea took shape—coagulated, actually—when Jim met Harold, a fifty-five-year-old millionaire who sustained himself on the twin pillars of lechery and alcoholism. Harold was the son of wealthy and crusty old landowners before whom he lived in mortal terror. For his personal fortune of some three million dollars was tied up in lame-brained business ventures which threatened continually to fail, and if his parents learned of his lifestyle, they would cut him off without a penny in their will. He was without ready cash most of the time.

Harold was surrounded by leeches and sycophants, people who understood that a fool and his money are soon parted. What it took them, and me, some time to learn was that this was such a fool that he was permanently parted from the bulk of his money, and had but the merest leavings to play with. He did nothing but promise futures, and this ought to have made me suspicious. But like the others, my venal vein began to throb, and critical intelligence became infatuated with this pigeon. Two in the bush got to seem mighty attractive.

This was the nature of the crew that populated the club. The essential idea around which the club was supposed to operate was a simple one, and in all fairness I must note that, were it anyone else but Jim running the place, it might actually have got off the ground. The Bay Area is peopled with thousands upon thousands of couples who, for one reason or another, have unsatisfactory sex lives and are ready to try drastic measures. They have seized upon the notion that more is better and, in one of the saddest marches since Napoleon approached Russia, have embarked upon a program of sexual expansion.

Now, there is a germ of validity in that approach. It is the same notion which fired Pan some fifteen years ago when he started Kerista. The difference lay in the fact that Pan had no fiscal motives involved in his scheme, although his mode of being warped had equally baroque ramifications. Pan is a great bear of a man, looking more and more, as the years go on, like an Old Testament patriarch. Since he has a brilliant mind, since he is thoroughly uneducated, since he is intolerably right-wing in his politics, and since he can chew LSD tabs like candy, he started a Utopian factory, spinning out the world's most grandiose schemes since the days of the Socialist Utopians in the middle of the nineteenth century. His name should rank with Butler and Bentham.

I made my first contact with him and with Lad, the pied piper of the love movement, through an exchange of letters when they had bought land on Roatán Island off British Honduras and were setting up the headquarters of a worldwide commune and hip travel agency. The notion was that there were hundreds of thousands of communitarians all over the planet, and if they could identify with a single organization, it would be possible for any of them to travel over the entire globe, visiting their spiritual *landsmen* who were recognizable as members of the family.

Concurrently, the sexual mores of the old civilization would break down, and new possibilities of mating and matching would come into focus, creating a milieu of total sexual liberation.

There were two difficulties. First, the very nature of the hip civilization involves its total unwillingness to identify with *anything,* much less a fanatic travel agency. Second, Pan is one of those men who are quite lovable but who have trouble getting laid, so his sexual libertarianism was always laced with a kind of resentment and urgency.

At one point, through their sheer novelty and the force of

Pan's personality, Kerista was managing a hopping commune in the East Village, and staging orgies for various screen stars who found the whole trip amusing and pleasingly decadent. But they were busted for dope and indecency by the stalwarts of the New York vice squad, and Pan moved to the Coast.

I met Lad for the first time then, at four in the morning on Avenue B and Third Street, as I was walking with Susan Ashton, then head of New York's Sexual Freedom League (although, alas, she couldn't come). I heard the sound of bells, and turned to see Lad, with his eternal flute and drums and jingling knapsack, heading west. As always, he was handing out mimeographed sheets on which he, again, once and for all, explained Everything and gave detailed instructions as to How It Can All Be Straightened Out. He remembered the letters we had exchanged and we rapped a bit before he disappeared into the night, forever, as I thought.

But one afternoon, at the Experimental College, I met Pan, who also, to my amazement, remembered our correspondence. He was now married to a black girl, illiterate and right up from Georgia, whom he treated as a slave in the grand old tradition. She seemed to find the treatment tolerable, and was content to raise their two children and keep the house, worrying mostly that he didn't spend the entire welfare check on dope or publishing the *Kerista Tribe,* the monthly movement newspaper.

Pan had aged. He had grown cranky. And he was having the most difficult time getting his sexual scene together, since his old lady was as physically unattractive as he was. But his mind had become a thing of wonder. Give him a few joints, a sympathetic ear, and he could spin out visions that would bring tears to your eyes. He would boggle the sensibilities by, in the middle of his fantasies, insisting that we "bomb Hanoi," but I have long ago learned that people's political prejudices are largely reflex actions and should either be ignored, or dealt with through immediate violence.

Kerista had transmogrified into an interesting organism, something that Pan could not recognize, since he still had hopes of an actual organization, with files and dues and obeisance to the Kerista Pope. But what had happened was that over the course of a decade and a half, some several hundred people had come to know one another slowly and well, through one or another project. There had been a continual cross-fertilization, a slow exchange of partners, a mutual assistance. And it had become a real family. And Pan was the unquestioned father of it. Like many fathers, he was roundly cursed and loved, ignored and listened to. Sadly, he still lived in the hope of his dreams, while he missed the stunning beauty of his actual accomplishment.

Harold, unfortunately, had none of Pan's humanitarian scope.

The people he appealed to were inverse Puritans, those who still found sex salacious but couldn't admit that to themselves. They were still being cute or heavy about it, a variety of closet tramp. The more decadent ones, such as lived in Muir Woods and Palo Alto, had put together a fairly discreet scene, and were content with enlarging their sexual circles to six or eight people. They were the type who fucked by scenario. But most of the married equivalents to single bar-hoppers had a different problem: how to meet other "swingers."

One way was to answer the sex ads in one or another of the specialized papers or magazines. But this entailed certain difficulties. What if one met a *real* sadist? Or what if one arranged to meet another couple, and found them unattractive? How to extricate oneself gracefully from the situation? Or worse, what if one met someone with a really vile perversion, and found oneself digging it? After all, one wanted to be wild, but not too wild. Middle-class morality is very pervasive.

There were a few bars that specialized in this sort of activity, but they were in the Los Angeles area. The swingers had not yet worked out as successful a subculture as the homosexuals, and couples-cruising was an unformed art. It was at this point that Jim had his Idea: why not a club for swingers?

He advertised in the trade journals and set it up as follows: a couple would come for an interview, and if accepted, pay a yearly registration fee. For this they would be able to come to two weekly parties, and have access to subsidiary services, such as party pads, etc. At the club, couples would be assured of meeting only other couples with similar interests, and the screening service would keep out the more dada types. Also, there would be a lightly suggestive ambience, so that one could look others over without pressure. On the face of it, it was an intelligent program, complete with socially redeeming value.

It ran aground on the shoals of reality. First there was the granite personality of Jim to contend with, his ability to discourage anyone with any degree of sensitivity from joining the club. Then there was the venality of the people who worked there. Also, the fact that Harold kept running out of cash at times when crucial investments were needed. And finally, the customers themselves.

For the concept of swinging is based on the supposition that a couple have got it so together, are so filled with love and respect for each other, have such a perfect sex life, that they spontaneously break the bonds of the twosome and reach out to include others. For the people who went to places like Vantage, nothing could be further from the truth. They were, almost to a person, characters out of Albee. Tight-mouthed, loose-assed, bickering, jealous deadheads who didn't have enough energy to follow the simplest debauchery to its logical conclusion. Not one of them could have tied de Sade's shoelaces or understood the depth of *The Story of O*.

As in every other human endeavor, the constitutionally strong, attractive, wealthy, and successful were off in some private corner, having their orgies, while the losers groped around the public places, searching to be found.

I sat across the desk from Jim and tried simultaneously to sell him a bill of goods and find out exactly what his scene was; I met the rest of the crew: Ellen, a delicious Taurus heaving into junk; Margit, a black Aries of twenty-six who worked hustling drinks in the jazz clubs, and must have been the world's most unconscious dyke; Madeleine, Jim's wife, a long-suffering woman of exquisite emotional sensibility and extreme social deprivation (I later took her on her first acid trip and had my mind blown as her Cancerian personality emerged and she kept saying, "I am the mother, I feed the bodies, the minds must grow."); Ralph, a pimply would-be orgiast who got the job of putting out the monthly newletter, with interesting titbits for all the swingers; and Evelyn, who had a permanent crash-pad in the outpatient clinic at Marin General Hospital's psychiatric wing; and the to-be-expected mélange of petty thieves, unsuccessful whores, déclassé hippies, and strange floaters.

It was several days before I met the Man. I was going by the name of Yen at the time. I had dropped acid with Pan about a month earlier, and in a burst of affection, I told him I wanted to "join" Kerista. He was outrageously happy. I was his first convert in almost ten years. The first thing that had to be done was to get me a name, it being a Kerista rule, derived from an early vision of his, that everyone in Kerista must have a name with only three letters in it. We repaired to the Ouija Board, placed our fingers on the pointer, and Pan rolled up his eyes. "O great ghost of Gurdjieff, guide us in finding a name for this new member of our Tribe," he said. I smiled inwardly, thinking about what old Mrs. R. would say if she could see the scene. The Board did its usual magic, and the letters emerged...Y...E and then a long hesitation. Was my name to be Yes? It was a glorious vision, but the triangle scooted past the S and went to N. YEN. I was delighted. Yen, as the dictionary points out, means a desire, and the phrase which crystallizes the Scorpio nature is "I desire," so that much of it checked out. Also, Yen is the standard Japanese currency, and I had been in Japan for two years and did much of my identification with that culture. Then, spelled backward it was NEY, pronounced "nay," which was no. So the name became NO spelled backward. Finally, it had a devastatingly exotic ring to it.

And it was with no little self-conscious suavity that I stood before the bed of the millionaire and said, "My name is Yen."

He looked at me with coolly appraising eyes which, because of the booze in his blood at the time, had trouble focusing. But I saw his posture immediately. This was a man who for all of his life had people approach him hat-in-hand. Although he was superficiality itself, he had learned that in social interaction he need do nothing but lean back and let others perform. As an endless stream of people did, in fact, do. He had the place, he had the bread, he had the power, and had to do nothing but be there, like a magnetic spider.

In all fairness, I must note that there was no malice to the man. He was merely spiritually corpulent, inane, and mentally fuzzy. Yet he did know how to appraise the motives of others in relation to himself. I decided that my tactic ought to be to confront him harshly, for I calculated that he was basically a passive homosexual and wanted nothing more than to be controlled by another man. But my functioning tripped up my reasoning, and I ended by flirting with him instead. This was as successful for the short run, because I knew how to handle him, and he knew that I knew the game we were playing. His eyes flashed and he said, "You are a very shrewd person, Yen," and I flashed back, "Like yourself, Harold."

But shrewd I wasn't, for he never gave me his money, only

his funny paper. We talked about my role at the place, and it was decided that I was to serve as a psychic host for the weekend gatherings. Since the people who came were largely guilty, games had to be provided to warm them up. The women working for the club had the function of walking around in see-through gowns, serving drinks, and acting as models for body painting which, it was hoped, would spread to the wives present.

I was later offered the same job by the San Francisco Sexual Freedom League, at the Ashbury Street headquarters. But the scene there was even more deadly than at Vantage. It was the large basement room of a private house, and each Wednesday, dozens of couples would come for a sexual cocktail party, sipping martinis and making small talk. One portion of the room was sealed off by hanging blankets and partitioned into cubicles behind that. The bit was, you flashed on someone you wanted to fuck, and if there was mutual agreement, you went behind the wall and did it. It was as ribald as a group of preteen-agers playing spin-the-bottle.

At least the decor at the club showed more imagination. Harold did all the decorating himself. The entire third floor was a large room, some forty by fifteen feet. He blacked out all the windows and then hung, laid, and suspended about a thousand dollars worth of ersatz Middle Eastern junk. There were gaudy overstuffed throw pillows, pseudo-Persian rugs, hideous little wooden sculptures, and fake bronze gongs. Indescribable posters lurked in the shadows. To the side of the main room was the master's bedroom, equipped with madras cloths hanging from the ceiling, blinking lights, and a Playboy bed. Beyond that was the kitchen and dining area, which held a jukebox, a bar, and a set of weights. Aikido classes were given there on Saturday mornings.

My workshop series ended in disaster the first night when Evelyn's schizophrenia was precipitated by the relaxation exercise, and she began freaking out by screaming and running wildly through the halls. After that I quickly joined the mood of the others who worked there, a kind of depressed lassitude. I began making it with Ellen and she stopped crashing at the club and moved in with me to a room in the Haight in an apartment we shared with two Kerista rejects. He was a New York Jew trying to be a West Coast Gentile, and his old lady was right out of Olympia Press. At the time, he was using her as a model for beaver flics. In the same pad were two homosexuals, one a cheerful chipmunk who stayed stoned, worked in the post office, and spent most of his spare time at the baths. The other was a serious interior decorator from Ontario, and he had built a complete environment in one of the rooms, out of tinfoil, strobes, mirrors, and Christmas tree lights. It was a pleasure to take mescaline in there, listen to his Laura Huxley recordings, and pass around an inhalator of amyl nitrate.

We became friendly with Jocelyn, who worked as the accountant, and who hadn't written down a single number in two months. She was making it with a Navy jet pilot, and they were vicariously interested in swinging. We got stoned at their place one night, in the middle of the Navy officer housing. His pad had a ghost and for a full half hour we watched it shimmering in the corner and making the rooms as bright as sunlight. We smoked some heady grass which a friend of his had just flown in from Vietnam, and he regaled us with tales of the military mind. His conversation was studded with jokes about "nukes," or nuclear weapons, and he described how beautiful it was to get really high on hash and watch the colors of napalm bombs as they exploded on Vietnamese villages. He once and for all disillusioned me of the idea that to smoke grass makes one a better person; the weed simply makes monsters more monstrous. Oddly enough, however, he came across as a likable person, friendly and sophisticated, with no illusions about the nature of his work. He provided me with one of my strongest insights into the computer mind, that modern mutation in man which will devise the most efficiently horrible means of destroying life on the planet without a single concern for the suffering involved.

It was that night that Ellen got onto one of her junkie rides and took me along, wanting us to promise a suicide pact. She said that three of her friends had gone to a mountain top two months earlier, and did the final nod-out. For a moment, I didn't know whether she was speaking metaphorically and then realized that they had indeed committed suicide through psychic agreement. One level of my consciousness saw it merely as another manifestation of the Dance of Shiva and nothing to get concerned about; but the rice-and-beans portion of my being was horrified. My feeling is that life is once around for each of us, and there is something amounting to a sacred trust for each of us to live it most intelligently, most lovingly, most honestly. I am given the creeps by people who think, somehow, that death isn't real. It indicates that they think life isn't real. And it is unfortunate that the spate of translations from the East has given them the jargon to justify their inability to wake up to the reality of living.

The fucking we did that night was grotesque. At one point we would be locked in ecstatic embrace, and then, as in a Gothic novel, some nauseating nameless Dread would seize us, and we would freeze in position, for as long as twenty minutes, staring at one another in reptilian loathing. The poppers we were using only intensified the experience, and none of it was helped by the presence of the ghost, or of the boy bomber in the next room. Yet, despite all the horror, it was one of the deepest experiences I can remember, for through all the twists and turns of that grisly ride, Ellen and I hung in there together, in a wide and moving communion.

As it became clearer that the club was not going to make it, Harold became even tighter with money, and most of the salaries were cut or done away with altogether. Some of the people split and the rest of us broke down into small sub-groups. The club became more of a crash-pad and place for meeting. One night I took Ellen, Margit, and Madeleine to Tina's house where we all dropped acid, strawberry barrels being the brand at the time. Tina was a sometime lover who was having a long thing with her therapist in Berkeley, a Jungian she went to see six mornings a week. She got up at five in order to get there for a seven A.M. appointment. It had been going on for almost two years, and there seemed to be no change except that he was some ten thousand dollars richer for it, and her parents, who were footing the bill, got a sense of helping their daughter.

By mid-evening, my clothes had come off, I had entered a barking contest with Tina's dog, and was in an intense fight with Margit for the attention of the other women. She leaned her Aries dyke vibes into me and practically seared my eyeballs. Like any smart Scorpio, I laid back until she was off-balance, and then shot bolts of vibrant energy into her solar plexus. But she was unbelievably strong, and after an hour of struggle I said, "Look, I'll split the chicks with you." She refused to cop to what was going down and the fight simmered into a long night of silent antagonism.

Personal hostilities meshed with financial crisis, and the club came apart at the seams. I was in a state of growing and frazzled desperation. The constant worry about money was draining my inner resources. It was inconceivable that I should go to work; I simply wasn't in any shape to go downtown and meet the Man. If I had gone into any office or employment bureau as I was, long-haired, wild-eyed, speaking what seemed to be gibberish a lot of the time, they would have freaked. And I had once and for all rebelled against the notion of putting on the "nice young man" act, pretending to be obedient and docile, selling my birthright for a mess of decaying culture.

The circumstances under which I was taking dope were making me crazy. One night I even stupidly dropped acid and went to the Carousel, a plastic rock palace, and had my sensibilities ripped off by the carrion vultures who swarm to such places to feed off the music and human vibrations.

And once again I could feel familiarity slipping from my grasp. The thing is that there is a way of perceiving existence that has no description in any symbology whatsoever. All the yogas, mantras, yantras, and religious cookbooks are nothing but a set of exercises which are supposed to put your head in that single place where the *understanding* takes place. The problem is, if you ain't got it, you ain't got it. And if you read about it, you can con yourself into believing that you do have it. Especially if you take a psychedelic. For a short time you sail into a self-induced Nirvana and think you really understand what the whole trip is about. But as Krishnamurti points out, "Reality is not an experience."

At one point in my inner and outer travels, I emerged with the phrase "the mysterious familiar," which is a personal literary tag to remind me of what I am always forgetting about the nature of things. It is to say that what *is,* is essentially mysterious. There is no one, there never has been anyone, nor can there ever be anyone, including the total Overmind of all Being, who has the foggiest notion why anything exists at all, and all speculation in that direction is as futile as it seems to be ineluctable. However, to live in that state of awareness all the time is a shortcut to madness, and while it may be a glorious insanity, it is not worth the agony, not to me at least. Nietzsche, obviously, thought otherwise; Artaud had no choice.

The alternative is to see what *is* as familiar. Being mortal and finite creatures, we seek refuge in the known. We cease contrasting that which is before our eyes against the backdrop of nothingness. We forget the void. The sky, the sun, the bird, the self...these are things we know from birth, we accept their existence unquestioningly. But in this state, we lapse into habit, our perceptions dull, and we enter a period of stagnation. In short, we fall asleep and join the rest of mankind in its round of walking coma.

Between the two extremes of sleepwalking and insanity, there is simple perception, a seeing in innocence. One can look at a tree, and see it always for the first time. To see without the symbol, without the associations, so finely, so purely, is probably the highest good. But to sustain such a state of perception requires enormous energy, of the type that I was wildly squandering in my metatheatrical madness.

Now I was sliding into an area where all context is stripped away, and there was no way to get a fix on my actions. Which is not to say that I was acting spontaneously; it was more like a drowning man thrashing about to find something to hold on to.

Evelyn and I began hatching schemes to blackmail Harold. She would seduce him and I would come in with a camera; or I would seduce him and she would come in with a camera. Or we would beat him up and steal his video set-up and jewelry and car and threaten to kill him if he gave us any trouble.

Harold became restless. His taste for new bodies and faces was making itself felt and he was itchy for a new set of conquests. The people around him were beginning to openly despise him, and he needed to dangle his millions before a different set of eyes. At one point, he opened talks with one of the motorcycle gangs, the same people who had stabbed Stanley the Astrologer in front of the Donut Shop. He cut off all money from the club and we knew the end was near. It was simply a question of when the properly attractive hustle was dangled before his eyes. And it was then that Esalen made the scene.

Esalen is a quintessentially American phenomenon of the middle twentieth century. As a mixture of therapeutic effectiveness and shallow hucksterism, of sincere humanism and power mania, it finds no equal on the entire social scene. It began as the private home and grounds of one man, who started a conventionally wealthy-man's trip of inviting his friends to his country estate. After a while, his friends invited friends, and within a few years, there was a very quiet groovy scene going on, against the glorious backdrop of Big Sur, and centered around a hot spring bath in a cave overlooking the Pacific surf.

However, through some mechanism or other, the people there

got the idea to turn the place into a human growth center, and they began to attract a long list of defectors from the psychoanalytic and psychotherapeutic communities. The Freudian Empire was in shambles, and the new therapies weren't filling the gap left by its downfall. So modestly at first, but with increasing momentum, Esalen began its series of workshops in sensory awareness, sensitivity, encounter, massage, "meditation," bio-energetics, and that entire range of techniques which has come to be known as "the Esalen approach."

But a strange change took place once the place stopped being a natural home for a group of friends, and became a business. Soon, Esalen began to sell sensitivity, to charge stiff fees for joy, and maintain waiting lists for awareness. They came at the proper historical moment. Therapy had sunk to such a level of pomposity and granite stupidity that no serious or hip person could take it seriously. And on its dead body, Esalen, like a great vulture, nourished itself.

The pioneers of that soon-to-be psychedelic Grossinger's stumbled onto a seeming truth, that if one lays emphasis on health, on growth, on joy, it is a more effective means of dealing with mankind's ills than by delving into the pathological aspects of the personality. And if it had remained merely a corrective to the older forms of psychiatry, it would have been a reasonably healthy manifestation. But, as with all things, it was organized, ritualized, jargonized, and finally turned into a religion. It went rapidly from Bill Schutz's workshops called JOY, to Stu Miller's workshops called MORE JOY and stopped just short of SON OF JOY. The fact that a human emotion was sold the way the detergent of the same name sells its washing power did not seem odd to any of Esalen's founding fathers.

Also, the community remained silent on the fact that going into a room full of naked strangers, being led in a massive group grope, and running out among the breathtaking grandeur of Big Sur will turn anyone on, and has nothing to do with the supposedly theoretical underpinnings of any psychological approach. Easlen's major crime came in refusing to cop to the fact that all they were doing, essentially, was providing tired and uptight middle-class America with mild orgies and a vain hope for a fuller life. They have never spoken about what happens when the Esalenized person steps back into his web of conditionings, into the fall of his civilization, with its wars and corruption and poisoning of the water and air, and its ethic of violence and greed. As with so much of the California scene, no one there seemed to have the historical perspective to see themselves not as a cure for society's ills, but merely one of its more vulgar products.

On they went, charging higher and higher fees, with Bernie Gunther helping people to discover that feeling the bodies of young girls would make you come more alive, with Betty Fuller leading giant workshops, with some five hundred people at a time processed through a four-hour pastiche of "growth techniques." The initial sense of family had disappeared, and big business took its place. Esalen became a groovy-factory manufacturing jollies. It even formed a "Flying Circus" to go around the country, "to introduce the Esalen techniques," as though intimacy and true sensitivity and flexible intelligence could be taught through "techniques." It held a weekend bash in New York City where some six thousand people paid almost a hundred and fifty thousand dollars to see the Esalen heavies put in a two-hour appearance apiece. Therapy transmuted to show business. And always, in the background, the sound of cash registers clanging.

Concurrently, hundreds of growth centers, spurred on by the Esalen success story, sprang up like warts around the country, and anyone who had spent a few hours with an Esalen teacher, or had been processed by an Esalen teacher, called himself a group leader, and the encounter madness began. Esalen made matters worse by setting up a "leadership program," whereby one might spend a month getting stoned at Big Sur and then go forth as an "Esalen-trained leader."

Esalen's chief general hit the benefit trail, and by the end of the decade had insinuated the Esalen mystique into almost every organization having even vaguely to do with personality change. Their latest conquest was a visit to England where they spoke of the growing success of "the movement."

Sadly, although none of them is any better or worse a human being than anyone else, they have given birth to yet another ism, another form of regimentation whereby people can hypnotize themselves. They have become the American-born version of the Tibetan hierarchy, for while they seemingly transcend politics, they are most influential in guiding much of the tone of the nation, much of its texture. Whatever the political outcome, Esalen will be on top. If the money is right, one can picture them just as easily leading sensitivity groups for the Weathermen as giving massages to Air Force generals.

At the club, Harold was visited by Esalen's San Francisco agent, who had been tipped off to Harold's scene, and had joined the line of those who wanted to clip him for some bread. But they had good bait. Harold and one of Esalen's big guns, it turned out, had been fraternity brothers, and Harold was flattered that the great Esalen chief remembered him. Esalen was trying to get him to buy them a house for their city headquarters, and were promising him lifelong admittance to all workshops, prestige, and orgies at the baths. It was the first time I saw Harold lose the calculating look in his eyes.

As Esalen moved in, I realized it was time for me to move out. One night, when most of the others had gone, Ellen and I dropped acid and stayed in Harold's bedroom to ball. We were deep into fucking, when there was a heavy pounding at the door. It was Margit. She had come upstairs and found the door locked. She screamed to be let in. Her worst nightmare was coming true. The man she hated and feared was fucking the woman she dug, and she was on the outside. Half out of malice, and half out of exuberance, the fucking got wilder and louder. We began making animal noises, and making the big bed squeak with our thrashings. Margit went to a back entrance and came in through the bathroom window, but not carrying a silver spoon. She burst into the bedroom and stood there, glaring. We ignored her. We fucked until we finished, with her watching us hatefully. And then, slowly and deliberately, we sat up and stayed in one another's realm of attention, pointedly leaving her out.

Finally, she came forward and sat at the edge of the bed. I turned and looked at her, full in the eyes and with no reservations. For a minute she held my gaze and then said, "All right, you win."

"I was never fighting you," I said.

"I know that," she said, "but I couldn't help myself."

The rest of the evening passed in normal acid waves. And at dawn, Ellen fell asleep while Margit and I went up on the roof to watch the city come to life. A little later, I went to Chinatown to buy groceries for breakfast. Walking through those silent streets, with the brisk solemn Chinese beginning their day taking down wooden shutters from the store windows, throwing buckets of water over the sidewalks, I felt a peace that rarely comes during a lifetime. When I returned, Margit put her arms around my neck and said, "Let's be friends."

"Sure," I said. And we made a giant breakfast.

Soon after that, Ellen met some musician friends on their way to New Mexico, and split with them. I stayed for a while in the mad-tea-party house on Waller Street, and had nothing to do with the club until a few weeks later, after having dropped some acid, I climbed up the stairs to the top to find Harold, very drunk, wallowing in bed. He told me some stories about two young hippie girls who needed some money and had come to see him. "They were very nice to me," he said in that oily way he had whenever he was referring to sex, "so I gave them ten dollars." All the compacted degeneracy of the scene rose up in me like vomit, and with the energy I had from the LSD, I entered into a long seduction scene with him, at the end of which I got him to go down on me. I gave him some poppers while he was doing it so the experience would be burned into his psyche. And afterward, I demanded money from him.

"I don't have much," he said.

"Let me see," I said, grabbing his wallet from his pants. He had only two hundred dollars, and I took that.

He looked up at me with fear and excitement. "That was very...nice," he said. "I've never done that before." He paused. "Can I see you again?" he asked.

"For that, you don't need me, Harold," I said.

"Do you know...someplace I can go?" he asked.

I looked down at him. "Sure," I said. "Go find a urinal."

6.

As though following some predetermined curve, the next day I moved from the Haight pad to North Beach, and found a room in a place called, appropriately enough, the Circle Hotel. I paid the sixty dollars month's rent in advance to a prototypic Irish landlady who was absolutely inured to the worst the species had to offer. Over the years she had come to view prostitution, drugs, murder, freak-outs, police raids, robbery, despair, and suicide with the calm of a Buddha sitting by a riverside chanting Om. She was an adept in the yoga of business, and had achieved her enlightened state through a thorough understanding of the dollar. One rented a room, one paid the specified price, and short of burning the hotel down, one was free to do whatever one liked. As far as I could see, she made no value judgments, cared not the least for anyone's opinion of her, and treated mayor and criminal with the same scales of justice. I have met few people I have more fully trusted to be totally consistent within the parameters of social interaction. She had a husband, or boyfriend, but his sole function seemed to be to check on rooms after people had left. The only times she spoke to him was to give orders, and I never heard a single word pass his lips.

The room was classic. Twelve feet by twelve feet, a rusted sink, a peeling dresser, and a squeaking bed complete with wrought-iron headboard. One entered from a long hallway that opened onto twenty similar rooms on each side of a complete square, making some eighty inhabitants to a floor. My room being on the inside, I could look out the window to a concrete courtyard, and the scores of other windows from which all the transient and already lost souls looked back.

When the landlady's husband left after taking me to the room, and I locked the door behind him, I was totally without an identity. For one of the many times in my life, if I had died on the spot, there was not a single person around who would know what my name was, or how to contact next of kin. Of course, I signed in under a pseudonym, writing "Augustine Tocco," with a flourish in the registration book.

I don't think I had any thoughts at the time. Living with others had become intolerable. And I didn't have enough money to take an apartment. And, most important, I hadn't the slightest idea of where I wanted to go. All the guidelines which help an obsessive-compulsive over the hard spots were gone. Subjectively, I was one of the damned.

My possessions, by this time, fit into a knapsack and small suitcase. This was a long way down from the apartment full of clothes and appliances and furniture and books I had had in New York less than a year ago. But now I took out a half-dozen books, a few pants and sweaters, my hash pipe, and some of the cloths I had learned to carry with me. One of the women passing through the Waller Street commune had just returned from India and had taught me the poor man's interior-decorating trick: three madras cloths, four holy pictures, an incense stand, and a small rug will turn any dingy room into a comfortable space.

I sat down to take stock. About four hundred dollars left from the stash I had come west with plus the two hundred I'd clipped from Harold. I had already sold my car. I was totally disillusioned with all the salvation scenes, and had had my fill of hippies. It was impossible to go back to the straight world, but I had lost my way among the dropouts. I continued to sit. I stared at the wall. Two hours passed. I began to feel as though I were getting as moldy as the woodwork. I wondered if I would just grow old here, become one of the thousand nameless drifters who slowly sink into social oblivion.

Perhaps I would become a bum. And with that thought, the first flash of my new insanity began. For somewhere in my private lexicon of folk heroes, the bum had always held a special place. Every now and then, while walking through the Bowery or one of its equivalents in other cities, I would meet a bum whose inner dignity burned through all the dirt of his rags. Perhaps a man with white hair and craggy features, with a fine intelligence in his eyes. A man who is aware that he is absolutely at the bottom of any social classification, despised by almost everyone who sees him. And yet, from the vantage point of sheer hopelessness, a fierce pride is born. The knowledge that he owes nothing to anyone, that he lives simply by what he can beg, and if he can beg nothing, then he starves. A man who sleeps on the streets in winter, knowing that he may freeze to death before morning. A man, in short, who has discarded all the pretenses of the world, and lives in the existential moment of breath. And of course, except for those very few bums who have the education and strength to transcend the judgment of everyone around them, these broken products of a sick culture come to see themselves as mere bums, and lose the single thing that a human being must maintain if he is to remain human: an unconditioned sense of inner dignity.

Yes, I thought, I would become a bum. I would drift through the streets in rags, silent, gentle, spit upon by all except those who could see through my disguise, those who would come to sit at my feet and learn from me the wisdom of poverty and self-renunciation. My eyes grew moist as the image took shape in my mind. I wanted to wax out on it, but heard my stomach growling, and decided to go to the MDR for a roast beef sandwich, and from there continue my plans.

But as I was leaving the building, I heard a familiar voice saying, "Far fucking out." I turned, and it was Tommy Simon standing there, and a new phase in my life began.

Tommy was six feet tall, black, beautiful and gay. I had met him in New York; I was an editor and he had worked as an art director. At the time I was not fully enough in touch with my own homosexuality to understand his scene.

Tommy and I were friends in the way that someone who is gay can be friendly with someone he digs, but who had not yet fully come out. I lent him money, he bought me dinners, we sometimes went to movies together. One day, bored and restless, I went to his cubicle to see him. He was out on a coffee break, and since he owed me ten dollars, I amused myself with a practical joke, leaving him a note which read PAY OR DIE with a black hand copied on it. There must have been some kind of psychic transfer which decided me on that particular joke because, at the time, he was some five hundred dollars in debt to a loan shark in the East Village, a man who was a minor Mafia lackey. I am told that when he saw the note he literally blanched. Of course, he learned that I had done it, quite innocently, and wreaked a peculiar kind of revenge. The next day, when I returned from lunch, I found that every single thing in my office had been Scotch-taped to everything else. Drawers, pens, typewriter, curtain, light switches, window handles, chairs...everything in a single web of sticky cellophane. I thought it quite funny, but the vice-president, a man who kept twitching his shoulders back as though he were a West Point cadet being criticized by an officer, looked at me suspiciously for weeks afterward.

Tommy had left for San Francisco shortly after that, and I thought I had lost touch with him forever. But here he was, with a new moustache, his hair dyed red, and looking absolutely ravishing in bell bottoms and cutaway shirt. "What are you doing here?" we said simultaneously.

So we went for a drink, told our respective stories, and found to our surprise that he lived at the Circle, too. At the time he was working in an art supply store by day, and at night working on a series of collages, shooting speed, and doing a lot of fucking.

After several hours at the bar he leaned over and said, "You have any plans for tonight?" I suddenly remembered that I was going to get a sandwich and contemplate my future as a bum. "I was going to get something to eat," I said.

He smiled. "I'll get you something to eat," he said. "Come on."

I followed him out and we went to the drugstore at the edge of Chinatown and bought a box of amyl nitrate. This was before the whistle was blown on the popper scene, causing prices to soar, and the things, ultimately, to become unobtainable without a prescription.

We left, and headed down Broadway. "Where are we going?" I asked.

"To the baths," he said.

My memories of the baths were from the two cesspools of blind lust I frequented in New York. It wasn't until I returned from the Coast and revisited them with a new perspective that I learned how to find sapphires in the mud, how it is possible to soar into the greatest ecstasy when one is at the depths of degeneracy. But at that moment, I recoiled. I was in no mood for urine-caked hallways and paint-peeling walls and dribbling old men. Tommy must have read my thoughts. "Wait until you see the baths here," he said. "It'll blow your mind."

We went under the overpass of the expressway to the warehouse district and entered a discreet door with the one word on it. Inside, it was pure Hollywood. Richly carpeted floors, a color TV in the lounge, a clean, lively atmosphere, with all the attendants being pretty young boys. The rooms were impeccably fresh, and even the johns were spotless. And roaming up and down the halls, dressed only in towels around their waists, were the loveliest of San Francisco's fairies.

We each took a room, and I met Tommy in the lounge. "It's beautiful," I said. "You haven't seen anything yet," he said, and taking me by the hand, led me upstairs.

Up we went, past the sun lamp room, past the weightlifting room, down a long, dimly lit hallway, and turned a corner. At first, I thought we had gone into a pitch-black space. I stood there a long moment, peering into the darkness, and gradually, as my eyes accustomed, a scene out of Doré burned into my eyes.

There, under a lamp that gave off but a few photons of light, in a round room with a diameter of about twenty feet, were some thirty or forty men in a great writhing pile of bodies. From their center came the continual sound of heavy breathing, groaning, sighing, all punctuated by cries of passion and pain. Almost the entire room was a circular leather couch, perhaps two feet high, and around the couch was a narrow walkway. Men posing like characters in the stud magazines leaned against the wall, while their counterparts knelt in front of them, variously sucking and licking and biting. Here and there, a figure would tumble off the couch, lying half on, half off, doing something into the mass of bodies and being done to by one of the men in the ring outside.

Tommy turned to me and smiled. "Something else, isn't it?" he said.

"Let's go," I said.

And we took a popper apiece, broke them, filled our nostrils with the heady fumes, and dived headfirst into the sea of bodies. The next fifteen minutes had no description, simply because there were no discrete units of activity. It was all touch, all liquid, all sound, all excitement, all images. During that time, I went through every imaginable variation on the physical homosexual act imaginable. There was neither the chance nor the inclination to take any of them to their full conclusions. Rather, it was a sort of smorgasbord, with the joy coming in the many different flavors and sensations. It provided me with the single most glorious moment of total anonymity I had ever experienced in my life, and when I finally crawled out, I felt as though I had gone through a baptism of orgasm.

I went down to the lounge and had a Coke and a cigarette. Within a few minutes, Tommy joined me. We exchanged conspiratorial smiles. "Nothing like that in New York," he said. "Amen," I said.

He looked at me. "Let's go to my room," he said. My stomach dropped, and I lowered my eyes. I was still at the stage of pre-coming out where I was too embarrassed to make it with someone I knew. I could only do it with strangers. "I can't," I said.

"Can't?" he asked.

"Won't," I said.

"Well I'll be fucked," he said.

"That's the way it is right now," I said.

He stood up and blew out a lungful of smoke. "Later, baby," he said.

I stayed for a few more hours, used up the rest of the poppers, and had sex with perhaps a half dozen men, not one of whom I can remember. And at three in the morning, my head aching from the drug, my soul sick from excess, I made my way back to my room.

Perhaps, if I had just gone to bed, things would have been better. But I needed some comfort, and picked up one of my books, a thing I had found at Clear Lake called, pretentiously enough, *This is Reality*. It was a handbook of meditation techniques based on the principles of Kriya Yoga. It was written, although I didn't know it at the time, by a southern Baptist minister from Florida who had studied with Paramahansa Yogananda, one of that great stream of popularizers who had flooded our shores. Like so many of the self-proclaimed gurus who wend their way from India, Paramahansa was selling a superficial distillation of a very advanced practical psychology which had its roots in a totally different culture from ours, the practice of which assumed that the student had mastered a score of lesser yogas. It had taken root as a spiritual equivalent of the get-rich-quick mystique which feeds the American mentality, a promise of instant enlightenment. The great yogi's death came, it is told, via a heart attack as he sat with a mouthful of roast chicken at a banquet given in his honor. His body still hasn't decayed.

By the time the minister had watered down the already weak brew, his book emerged as a screaming parody on the whole idea of meditation. Of course, in my current state of mind, I took to it voraciously.

Basically, it was a system of self-hypnosis. One sat in a chair, regulated one's breathing, and "felt" the energy going up the spine to the crown of the head. The book listed a series of recommended visions and sensations which were to accompany the exercise. It was supposed to be a kundalini yoga on the astral plane.

So, for the remainder of that night, and for the two weeks following, I alternated my time between freaking out at the baths, and spending hours practicing those venerable techniques. I should like to have a psychiatric description of my state of mind at the time. Certainly, it fit no categories I am familiar with. After a breakfast of bacon and eggs, and a quick trot through the pages of the *Chronicle,* I would return reverentially to my room, nodding hellos to my fellow debauchees at the hotel and then dutifully enter what I thought to be a mediative state. I can remember getting all sorts of flashes and buzzes and odd insights, and simultaneously wondering, Am I doing it right? Am I really getting enlightened? My critical faculty had been totally eroded, and I was completely at the mercy of blind whim.

Tommy hadn't spoken to me for some time after that night, but one evening I ran into him on the stairs. There was a moment's awkwardness and then the tension melted. "Come on," he said, "I'm going to score some speed."

Speed! Despite all my seeming hip concerning drugs and my familiarity with the psychedelics, the word struck a chord of fear into my heart. The house of speed freaks I had once visited in the Haight forever warned me away from the drug, for its end result seemed to be a kind of walking death, an endless regression into the folds of the ego, until nothing was left but a strident voice insisting on being heard. On the other hand, the principle of try-anything-once was a guiding string through my life, and the time seemed to be right.

I went with him.

The dealer was a round, soft black faggot of about forty-five who seemed to radiate a calm peace. With him were his lover and a thin red-haired whore. She was walking up and down, agitatedly talking to herself about a date she had later that evening, and seemed to be arguing about some fine point of prostitution ethics, which totally escaped me.

Tommy bought a small white packet and then gave the man an extra three dollars. "Give him a hit," he said, pointing to me.

A current of sexual excitement ran through my legs. I sat down. He spooned out some more of the powder and mixed it with some solution from a medical-looking bottle, and then sucked the mixture up into a syringe. I held out my arm. The needle entered. For five, ten seconds, nothing happened.

And then, suddenly, I was washed over with the most breathtaking waves of love I have ever experienced. My heart swelled and my body tingled. My mind became clear on the spot. There wasn't a trouble in the entire universe. All people were brothers and sisters. God was All.

I looked at the man in front of me. Great affection poured out of me. It was he who had brought me this miracle, and I stood up to embrace him. I felt as delicate as a hollow egg, as gentle as a spring breeze, as warm as candleglow. I leaned forward and kissed him on the forehead. "Thank you," I said. He seemed not to notice. I suppose he was bored with virgins.

Immediately, the spiritual flush condensed into sensuality, and when I turned to face Tommy, the sensuality exploded into sexuality. I burned with passion. "Ready to go?" he said.

We went back to his room, and while he locked the door and fixed himself a hit, I took off my clothes and lay on the bed. In a while, he undressed and turned to face me. I lay there in absolute calm, in total self-possession. I felt as though there could never be any confusion again for me. All the static which normally interferes with thinking and seeing was gone. All sense of urgency had left. Now was forever. I imagined I could stay in this spot for all time, being content simply to breathe and eat, and fucking whatever beautiful people came by. Speed! I had found my drug. It gave me all the things I had searched for in the psychedelics and never really found. Also, there was no nonsense with hallucinations and pseudo-cosmic insights. It was clear and immediate reality.

As soon as I thought the word, the two weeks of working with the book sprung into my mind, and I began running through all the practices, doing the astral kundalini. Only, now, with the drug giving me the energy, I could really do it! I became the baby Krishna, cuddly and omniscient, ready for a roll in the hay.

And then Tommy joined me. His skin glowing purple and bronze in the red light, his face an African mask of terror and joy, his body sleek and muscular, his cock a sensitive rigid pole of unendurable beauty.

And then we made love. We did nothing spectacular, nothing that men haven't done with men millions upon millions of times through all the ages. Yet, with what concentration, with what exquisite edge of sensation, with what surges of affection! I explored every inch of his body, and surrendered totally to myself in him. Narcissus had found an image more substantial than his reflection in a lake.

When, finally, after aeons of foreplay, he took me in his arms, kissed me, and penetrated me, I broke through all the barriers of shame and repression which had forced me to seek only the embraces of strangers. Again and again, as I rolled through the changes of desire and fulfillment, as he sank deeper and deeper into my flesh, always surprising me, always finding another level when I thought he could go no further, as I moaned and bit his ear, I would suddenly open my eyes and see his face, not the face of a stranger, but the face of a friend. And the friend was a man!

Once and for all the taboo of homosexuality was broken, and I realized how natural, how easy, how rapturous it is to give oneself up to the sweet closeness between people, to taste the richness of sex with them, and not once care whether it is a cock or a cunt which is giving pleasure, whether it is a man or a woman who is the vehicle of such great transports of joy.

We fucked for hours, and the cycle came to its natural end. Afterward, having taken the active role, he was restless. Having taken the passive role, I was ready for more. He split, and I got dressed. The speed was still working in me, although I was starting to bounce down.

I was still horny and began raiding the bars for scores, and spent several hours tricking in the backs of cars and alleyways. And after several hours of that, back on the darkened streets, I began to feel the dregs of the trip, the crash. I had not realized how euphoric the drug had made me feel until, when its effects began to wear off, I experienced the actual world as a dull, dirty, and infinitely boring place to be in. It is at this point that there is a temptation to shoot up again, to recapture that initial glow. Of course, one can continue to do this for days, weeks, even years. The result is the familiar burned-out speed freak that has become a part of our new folklore. And I almost yielded to that temptation, except that all kinds of warning bells went off in my head. It was at that moment, strangely enough, that my two weeks of Kriya Yoga came to the rescue. I decided to use the remaining speed energy working out on the techniques. I couldn't go back to my room feeling the way I was, so I went to the Haight to crash at the Waller Street pad.

The place was fairly empty and I was able to cop the hammock for the night. I lay there, staring at the ceiling, going through my paces. Slowly, my eyes closed, and a most peculiar thing happened. I slipped, without any premeditations or foreknowledge, into the yoga of the dream state. This is described by the Tibetans and consists in learning how to remain conscious while asleep. This may sound mystical to anyone who has no imagination in these matters or who had not experienced it himself. Actually, it is quite simple. It merely involves activating consciousness at the muscular, cellular, and molecular levels (and in some instances, on the electronic level, but I was not to find out about that until a few months later). Then, one brings the conceptual consciousness to a single pinpoint, and while the "body" is totally asleep, the "mind" continues to register impressions. It was during this time that I "saw" my dreams, that is to say, saw the actual mechanism of the mind as it produces dreams, sat in the projection booth or the unconscious, as it were. This persisted for some time, and made up a complexly interesting experience, until my energy fell below the necessary level to maintain this clarity and multiplicity of perception, and I lapsed into normal mundane sleep.

The next morning I woke up in the ninth circle. To the degree that everything had been exhilarating the night before, it was enervating in the morning. I remembered everything and regretted nothing, but I felt that I could never experience such a scintillating state again without shooting speed. And it seemed that the gray world I now faced would last forever. I had no sense of its passing, as all things pass. The people around me seemed distant, and I couldn't blend with their marijuana vibes. So I took off for the hotel again.

I went into my room and sat at the edge of my bed for an hour. Then, woodenly, without thought, I went to the sink. I looked at myself in the mirror. It was like an automaton regarding itself. I went to the dresser, took out a pair of scissors, went back to the mirror, and methodically began cutting my hair off. When I had clipped it as close as I could, I lathered my head and shaved it with a safety razor until my skull was totally bald. I washed the suds off, dried the dome with a towel, and stared uncomprehending at myself for a very long time.

I was without the slightest ability to recognize my own face.

Hurriedly, I went out into the street. I didn't want to be around scissors and razors any longer. I didn't feel suicidal, but neither had I felt like shaving my head. It was wise not to take chances.

"Look," I reasoned to myself, "you haven't got the slightest notion of who you are, what you are doing, or where you are going. At this point you seem to be in real danger of getting heavily into speed and a sure-to-be-disastrous affair with Tommy. You are also sitting like a loonie trying to find enlightenment in a book. And just an hour ago you shaved off all your hair. Now, under the circumstances, what do you think you should do?"

The other half of the schizophrenic dialogue provided a quick answer: "Leave!"

"Very good," said the first half of my personality. "Where?"

And from some psychic pit deep in that portion of my mind which taps into the collective unconscious there came a single word: "Tucson."

"Tucson?" I said. "What's in Tucson?"

But the voices of the gods kept silence.

I found myself walking once more to the Haight. Outside the pad on Waller, I found Gerard working on his truck.

"What's happening, Gerard?" I said.

He looked up. "Jesus Christ, what happened to your head?"

I appeared nonchalant. "Oh, I was getting too attached to my hair, so I decided to get rid of it."

A look of admiration crossed his eyes. "Far out," he said. And although I didn't know it at the moment, the seeds of another myth had been planted in my head.

"Fixing the truck?" I said.

"Yeah, I'm splitting tomorrow," he said as he lowered his head under the hood.

"Where to?" I asked.

He looked back up. "Mexico."

I wasn't too sure where Tucson was, but I knew it was in the direction of Mexico. The coincidence was too perfect to ignore. "Mind if I come along?" I asked.

"OK. But don't bring too much stuff. There's four of us already."

"I have just a knapsack," I said, mentally discarding my suitcase.

"Fine," he said. "We're leaving early tomorrow morning."

I went back to the hotel, packed one pair of pants, one sweater, one toothbrush, one book, a hunting knife, the remainder of my acid, and bid fairwell to the Circle Hotel. The next day, I headed south.

7.

With Gerard and myself were Diane, Mark, and Julie. We went down Highway 1 in Gerard's panel truck, painted dark blue to cover the Buddhas and psychedelic eyes and rock candy mountains it had sported in San Francisco. The idea was to get as inconspicuous as possible to avoid a bust in Mexico. We had enough dope stashed in the vehicle's roof to put us all away for ten years. Mark, who spoke Spanish fluently, was going to take us through Mexicali at night, where, with some polite talk to the guards and twenty-five dollars, we wouldn't be searched.

Their notion was to drive all the way down to British Honduras, where Gerard would buy land and they would start a farm. The idea erased Tucson from my mind. Diane had a satchel full of seeds, and all the way to the border fed us on germinated rice and wheat germ cookies. Julie was sheer waif. She had been traveling the country for two years, carrying only a flute. All the time I knew her she wore the same jeans and shirt, and went barefoot. She hardly spoke, but was always smiling and dancing and playing the flute. We had spent one night fucking, and the next morning I felt as though I had been making love to sea foam, very beautiful, very insubstantial.

As far as Santa Barbara, there was no trouble, and we spent the night there with friends of friends. But the next morning, everyone woke up freaky. It may have been some planetary influence, or too much raw rice, but where we had been easy and warm with each other, we were now rank with suspicion. The truck filled with friction.

We should have stopped until the thing straightened out, but we got hung up in L.A., getting tourist cards for Diane and Julie. And after four hours in that unreal place, we were filled with a panic-laced need to get out of the country. We decided to drive until we were in Mexico.

It got dark and cold as we sped toward the border, and the countryside began to look menacing. We headed down 86 to Brawley and then began that long lonely ride down 111 to Calexico. When we stopped for gas, it was like a scene from *Easy Rider,* long before that film was put together. With my shaved head, Gerard's Jewish locks, Mark's beard, and the braless chicks, we exuded paranoia amid the close-cropped hot-rod types hanging out in front of the nearby diner.

Our fear backed up among ourselves, and we were feeling a great mutual hatred. The sense that everyone wished we had never started the trip was thick, and we rode in heavy silence. The cold night wind whipped through the old truck, and it was impossible to get warm. By the time we got to the border station, we were almost welcoming arrest. But Mark's plan was a good one; he had been this route a number of times and the scene was cool. We moved on, grimly pushing south.

We pulled into San Luis about three in the morning and decided to crash in one of the hotels. Exhaustion and cold had reached critical levels. At the hotel, Julie flipped out and claimed she was going back to California in the morning. Gerard took me aside and told me that he wanted to spend the last few hours with her, and since Mark was making it with Diane would I mind sleeping in the truck to guard the stuff.

At first I didn't care, but as I lay there, shivering and feeling sorry for myself, I got more and more angry, and when dawn broke I put my bag together, hitched north, and found myself in Yuma, Arizona. Destiny had me by the scruff of the neck. I bought a ticket for Tucson at the Greyhound Bus Station.

But a half hour hadn't gone by when I looked up to see Julie standing in front of me. She too had hitched a ride, and found herself dropped off in the same place. She had the address of a friend in Tucson and had decided to go there, independently of my saying anything to her. I bought her a ticket and together we headed toward the unknown city.

The first flash was disappointing. A downtown section that could belong to any small-sized city. The bus stopped outside a taco joint that was the Southwest equivalent of a cheap pizza parlor. We asked directions for Sixth Street, and began to walk toward the bookstore where her friend could be reached, a place called Mandalia.

When we arrived, the store's owner, an astrologer named John Soames, was giving a class in celestial influences. John is a six-foot, thin, bisexual madman who rarely speaks English; everything he says is in astrological terminology. He has a long wispy beard, hair below his shoulders, and sports Merlin robes. My first feeling was wonder that such a person could not only exist, but flourish, in Tucson, which I imagined would be totally straitlaced.

I sat in a corner while Julie went in search of her friend. I didn't realize that my appearance was so odd, and only later learned that a shaved head usually meant that one had been busted in Mexico. After a while, however, a young and earnest boy came up to me, sat cross-legged and said, "Are you a yogi?" There was no reason why I shouldn't be. "Yes," I said. "What's your name?" he asked.

I looked out the store window and saw silver clouds scudding past the sun. "Cloud," I said.

"Far out," he said.

I sat while John ran through his rap, and met Mortimer Sand, a pacifist from Vermont, working now at the Peace and Freedom Party Headquarters next to the bookstore. I asked him if he knew of a place to crash, and he offered to let me sleep at his house, where three other people were staying. I thought Julie would come with me, but she found her friend, who was living in a Tucson equivalent of the Waller Street pad, and since I had had enough of that kind of scene, I parted ways with her. I moved in with Mortimer and Wanda and Doug and Susan and their one-year-old daughter.

To understand that time, it is necessary to grasp the texture of the place. The city is on a broad, flat plain which is ringed by mountains. In the summer, the temperature goes up to over a hundred each day, and in the winter simmers along at an even seventy. Most of the time, the sun rises in the morning and sails through a totally clear sky all day long, only to set in a cloudless sky. The effect of having that much startling sunlight beating down without relief is to make everyone who lives there, from the youngest hippie to the oldest shopkeeper, a stoned *head*. In Tucson, everyone is high.

There is a legend among the Indians that when the world suffers its next cataclysm, which should be any day now, Tucson is one of the places which will remain untouched. It is easy to see why. The ground is hard desert floor, and the surrounding mountains are like the shields of the gods. Now, for some obscure reason, the place is also ringed with ABM's and other pseudo-defensive paraphernalia. The inhabitants are safe not only from acts of nature, but also against the devilish Rooskies.

In all, the city had a great sense of security, and my reactions of familiarity were flashes I was receiving from childhood, when I grew up in the Mafia enclave of East Harlem. What I remember most pointedly from those days was, that while gambling and narcotics were rife, no violence was allowed. The men who ran the great crime empires had no desire to bring in heat on the basis of petty crime, so they assisted the police in making sure that all the civil laws were strictly kept. In fact, I have never had any trouble with police, since from earliest days I saw them as foreigners (they were usually Irish) whose function it was to walk peacefully up and down the street, accepting small bribes to look the other way when there was a crap game, or when the local merchants sold firecrackers for the Fourth of July.

In many ways, it seemed the ideal condition. For gambling and drugs are relatively harmless pastimes, and such indulgence seemed a small price to pay to insure that there would be no beatings, stabbings, muggings, rapings, murders, or other crimes of physical violence. Of course, this is a purely right-wing selling point, and was the major vehicle for the Nazi appeal to the masses, as is the law-and-order appeal in our time. The one thing necessary for it to work is that the neighborhood or city or nation be totally assimilated, in terms of race or nationality or religion. This is why the Nazis had to kill the Jews, and why the Italians fought such bloody wars with the Puerto Ricans when they moved in. Crime inside a "family" is always less vicious and damaging than crime between alien entities.

For the first few weeks, I spent most of my time exploring the land. Mortimer would take me in his VW van to the Indian reservations, to the great stretches of desert to the northwest. One afternoon, we drove for three hours through an Indian land and came upon a small village with about twenty horses, and assorted corrals. It was about six o'clock and smoke was rising from the chimneys. The sky was absolutely clear, the sun shining in perfect stillness. The land was hilly, with huge barrel cactuses growing every ten feet or so out of the caked earth. And everywhere, there was a deep silence. Not a sound. My ear reached for the smallest noise, and found nothing. I wondered for a long time what it must be like to live here, in this village, where the sense of timelessness was as palpable as the rocks below one's feet. I got a flash like the one I had received the first time I stood at the rim of the Grand Canyon, of the utter vapidity of civilization, of the immense vain pride and pretentiousness of man, who in a few million short years thinks he is some ultimate value in the scheme of creation. Here, in the desert, where the tens of millions of years of geological time are constantly staring one in the face, where the great sweep of eternity paints the world with both strokes, it is impossible to be anything but humble, unless one is the typical American.

And, less than a hundred miles away, in the heart of Tucson, the self-indulgent madness continued.

The house I was living in was tied in with a loose family of perhaps a hundred people who had roots reaching back many years. They came mostly from Los Angeles, and now formed a thin line of houses and farms and stores from the coast to the desert. As with so many of these families, which are tied by spirit and not by blood, there were no clearly defined limits, and people drifted in and out. One always found somewhere to live, one always found some way to make work. In Tucson, two establishments formed the heart of the family, the Mandalia and the Grainery, an organic food shop. Within three months, I had floated in and out of all the subdivisions of the group which revolved around these two nodes, and even taking off with the gypsy wing, led by Gilbert and Eve.

Gilbert is a beautiful man who has also decided to live a life of poverty. He panhandles and begs, sometimes does odd jobs, but mostly goes without money or possessions. Like the Ernestos and Julies of our time, he is totally free, traveling wide distances simply on the basis of his being. I have run into him in Oregon and Mexico, and he is always the same, always smiling, always willing to help.

Eve used to be a cripple. She had a birth defect which shortened and deformed her torso and left her no more than four feet tall. Half of one side of her rib cage is missing, and for a long while she thought of herself as a hunchback. Until she met Gilbert, who, upon seeing her, immediately understood the beauty in her. I went camping with them in Sabino Canyon one week, and one day, as I was smoking catnip by the water hole, saw Eve go in swimming. She was nude. Her legs are perfectly formed, and her face and breasts are those of a lovely woman. What a shame, I thought, that she is crippled. And then, she looked up at me, and smiled, and in the radiance of that smile, in the joy of her eyes and the purity of her heart, refined by so much suffering, she glowed with transcendent beauty. Her disfigurement disappeared. It was literally impossible to see her in any way as ugly. And then I realized that we judge ugliness only by comparison with some standard we carry about in our heads, and that any human being who is whole within himself or herself is beautiful by virtue of being whole. And then I saw what Gilbert had done for her; he had taught her how to see herself as a whole human being. I found that tears were streaming down my face, and then Gilbert came up behind me. "She's beautiful, isn't she?" he said. "So are you, brother, so are you," I said. "Praise be," he said.

It was a blessed time, rising in the early mountain morning amidst the trees and streams, loved by the sun and the warm hearts of those people around me, and climbing to the high spot to overlook the vast and silent desert. If I had had any sense, I would have pitched a tent and remained there. It was there that I came into contact with the true invisible underground of America, the psychedelic hoboes, dark men who travel light, who move from camping ground to camping ground, going into towns only under dire necessity, roaming the deserts and unmapped portions of Idaho and Oregon, men without names, men content simply to exist, and to keep their own counsel. To sit by a campfire with some of these men is to understand how utterly shallow we others are, we who measure our worth by the weight conferred upon us in social terms, who need constant reassurance, constant contact, constant commentary.

Back in the city, it was the old set of games. Since I was an educated stranger with a shaved head, there was a certain amount of curiosity about me. Since I had some of those talents which were necessary to the burgeoning burghers of the Aquarian Age, my help was sought. Since I once more fell into a self-created myth concerning my role in the situation, I made matters worse. In short, I started to get involved in Tucson city life.

It was at this point that the many socially conditioned facets of my personality began to feel a pull from the miniature culture which any city is. Julie had since danced off into the mountains and I saw her from time to time as she came into town to take a bath or rustle up a few dollars. Aside from her, I had no links from my past to hold me down; I was, insofar as my public face, a *tabula rasa,* ready to be imprinted, and before I left the area, I got involved with everything from the revolutionary wing of the dropout community to the politics of the Methodist Church.

My relationship to the family was tenuous. They were willing to allow me in as a friend, but enough suspicion remained to keep me at a distance. Don, who ran the food store, was on the run from the Feds for draft evasion. He later turned himself in because, after five years, he got tired of hiding. At the time, however, any new person was suspect. John, another Scorpio, was the spiritual head of the clan. He resented my own Scorpio personality and the fact that, once I began to give relaxation classes, I pulled in bigger crowds than he did for his esoteric lectures. Also, an underground paper was being born, and in general, a "scene" was being created, and the accompanying tensions were making themselves felt in personal relationships.

I also got a strange political education in Tucson. For the first time I got to talk to real right-wingers, and found most of them to be not the monsters I had imagined. Of course, I never met any of the Minutemen who practiced their maneuvers to the south, or any of the other real crazies. Rather, the average Southwest conservative.

I once rode on a bus with a crusty old-timer who kept looking sideways at me. Finally, he said, "You're one of them hippies, ain't ya?"

I smiled. "Yes, sir," I said. I couldn't deny it, looking the way I did.

"You're all the time having wild sex parties and not working and taking drugs, ain't ya?" he said.

I thought about it a moment, and said, "That's right," since it *was* an accurate précis of our life-style at the time.

"I don't much hold with all that," he said. Then he paused a long time and added, "But so long as you don't come do it on my property, you go right ahead."

I marveled at the succinct wisdom of it. Here, where there was still enough land for a person to maintain his privacy, it was possible to be very liberal about life-styles. Here, where the heat made life pleasant, even the slums were more than tolerable. The black ghetto of Tucson makes most middle-class white sections of Queens seem like hovels. Again and again I ran into that attitude. Even the police had it. Drugs, for example, were widely tolerated. It was almost impossible to get busted unless one started dealing in hundreds of pounds. The idea was that as long as the Feds weren't dragged in, local problems would be managed according to local limits of tolerance. It was possible to walk down the street looking like a freaked-out Tiny Tim, and one wouldn't receive so much as a sideways glance from the cops. But if one crossed against a red light, one was immediately stopped. The point was, obey the civil law, and your private life was pretty much your own concern. In all, it exhibited the most intelligent approach to practical politics I had ever seen in this country. And I am convinced that the one thing which made it possible was the simple fact of having enough geographic space to live in.

But this wasn't to last long. The exploiters were moving in. Tucson's population had gone from 30,000 to 300,000 since the end of World War II. And from the right and left the vultures gathered. That foulest of all forms of animal life, the real estate developer, was beginning to eye the vast stretches of unspoiled desert, converting natural beauty and ecological survival into the numbers of dollars that could line his pocket. And his cousin, the scene-maker, was beginning to see the vast stretches of peace and quiet waiting to be inundated by noise.

I am not arguing that there should have been no change in Tucson. Certainly, it has its share of injustice, poverty, racial prejudice, provincialism, and sheer human stupidity. But that existed everywhere. Tucson had one advantage; it was still clean. To move in and raise the dust in the hope that something better might emerge from the ensuing chaos is the kind of maliciousness reserved for the emotionally childish. And so it began, with the first traces of Los Angeles pollution visible over the far horizon, and the thin dust from the copper mines settling over the valley, and the illiterate yellow journalism of the underground press starting up.

Before any of that got to me, however, I was having food problems at the house. I have since become a vegetarian for simple aesthetic reasons, and after having learned what is done to meat before it reaches the plate. But at the time, I was ignorant of most nutritional lore, and like many others on the dropout trail, ate out of a mixture of religious, ideological, and economic conditionings. The people in the Grainery were split into two major camps. Half were macrobiotic, half were fruitarians. And they were all fanatic about their own scene. Since I was trying to ingratiate myself, and since I wanted to experiment with different diets, I ate whatever the clique I found myself with was eating. But sometimes I would slip, and then the trouble began.

Tony, for example, had been living on watermelon for three weeks. He claimed that rice made mucus in the intestines. And when he and I went on a four-day hash binge together, I subsisted entirely on that fruit. But on the fifth day, when I went to the store, he wasn't there, and Al was cooking up a delicious pot of brown rice, sesame salt, tamari, and onions. He invited me to join him, and I sat down to dig into the delicious stew. Halfway through, I heard a sound behind me. I turned and saw Tony's face, two inches from my eyes. He was white with anger.

"MUCUS!" he shouted into my ear.

And then he grabbed a handful of rice and squeezed it between his fingers until it had turned into a pasty pulp. "That's what it does in your stomach," he hissed. I felt the food in my stomach like a great squishy rock, and simply put my bowl down, my appetite for rice squelched for a good two weeks.

On the other hand, I had my hair almost turned white by Don, who described in detail what happens to fruitarians who don't get enough protein.

Mortimer was a purist, eating only avocados and sunflower seeds, quietly despising anyone who gorged himself on any unnecessary food. He would go on at great length about how the two of them gave a man all the elements of nutrition he needed.

There were splinter wings. Two people insisted that no food be cooked, and when they were at the helm, I dutifully munched raw rice and carrots, and sprouted soy beans.

To escape the food commandos was a chore, and one morning I was awakened before dawn by sounds in the kitchen. It was

Susan making scrambled eggs. She looked at me with terror in her eyes, as though she were a witch being discovered making a brew by an Inquisitor. Tears sprang to her eyes. "Don't tell them, please," she said. "It's for the baby, it's not for me. Believe me, the eggs are for the baby. She needs eggs." My mouth watered. "Can I have some eggs?" I said. A conspiratorial gleam came into her eyes, and together we hunched in the corner of the kitchen floor, scooping the most delicious scrambled eggs I have ever eaten into our mouths.

Another time, I was awakened at two in the morning by John. "Come with me," he whispered. I got dressed and followed him out to his car. "Do you want an ice cream soda?" he said. I looked at him, blinking. "I know this sounds stupid," he said, "but I have to have an ice cream soda, and I really feel guilty about it. Will you come with me?"

So we sped off into the night like thieves, to one of those horrible all-plastic all-night diners, where we gorged ourselves on cheeseburgers and ice cream sodas, and then drove to the top of Mount Lemmon, to smoke grass, belch in great contentment, and watch dawn break over the desert.

At this point, three things happened simultaneously. John decided to have a celebration under the stars and asked me to do a relaxation meditation, someone came up with the idea of starting a free university, and I got involved with the Methodist Church's painting party at an orphanage in Mexico. They came together over me in an odd mélange which served as the prelude for the event which was to open Tucson up to the rest of the nation's movement.

The house I was staying in had an immense back yard which lay under the majesty of a great fig tree. The tree was bare when I arrived, but by April had come out in a lush coat of deep green. For several weeks we put up posters on bookshop windows and the other attention spots in town. We planned a joint venture between Mandalia and the Grainery, with plans for a big macrobiotic spread in the yard, readings from Dane Rudhyar, a talk by John, and a relaxation session led by me.

Tucson is a place that breathes the religious spirit, although formal religion there, as everywhere, has degenerated to empty social ritual. The hippie community especially, with its affinity for the Indians and its taste for peyote, imbibes the atmosphere of holiness with a fervor which verges on the embarrassing. The difficulty, of course, is that they have neither the framework nor the actual ethnic roots to understand the source from which they draw the inspiration. With them, also, there is something more of the artifact than the substance.

The day of the happening was brilliant, perhaps the thirtieth straight day without a cloud in the sky. I went for a long walk in the nearby scrub country, and spent the time with my thoughts, as inchoate as they were, and smoked a lot of grass. There is a faculty to my mind which exemplifies the dictum once taught me by an old psychology professor at Brooklyn College, to wit, "Any logical system brought to its logical conclusion ends in self-contradiction." With me, if I begin with a premise, I can follow it step by step, as in a Euclidian demonstration, and although each step is impeccably right formally, I often end like the existentialist who has proved that he doesn't exist. This is the core of madness for me, and the most maddening aspect of it is that from the vantage point of my own cerebration, I can't understand why my position seems odd to anyone else. At such times, I can't understand that somewhere in the chain, a qualitative change has taken place which has removed me from the common view of mankind. Of course, that way lies both enlightenment and insanity, and which of those two poles one experiences oneself to be hoist upon depends on the degree of inner clarity and strength one maintains.

Thus, by the time I returned, I found myself believing myself to be the savior who would dispel the clouds of illusion from the minds of the unwary and lead the children to Tillai. At that time, I had been reading Huang Po, and the iron centeredness of that crusty old villain had me in a psychic cramp. I had become bored with all the shouting about the Age of Aquarius and the constant cant of all the pseudo-systems which had become so popular, and I was ready to "point directly at Reality."

The dinner was a smashing success, and after a while, there were about a hundred people, stomachs full and pleasantly stoned, lying on the grass looking at the darkening sky. I let the environment work its magic, and then began a new variation on the rap which has become a leitmotif to my life. Relaxation was easy to induce in such a setting; by now, the sky was black, with prickles of light. There was no moon so the effect was that of staring directly into the galaxy. I knew this much, that everyone there was in the usual waking hypnotic state which doesn't receive the full impact of the fact of the overwhelming thereness of the world. So my trip was simply to bring the awareness of the group into sharper and sharper focus.

The technique I chose was quite simple. I told a fairy tale, an as-if story, concerning the actual setting. "Pretend we are enigmatic creatures, strangers to ourselves, and mystified by what is about us. Pretend that we are staring through an infinity of dimensions to an incredible landscape, a universe of blazing centers of light. Pretend that we are people, looking at the stars. And now, remove the veil of pretense and actually look, see what is before you. Behold the stunning splendor of creation."

It was corny, but I was playing the sticks. I don't know what it did for most of the people there, but I did receive invitations from young ladies to escort them to their beds, and I went home that night with a girl named Georgia.

Also, a man who looked like a professional traveling pseudo-revolutionary came up to me and asked whether I would like to begin a free university in Tucson. Now, I had been through the mill at Experimental College, and had known Francis Schick when he operated the Free U on Fourteenth Street in New York, before the Maoist crazies threatened to put him in front of a firing squad to pay for his anarchistic bent, and at this point in time and space it seemed to me that I would make the ideal founder of a school. I envisioned something called "The School of the Southwest Sun," where we would teach the value of pure air and food and water, and meditation, and where we would discover the true religious foundations of man. I didn't know it at the time, but I was prefiguring the whole ecology flap by about two years.

The problem was to get backing, and during the next week, while I pondered where we might get funds, I fell in with one of the Christian youth centers which serviced the University of Arizona.

It was a classically nondescript religious function, replete with blond boys and girls, and hapless ministers. As with everything in that city, it held surprises. One of the ministers had been a drug-taking jazz musician before he found his own form of God, and another was a Hebrew scholar, and a third was a gently disillusioned man who realized the full depth of his own futility. There was something about the thorough naïveté of the young people there, however, which entranced me. I had never known people like that in my life. The one word which describes them, and which points to a quality which had always fascinated me, is purity.

They approached everything with clear, frank eyes, and in everything from sex to dope, although they had clearly conditioned postures, they were never prudish or small. They seemed to be able to take life as it is, without judging others for the way they approached life. They were involved now in a charity project, involving bringing a couple of hundred gallons of paint to do an orphanage which a Mexican laborer had spent twenty years building in his spare time. It seemed, for me, as good a way to get to Mexico as any, certainly less complicated than the last time I tried to get there, so I signed up.

The trip south was made tolerable only by my ability to appreciate things in their purely phenomenal aspect. I sat next to the minister's wife, a woman of quintessential vapidity, and within ten minutes had exhausted all possible conversation with her. The others in the car were even less interesting at first glance, so I settled back to enjoy the passing scenery. But after about six hours of traveling I noticed something odd. One of the girls in the front seat, Louise, had not said a word or moved her position for the entire time. I found myself stealing glances at her. Either she was in a light trance or a Buddha in disguise. Later, when I asked her what she had been thinking, she said, "Nothing. I hardly ever have any thoughts."

She had been born and raised on the outskirts of Tucson, by a pleasantly conservative schoolteacher of a father and a warmly efficient housewife of a mother. The single largest impression in her life was the stillness of the desert, and she had grown up without a single complication in her mind. She was not in college, was moderately intelligent—as such things are measured in our so-called educational institutions—and had all the proper attributes of a young lady her age. But for one. When she wasn't actively involved in something, her mind and body fell into automatic repose. An enviable state.

The stay there was odd. The man who had been building the place was a fanatic who said, upon being questioned as to why he had put so much time and effort into the project, "I do everything for God, and for Mexico," a patriotic sentiment I had seen only in history books. It gave me an insight into the growing power of Mexico as the next power center in our hemisphere after the

United States comes to ruin. I didn't enter into any deep relationships with any of the people except Louise, with whom I carried on a delightfully old-fashioned flirtation, but simply sharing the slow pace and hot climate of that nation brought us together in a gentle union. By the time we got back to Tucson, I was ready to approach the ministers about the Free U.

It was a mistake. The ministers had been looking for something to give their waning organization a shot in the arm, and this looked like it might be it. But they were extremely frightened of almost everything and everyone, including themselves.

At the third meeting, the dirty laundry came out. The lists of people who couldn't be offended, the organizations which would have to be consulted. They wanted no "political" elements in the school, and strict controls had to be laid down as to who was allowed to teach. I watched with horror as these educated and supposedly intelligent men, whose lives were theoretically dedicated to doing God's work, twisted and squirmed under fear of retribution, of having funds cut off, and of offending anyone down to the level of county dogcatcher. Very soon, all serious discussion about the actual Free U went out the window, and we were talking about the effect of even mentioning such a project would have on the careers of the ministers involved. It sickened me to see grown men crawl before their own cowardice. I was repelled, as I have hardly ever been, to watch them literally whine at any notion of freedom. They were the castrati of the dying culture, the living proof that Christianity is not only dead, but rotting.

I had gone in with ideas of actually attempting to give the young people, the hip and straight alike, a center where they could enter a no-bullshit relationship with each other and with those who felt they had something to teach, whether it be transcendental meditation or marksmanship. The notion was to let everyone crawl out from under the rocks and into the light of the sun, and let the people make their choice. I came out with the thin taste of bile as the meeting concluded with a resolution to make a resolution to further discuss the resolution to open a school.

Suddenly, I saw Tucson in a new light. That was why it was so orderly, so well-run, so much without conflict. It was a cemetery, and the one rule for living there is that none of the inhabitants show any sign of life. It was a city of the living dead.

I walked back to the Mandalia filled with gloom. And as I

approached the store, I saw four of the people from Peace and Freedom painting a huge sign over the storefront. I almost fell over backward. They had written: THE DEAD.

I rushed over to find out whether this was a psychic transference of the highest order, or some bizarre coincidence. It turned out to be both, but in an unexpected way. The entire sign was to read: THE DEAD ARE COMING. Referring, of course, to the Grateful Dead. Tucson was about to have its first rock concert.

The Peace and Freedom Party of Tucson was perhaps the single most innocuous political organization in the world. They had a store filled with revolutionary literature, held meetings all the time, went around saying "All power to the people," to each other, but weren't allowed to *do* a single thing. They, like everything else in Tucson, were allowed to exist as long as they didn't break any civil laws. This, of course, included demonstrations, marches, speeches, and blowing up banks.

But now they had a cause. One of the local boys had just received five years for refusing induction into the Army, and the concert was planned as a benefit in his honor, as well as to raise funds for the Party. It was to be held in the university auditorium.

For the local revolutionaries, it was a great step forward. For the police and political heads, it was an event to be closely watched. For most of the university students, it was to be their first introduction to live rock. And for the townspeople at large, it was an oddity to be interested in.

The store was in great upheaval. "Everyone will be there," John said. Not yet knowing the entire scene, I pictured a hundred scraggly hippies sitting in the front row. But yet another surprise was in store.

In the two weeks before the concert, many strangers appeared in town. Some were clearly narcs, and others were clearly dealers. Like a great tidal wave, the Dead were preceded by swarms of birds and changes in the atmosphere. All of a sudden, there was a great deal of dope around. Grass and hash were to be had for the asking. It wasn't even necessary to pay for it. Everyone had dope. Everyone was sharing. It was like the preparation for a saint's feast day. The people were beginning to whoop it up. Also, for the first time, there were large-scale busts. Fifteen people got picked up on the street on obscure charges. They were released the next day, but the warning was clear. The cops were watching. Like schoolchildren, we could have fun, but would have to stay cool.

On Mount Lemmon, ten people were busted for nude sunbathing in a totally isolated area. Once again the finger came down to point out the message. We were being reminded what the real power in the city was.

The day of the concert was like Mardi Gras. Peter came into town with a gunny sack of peyote buttons, and for breakfast that morning we boiled the cactus down into a strong tea, added honey, and sipped the heady mixture while sitting on the lawn. Peyote is, of course, a sacred plant among the Indians of the Southwest, and their reverence for its powers has extended to the young white dropouts. Peyote is never sold, for example. It is shared, and to ask money for peyote would be considered a sacrilege. It is quite bitter, and one must be careful to scrape off the whitish growth on top of the plant. Usually it is eaten with fruit, to cover the taste, but it can be made into tea.

It was the first time I had tried the sacred cactus in this form, and I had no way to gauge its strength. I drank several cups and after half an hour found myself pleasantly high.

For several hours afterward, I busied myself with a half dozen details, such as doing hatha yoga, reading, and making lunch. By afternoon, we had more tea, and I went with John into town to open the bookstore. He felt that with today's excitement, there would be a brisk business. The store was his cross and his salvation. He worried over it like a mother over her brood. Profit was always at the margin, and his struggle was between ordering books which would sell widely, and books which he felt should be exposed to the public. The entire store was a mine of esoterica, and served as a miniature replica of Weiser's in New York and Shamballa in Berkeley. If it had any fault, it was too heavy an emphasis on arcane aspects of astrology, But that could be forgiven, given John's specialty of study. The walls were hung with the usual madras cloths and gravure reproductions of Krishna, and the place was redolent of incense and rock.

And it was a busy day. I found myself behind the desk, selling books, rapping with people, and ducking in to the back every now and then for a hit on the peyote bottle. I got extraordinarily high, but it was the sort of high that builds very slowly and gradually, so that I felt more like I was sitting on a high mountain peak than balanced at the tip of a flagpole. It was in the organic nature of the peyote, and the slow crescendo of the day, that I lifted slowly to a point where it was difficult to estimate just how high I was.

As the hour for the concert approached, the tempo increased. And finally, about seven o'clock, ten or twelve of us finished off the rest of the tea and strolled over to the campus auditorium. As soon as I walked into the place, I got a complete flash on the true scene in Arizona. For it was filled with thousands of the most beautiful people I had ever seen.

The city *heads* were only the tip of the iceberg. Out in the hills, in the desert, in the ghost towns, on farms and ranches, lived the members of the larger community, the dropouts who had dropped so far out that they were invisible. And so invisible were they that they could live in the heart of right-wing America, staying pleasantly stoned, living simply off sunshine and fresh air and good food, and never be noticed; for they had become one with their environment. And now they were massed together, and while there was little in the way of freaky dress or hippie insignia, I could see in the eyes and the smiles, the gestures and voices, the true gentleness which had been the hallmark of the early Haight. America's love generation had been seeded back into the soil and was quietly living the good life in the last unspoiled areas of the continent.

I became the total impacted experience of the moment and zoomed immediately to the highest level of intensity of which I am capable. I went down front to find my seat, but found that the bookstore and food store family had all gathered in the space between the front row and the stage. Everyone was in costume. I was wearing my venerable red robe, a white cotton tunic underneath, a velvet cowboy hat, and shades. John looked like a wizard. The others were clearly from Oz.

The local head of the Peace and Freedom Party came out and gave a small talk, getting into the cat who was now in jail, and then introduced the Dead. As the curtains parted I looked around the auditorium. There were no police, no signs of control. And yet, there was a deeply felt order. There wasn't the slightest vibration to indicate that things would get out of hand that night.

The group began its thing, and we listened through the first piece. But by the second, it was impossible to keep still, and we started moving. By the third, we were dancing openly, and by the fourth we were going wild in the aisles. Now, when this happens, the group on stage pays very little attention and keeps on playing as though it were in a studio. But the Dead were sensitive and responsive, and they did that thing which is most gratifying in the world to a dancer, they began to make our movements part of the music, playing to us and with us, responding to our responses, working to reach climactic points with ours. In short, we became a dance-and-music ensemble. And the audience was totally sympathetic. Within an hour, the place was rocking. Perhaps fifty people walked out, unable to absorb the heavy vibrations which were beginning to saturate the walls.

And by the second hour, all distinctions had been broken down. The scene was all sound and movement. And then, Shiva descended.

Shiva is perhaps the grandest conception that the mind of man has ever created. Coomaraswamy, in his *Dance of Shiva,* spells it out in detail. To understand, to really understand the scope and depth of the Shiva concept, is to have a world-view which blends the artistic, religious, and scientific modes at their highest synthesis, and to clothe the resultant metaphor in some of the world's most sublime poetry. The entire history of the solar system is but a twinkling in the eye of Shiva, and it is his dance which destroys the cosmos in a grand conflagration which precedes the night of Brahma and the ensuing creation of the new universe. The dance itself is but metaphorical language for what science is recently reformulating in terms of its subatomic schema of existence.

Shiva dances and All is One. The male and female principles join, and in their union is born the entire manifest universe. All phenomena are but the flashing colors of the movements of Shiva's dress. All dualities are but the striving for opposites to drop their illusory aspects of either/or and merge into a glorious both/and.

That night, the group of us began to move as a single organism, losing all sense of distinction, forgetting time and place while remaining in time and place. And we discovered again the crushing joy of the dance, the highest and most perfect of all man's expressions, when the I and the Other become the One, and the One moves in an eternal round of ringing pain and pleasure, realization and sleep, creation and destruction.

The last piece played was "Let It Shine on Me," and I felt borne aloft by the waves of the music. The electricity sent my body into rapid minute spasms each time the electric guitar bent a note; the molecular level of my body felt its quick panting rhythm each time the harmonica shuddered down the scale; and the beat of the drum sent the vegetative flow thudding up and down my limbs and spine. I went through all the historical forms, played all the sexual roles, visited all the halls of the deities, and all in the pantomimic dancing exuberance of this thing called "I." The body was the vehicle that night; it was the rapture of the body which informed the mind. It was the yearning of the heart which stormed the heavens and conquered the hells.

Then, the music died down and Pig Pen began a rap. We settled down to a jogging swaying rhythm. At one point he said, "Do you ever wake up in the morning and don't know who you are?" Something in his voice caught my ear and I looked up at the stage. And found him staring down into my eyes. He pointed one finger and said, into the microphone so five thousand people could hear, "I'm talking to you." I almost fell back two feet, and felt the eyes of the crowd on me. The question circled through my mind. "Yes," I shouted. "You want to know what I do when that happens?" he asked. "Yes," I said. "Well," he said, "I always have a woman lying there next to me and the first thing I do is tap her on the shoulder and say, 'Hey, baby, come on over and tell me what my name is.'"

And then the group hit a mighty chord and rocked on toward the end of the piece. There was total pandemonium, and I remember the bunch of us leaping high into the air, throwing ourselves over the railing, and screaming and screaming as loud as I had ever heard people screamed, until the music came to a crashing halt, and the curtains abruptly closed.

Then, suddenly, it was all over. I stood there, stunned, as all the people in the auditorium began to file out. I waited for some return, some feedback, but there was only the empty stage. I felt as though I had suffered some monumental ripoff, letting all my energy and perceptions and vibrations be sucked into the air, to feed the crowd, to feed the band, and received nothing back. There were just a bunch of whacked-out musicians making a few thousand dollars in an uptight town, for a group of teen-age would-be politicos. Shiva hadn't descended at all. There was no Shiva, that was merely an idea. I had let myself be used, I had used myself, as psychic cannon fodder.

I looked around and saw that the family had also left. Of course, for them, this was just a wild night out. None of them would have taken the intense metaphysical journey which had wrung me dry. A great crashing took place, but I remained high in spite of it. The resultant state was dread. I left the campus and walked toward the bookstore. Everything had become alien. All the people were strange. There was no one there who even knew my name, who cared what I was feeling, who could comprehend what I had just experienced. I was free, and I was frightened.

There were people at the Mandalia and they were preparing to drive home. Half a dozen of the family were there, plus some others who were acquaintances. I got in the car and rode back in silence. I felt bitter and superior. I needed the people around me and yet I despised them. Worse, there was no way to make contact with them for we inhabited different universes. A dozen times I wanted to speak, and realized the inadequacy of words.

And then the idea hit me. I would not speak. I would not speak again. I thought of the boy in prison for five years. I would not speak for five years. I would write him a note telling him that I had taken a vow of silence for the duration of his imprisonment, and that by this vow he would know that he wasn't forgotten. Once again I stepped out of despair by the expedient of adorning myself with a myth of impossible proportions. Yet, it served the purpose, as would have any less baroque and grandiose neurotic defense. In these, as in most other matters, it is the style of the gesture which separates the artist from the run-of-the-mill psychopath.

The scene at the house was turgid. John and Ginny, Don and his old lady, and Connie, the tiny grain-fanatic, sat on one side of the room drinking tea and smoking grass. The other group of about five people sat on the other side, talking almost secretly among themselves. I went into the bedroom and wrote the note to the man in jail, and put it away for mailing in the morning. I felt elated once more, but didn't have the presence of mind to realize that I was simply following the waves of the drug and the environment, as helpless as a cork on a stream.

I sat midway between the two groups, and got heavy. I sank deep into my resolve and absorbed from it all the benefit which would have accrued had I actually carried out my plan. I got high on my self-delusion. It took perhaps some ten minutes for some of the people to notice that I was sitting there, very loudly being silent. Don called over to me and asked if I wanted a joint.

I waved my hand. "What's the matter, man?" he asked. "Ain't you talking?" I shook my head. Again I got up and went into the next room and wrote a note which I pinned to my chest. It read, "I do not speak, but I can hear everything you say, and will do my best to help you." And returned to my post.

The reaction that the note caused ranged from the feeling that I was stoned and on some kind of strange strip, to the kind of revulsion people often feel in the face of massively irrational behavior. But I did not flinch. Once again, I was forgotten by the others, and then a strange thing began to happen.

I could hear, not only every individual conversation in each group, but the thoughts and intents of all the people there. In effect, I was doing no more than paying attention to the total ensemble of relationships and communications in the room. This is no more than what a person ought to do all the time anyway, but it took that massive amount of peyote and the wild trip of the night to bring me to that point which the mass of mankind does not attain, and views with a suspicion of witchcraft. So low has our species sunk that we cannot stay tuned to all the levels of intercourse which take place, and we laughingly call the blind shouting we do at one another human speech. From my vantage point, I could literally see the shapes of energy as they shifted with the changes in focus and emphasis.

Don, who was generally thought to be inarticulate, turned out to be a brilliant talker. All that was required was to be silent and let him come to the end of his rap. He talked the way a musician plays, and to listen to him for content was as silly as trying to understand what a musical phrase "means."

I was able not only to sit in my own silence, but to pervade the room with silence, so that the words each person spoke stood out sharp and clear and it was possible to actually *hear* what that person was saying, stripped of all punctuation marks and projections and social-theatrical roles. It was a chilling experience to listen to the naked human voice in that way, and to realize that we are all always so exposed, all the time, in our voices and eyes and gestures and body postures and intentions. It is only necessary to pay attention and stop one's inner clatter, to silence the thought machine in the brain.

Then, although the two groups weren't talking to each other, I saw the subtle signals which passed back and forth. The people from the family were blind to that, but the other group gradually fell silent and began watching me listening to the other group talk, amplifying my perceptions with minute facial expressions. In short, they began tuning in on my wavelength. At one point, Don's rap filled up like a balloon over a cartoon character's head, and began floating across the room. I looked up and watched it sail overhead. One of the people in the second group saw me looking at it, and then saw *it*. He grabbed the person next to him and said, referring to me, "Do you see what he's doing!"

I smiled to myself. At last, I was being recognized. But just then, the balloon burst, and the room filled with confusion. Suddenly, everyone was talking at once and sharp-edged waves of paranoia filled the space. My mind, very vulnerable and sensitive, screamed in pain. I ran into the kitchen, found an iron pot, and returned with it on my head. The thing helped. Whatever the relationship between the metal in that pot and the vibrations in the room, it had the effect of blocking out all the jagged energy singing through the room. I added a signature to the note on my chest. It said, IRON HEAD. What a perfect name for a Zen master, I thought.

After a few minutes, things calmed down, and I heard Connie's thin voice in a clear whisper to John: "Do you think he's really crazy?" she said.

I saw the photograph of myself. Wild-eyed, red-robed, sitting in the middle of a house of crazies in Tucson, having made a vow of silence and now crowned with an iron pot on my head. The immense confidence I had just felt crashed, and emerged as its opposite. Suddenly, I didn't know who I was or what I was doing. Fear flooded my veins. But there was nothing for it and I continued to sit there, keeping up the front.

Several new people came in, and looked at me with raised eyebrows. One sat next to Ginny and asked, "What's the note on his robe say?" She looked up at me and said, "Oh, nothing at all." And everyone laughed.

Now the mockery began. The weakness I was feeling egged them on, and the room lit up with evil grins and condescending glances. I felt myself collapse, and lay down on the floor.

Then Don put on a recording of electronic sounds based on *The Tibetan Book of the Dead*. It was an attempt to record the sounds of breath and blood and heartbeat and fading consciousness that are heard in the ears of a dying man. I entered fully into the experience, and in my state of high suggestibility, I slipped into the state of expiration. I sank below the molecular level of consciousness and existed as a mass of electrons. I understood the universe, not intellectually, but experientially, as an electric phenomenon, and in a flash, the entire world of appearances melted like a rubber mask and was seen for the shadow show that it is.

And in the midst of this, a loud metallic laugh crashed across the room, and I sat up with a sob. I leapt through giant levels of consciousness in an instant, and it freaked me. Suddenly, I was convinced that I was actually physiologically dying. The usual thoughts went through my head. "I took too much peyote, I have strychnine poisoning," and so forth.

I jumped up and ran into the back yard, to be among the stars and trees and grass. If I was to die, it would at least be in the bosom of nature. I knelt down under the fig tree, and for the first time in years, attempted to pray. There are no atheists on bad trips. I felt hypocritical, for I had long ago discarded any belief in a personal God who listens to the words we think when we think we're praying. But I was desperate.

"Just let me make it through this time," I said, "and I'll never take dope again. I'll never pretend I'm a Zen monk again."

And as I prayed, a small thin voice in me said, "You liar. You know that if you make it through this one, you'll be back at the same old stand tomorrow."

The voice freaked me out. "Sshhh," I said to it. "He'll hear you."

And with that, a great ten-foot bookcase which had been brought out of the house and was standing solidly and in total stability by the side of the house, for no known physical reason, toppled over and fell onto the hard ground with a great resounding crash.

My hair stood on end. "All right," I said, "I lied. I'll be smoking grass again tomorrow. But just get me out of this one."

Then my spirit lightened, and the worst of it passed. I sat under the stars for over an hour, and then went back inside. The guests had left. I went past the alcove where John and Ginny were sleeping. John looked up. "Ginny can't sleep," he said. "Will you help me massage her?" It was clearly an invitation to a threesome. But Ginny was the one who had led the mockery of me earlier, and John had been no help at all. I was pissed off. I leaned over, drew their heads together with my hands, and leaned my forehead to touch the spot where their heads met. And then I took every bit of heaviness that was wracking my being, spewed it out of my third eye, and laid it right on them. They passed out immediately, and were depressed for three days afterward.

I walked into the kitchen. My vow of silence was growing unbearably oppressive. I got a flash on what it would be like to be locked inside my head for five years, never to let my voice out. I began to sweat, and went into the living room.

Don was still up. "Hey, man, want a joint?" he said. And in his eyes I saw actual concern, and remembered that he was the only one who hadn't turned against me, was the one who tried to communicate with me earlier in the evening. "Sure," I said. "Thanks." The words came out without thinking.

He smiled. "Hey," he said. "You're talking again. You had me worried for a while."

I sat and smoked with him a long while. The back of the nightmare was broken, and I felt waves of relief wash over me. Slowly, I returned to mundane perceptions. I took note of time and place. I made a resolve to telephone a friend in New York the next day.

Finally, Don lay down and fell asleep. I went into the bathroom, and curled up with my forehead against the cool tile floor.

"I'll just stay here until the dawn comes," I said to myself. For, no matter what else was insane in this universe, one thing was certain. The sun would rise. And with the sun, I would be all right again.

Within a short time, I heard the first bird sing. And then the sky grew light. And gratefully, I fell into a deep sleep.

A week later, I left Tucson.

8.

"JoJo left his home in Tucson, Arizona, for some California grass..."

And so it went. The Greyhound headed west, and I slept through the Mojave Desert. Breakfast in Los Angeles, sitting in a greasy spoon and watching Dada City come to life. Santa Barbara, and the first whiff of ocean, and then the long haul up the coast, watching the countryside change to green. Until a long cycle of thoughts later, I put my feet down on the concrete sidewalks of San Francisco.

My money was almost gone. I was burned black. I had lost fifteen pounds. And I needed desperately to recuperate. I slung my knapsack on my back, holding everything I owned in the world, and moved on up to Bernal Heights. I found Fred and Melissa at home.

Their game of separation and return had reached a crucial point. I arrived and immediately relaxed in the atmosphere of food, dope, and good vibrations which generally characterized their place. "I'm falling apart," I announced. "I need to stay here."

"Perfect," said Melissa. "We're going to Chicago to get married."

They had decided that since they would probably be living

together for a long time, they might as well get married in grand style, make Melissa's mother happy, and collect a couple of thousand dollars in wedding gifts. It was a form of polite robbery. Melissa's mother, whose fixed judgment on Fred was "dot bum," was less than overjoyed at her choice of marriage partner, but now at least had the chance to bully caterers, make countless arrangements, and crow before her relatives. I had met the woman once when she had visited Melissa some eight months earlier. She spent half an hour in the apartment, and when Melissa went to the store to buy some groceries, had come running into my place next door, grabbed me by the arm, and dragged me into Melissa's living room.

"Look at dis place," she said in the accent she had steadfastly refused to surrender after fifty years in this country. "Look at all dis shit." What she was referring to was the fact that Fred and Melissa had largely furnished their place with stuff they had picked up at the city dump. Most of it was the sort of furniture which, if refinished, would fetch nice prices as antiques. The style was funky. But Melissa's mother was adamant. "Look at how dey live." I was still sleepy, hadn't even been introduced to the woman, and wanted to escape from the scene. "It could be worse," I said politely. She drew herself up. "VOISE?" she said. "Vat could be voise dan to live like dis. DEAD could be voise."

And now the two of them were flying to Chicago to confront the dragon and come away with booty. They would be gone two weeks and I could have their apartment. The timing was perfect.

I saw them off a few days later, and then set about trying to find work. I went through the want ads in the *Chronicle,* with an ever growing sense of despair. There was nothing that didn't require some special dress or special skill. There seemed to be no need for retired Zen monks from Tucson.

But the next afternoon I went into the corner restaurant-bar, a kind of bohemian meeting place peopled by the entire spectrum of those living in the neighborhood, from hippies to Hell's Angels, from homosexuals to old Italians, from office workers to junkies. It boasted a good jukebox, fair prices, and an owner who had made the change from traditional to transitional modes. George was an Italian of about sixty who had dropped mescaline and grown a beard, and was able to expand the parameters of his awareness to make his place a home base for such disparate groups. He needed a dishwasher. It paid $1.75 an hour, free meals, and was only a two-block walk from home. I took it without hesitation.

It turned out to be the best job I'd ever had in my life. Unlike any of the so-called respectable jobs I'd had, such as teaching school or editing or doing therapy or translating, this one asked nothing of me except the labor of my hands. No one cared how I looked, or what I thought, or what my moods were. I was the lowest man on the ship, and with that position came a healing and blessed anonymity. It didn't take too long to learn the routine, and the actual mechanics of washing dishes involved a rhythm which soon became a kind of dance. I didn't have to talk unless I wanted to, and for that reason, my silence was a joy.

From six to eight, there was the beer-drinking crowd, and I had little to do except sweep and bring supplies from the larder. From eight to twelve, dinner was served, and I worked fairly steadily, doing hard labor for about forty-five minutes out of each hour. And from twelve to closing, it was back to beer and coffee, and the neighborhood regulars would come in. Almost always, someone would be playing a guitar or singing. And a few times a week, the Chicanos came in and made the air spicy with Spanish. When I wasn't working, I took long walks, or went to movies, or sat in the back yard and took the mild San Francisco sun. I got back into writing poetry again, and treated myself to a reading of the plays of Shakespeare in chronological order.

For the first time since I had left East Harlem, I felt part of a neighborhood. I got to know its gossip, its warmth and tragedy. Many of the young kids were deep into dropping downers and shooting speed, and I watched that entire generation waste away, for lack of knowing how to turn their energies into something that supported life, since nowhere in their society could they find a healthy channel for their youth drives.

Also, during that time, I met Abraham Rubin, a self-proclaimed Sufi master who looks, acts, and talks like an old Jewish tailor. I learned little about the details of his life except that he had traveled around the world many times, had been taught by Sufi and Zen masters, and was an "accredited" master in at least three schools. He actually had diplomas on his wall attesting to the fact that he was enlightened. But Abe was a goof. He was the kind of person who could pierce through to the heart of any given situation and understand the humanity of it instantly, but he was garrulous and cranky. He had a Sufi school where he presumably led young people into the mysteries of that sublime Middle Eastern way of life. On Sunday afternoons, he led his students in so-called Sufi dancing in front of hippie hill. Everything he did was once removed from the source, a mild unintentional parody on the real thing.

Still, Abe had a good rap. I went to his place a few times, to listen to his tales of confrontations with Zen masters in Kyoto monasteries, his travels through China and North Vietnam. "One thing I can tell you," he once said. "In any argument with a master from any school, a Sufi always wins." It was impossible to take him seriously, impossible not to love him. He wasn't what he claimed to be, but what he actually was, was so much more.

I got to know Paul better. Paul had taken so many drugs of so many varieties that he could hardly talk. His mannerism made him appear like an epileptic, and for a while I thought, as so many others did, that he was simply a ruined human being. But it took a while to see that as his body fell apart his mind and his heart got bigger. Paul's rap was largely unintelligible until one got into the inside of it, found its logic. And then one found the wisdom and humor of the man. His one line which has since proved a talisman to me at moments when I didn't know how to make it through was, "Stay with what you know."

Fred and Melissa came back and moved to a small town north of Mendocino. They were going to try to return to nature, away from the distractions of the city. I stayed in their place for over a month, and was feeling strong enough to make some new move, when Rita appeared once more in my life. She invited me to come stay with her in a small cabin in a redwood grove in San Rafael, north of the city. And on impulse, I quit my job and went.

It was an idyllic time, and the six weeks of it went a long way toward restoring my health and putting me in touch with my humanity once more. To wake up in the morning to the sound of birds, to step out into the majesty and empire of redwood trees, to have a substantial woman by one's side...life knows fewer more gratifying modes.

And then the letter arrived. It was from Georgia in Tucson. She was pregnant, on the basis of the one time we had made it together. I borrowed a VW from a friend and made the long journey back to the desert again. Leah had just returned from a two-week odyssey that ended with her working at a truck stop in Needles, and she wanted to get into the desert again, so she came with me. On the way south, we stopped to see Doris at her parents' in L.A. She had gone to Fred and Melissa's wedding, contracted hepatitis, and gone home to recuperate. At her place we found, of all people, Melissa. She and Fred had freaked out in their farmhouse, had had no friends to help absorb the shock, and had split up. Fred took off for Portland and Melissa went to visit Doris.

We spent a surrealistic evening in that house, with its countless rooms and swimming pool overlooking a smoggy valley. Doris' father was having a birthday party, and his guests were a dozen or so people who looked as though they had been sprayed with Krylon. The four of us stayed for a while, indulging ourselves in the fragmentary conversation, and then repaired to Doris' room to get stoned. The next morning we left, and Melissa decided to join us, so the three of us waved good-bye to Doris and the caravan continued.

The scene with Georgia was out of a bad movie. She was twenty-one, a warm and attentive girl, but very schizzy. The sensible thing to do would have been to have an abortion. But after three days in the Arizona sun, and with the overflow of good feeling that comes from being surrounded by three women, and a distinct failure of reason, I decided that Georgia and I would get married and we would settle in San Francisco. We got quite stoned, and headed for Nogales, where we spent an hour with some obscure Mexican official, in a room with a slow-revolving fan overhead, and filled out a long series of forms.

We went back to Tucson, where Georgia was living at the guest house of some wealthy people who had hired her to look after their cats while they were gone, and for a week we played in the swimming pool, smoked hash, and fucked. I went around renewing acquaintances, and enjoyed the city through the eyes of one visiting, not tripping out.

And then I had to leave, to get the car back. Also, I had an unspoken contract with Rita still hanging. I was now into my second legal marriage, the first one having taken place in Japan some ten years earlier, and annulled a year later. Life was once more beginning to edge toward a level of complication past my ability to deal with it. I left Georgia with the idea that I would write, and as soon as I got it together in San Francisco, would call for her. Secretly, I wondered how it would all turn out, for I was genuinely fond of the girl, as I was of Rita and for that matter, of Leah, and of a hundred other women I had known.

When I returned to San Francisco, chaos reigned. We left Melissa at the Tucson airport, from whence she was flying to Seattle to meet Fred, who had called and wanted a reconciliation. Leah and I pushed on, saw Doris again in L.A., and then spent two transcendental days winding slowly up Highway One, getting high on the grandeur of Big Sur. We stopped once to look down on Esalen to see if we could spit on the guard shack from the road. The night we arrived, Leah and I made love for the first time in half a year, and I returned to San Rafael in a good frame of mind, only to find that everyone was being evicted from the grounds. Rita was moving to San Geronimo, and I decided I didn't want to move with her. I crashed with Pan for a while until I could find work. I was ready to sacrifice anything to get a job, to put enough bread together to see whether Georgia and I might have a chance of bringing a child into the world.

I borrowed a suit from Charlie Winston whose wife and kid had shared my place for a month some time back. He was now teaching school, and making great efforts to look straight so they wouldn't fire him. I took a few of my remaining dollars, bought some shoes and a pair of socks, got a white shirt from Paul and found a tie in the garage under Fred and Melissa's old place, and was ready to step once more into the world of commerce.

I decided to try office temporaries. They are the most rapacious of the lot, but they always have work, and are not too scrupulous about the appearance of the people they hire. I typed up my résumé, rearranging the dates and leaving out half the jobs I had held so it would appear that I was a stable and serious person, and marched into the offices of Career Opportunities Unlimited on Market Street.

Doing the scene required no little acting skill or courage, for I was actually beginning to feel the bite of desperation. I believed the myth that one can't starve to death in America, but there was nothing in the national propaganda which guaranteed that one couldn't become a total wreck, barely subsisting, shunned by one's former friends, and thrown into jail with some regularity. The important thing at the time was that I had lost the *ability* to pull myself together in any meaningful way. I could only manage a bare disguise, manipulating makeup and costume to make me seem normal in the eyes of my fellow citizens, whose criteria were not based on compassion but on profit. America had no space for failures. And it was the mark of my personal failure that I had descended to the level of judging myself by the same standards Americans used, that is, could I hold down a job?

I sat in front of the interviewer's desk and played the role. She was a trim, tight chick of about twenty-three. Probably had a boy friend who didn't fuck her right, and lived in a two-and-a-half on Potrero Hill. It was odd to sit there, doing psychological and sociological analysis of the women I had to grovel in front of in order to get some menial job. I realized that just a few months earlier, when I was flying high, I could have hypnotized her, done pretty much what I wanted with her, and left at my leisure. Now, I felt as though my cock had been cut off.

My job skills were amorphous. Given the right costume, I could have walked into an executive editorial spot with a high salary. But there was almost no editorial work in San Francisco, except for house organs and trade journals, and I would have starved before taking another job such as I had at *Americana*. Luckily, out of everything in my life which I had learned, the thing that I took as most inconsequential came to save me: I could type eighty words a minute. This, in the eyes of the office temporary mind, gave me status. "It'll call you when we have something," she said.

That afternoon, she phoned in with a job that had nothing to do with typing skills, and at eight o'clock the following morning, I reported to the mail room of one of California's largest businesses. The last time I had worked in a mail room was in New York at the age of twenty-four, when a similar dip in fortune sent me scurrying for the least complex form of employment. The man in charge here had the exact same personality as my previous boss, that of a sergeant who knew more about running the base than the commanding officer. The firm, he informed me with no little pride, received and sent more mail than any other organization in northern California. The mail room was the size of a football field, and had scores of machines for collating, wrapping, stamping, sorting, and shredding. Some fifty people worked there, mostly women who were Mexican or Puerto Rican, and some ten boys ranging in age from seventeen to forty. For most of them, this was a career opportunity, and the day I spent there was a complete education in the mores of the déclassé lower middle class.

To call what we did there "work" is misleading, for work implies some necessity for intelligence. There, the machines did the work, and we served the machines. It was the sheerest drudgery. Daily, hundreds of thousands of envelopes were processed through, and half as many small packages. I was again informed, with some élan, that the workers were given two fifteen-minute coffee breaks, a full forty-five minutes for lunch, and received free hospitalization. At the end of one year, one received two weeks paid vacation. The place drove home the reason why the term "wage slave" has been expunged from the American vocabulary, although conditions were clearly an improvement over their sweatshop equivalent in the garment district in New York. The long window against one wall provided a stunning view of downtown San Francisco. I imagined that if one were basically robotic, this was not a bad job, and brought us one step further in our frantic attempt to emulate the civilization of the ants.

But it wasn't my scene. My call from the agency had indicated that this was to be a two-week stint, yet when I left that afternoon I knew there was no going back. I couldn't face another day of the routine, the empty eyes of the people there, and the benign deadly efficiency of the mail room boss. It was as though everything in the place, every human feeling, every fleshy vibration, had been coated with a thin veneer of plastic, so that we smiled and spoke like people, but were in reality mannikins, programmed to a single task.

The next day I showed up at the agency and asked for another assignment. The chick fixed me with a stare that let me know that I should be grateful for the chance she gave me—two weeks of work (and I flashed the stories of the Depression my father had told me)—and that my leaving the job was a black mark against me. I let my eyes fill with silent pleading, and she decided to give me one more chance. "Here's something perhaps more suitable for you," she said. "It's a computer programming company."

The next day I appeared at the offices of Amalgamated Electronics, a squat seven-story building with almost no windows, resolved in my heart to do better. I would show the agency that I could succeed. While part of me was able to laugh at my situation, the other part felt sick with anxiety. Living with Pan was a chore, and if I couldn't take it there, I really had no place else to crash, at least, no place where I would be received graciously, or which didn't entail some emotional contract. And I couldn't sustain another period of sleeping on the floor in the corner of some pad in the Haight. I had to make money!

The job I was given made the work in the mail room seem the soul of spontaneity. I was handed a pile of punch cards, and an equal pile of typewritten sheets. Each of the sheets had a more or less cryptic message written on it, and what I was to do was copy the messages onto the punch cards, printing in capital letters, putting one letter in each of the hundred squares on the cards. It was something such as might be given to a kindergarten student to have him practice the alphabet. I sat down, listened carefully to the instructions, feeling like one of the contestants on Beat the Clock. Later, I was to sense myself more like a chimpanzee in a bizarre psychological experiment. And still later, like a reject from a mental hospital doing the only form of work of which he was capable. I rolled up my sleeves, and began.

In a very short time, I realized that the work load was so planned as to keep me busy every second of the time. I didn't have to rush, but neither could I slow down. I had to assume the untiring pace of a machine. Looking around, I saw my would-be peers, middle-class college graduates, each in his or her own cubicle, bored, wan, trapped. Their job was to write the messages which I was copying onto the cards. It was as though we were the middle components of some insane conveyer belt, transferring dada messages from an obscure source to an equally obscure end.

I went into a light trance and worked straight through, being interrupted by a tap on the shoulder for lunch and for each of the two fifteen-minute coffee breaks. At one point, the pile of messages disappeared, and I ground to an abrupt halt. I looked up and realized that I had finished. I walked up to the lady who had started me off in the morning. "Are there any more?" I asked. She looked up, puzzled. "No…" she said. And then, "Are you finished?" She looked up at the clock; it was twenty-five before five.

She gave me the kind of smile that teachers for the mentally retarded reserve for their most industrious students. "You finished ahead of time!" she cooed. "Why, that's marvelous."

To my intense surprise, I swelled with inane pride. It was the first word of praise for an accomplishment that I had received in months. And it was for an honest labor, however mindless. I almost kissed her hand. "Can I come back tomorrow?" I asked hopefully.

Her face fell. "No, I'm sorry. That's all the work we'll have for a while. Our regular girl is coming in tomorrow."

We stayed like that for a long moment. Then she added, "But if we need someone again, I'll tell the agency to make sure to send you." She looked up at the clock again, and as though she were handing me a star for my report card, said, "Why, you might as well leave early. After all, you've earned it."

I walked out whistling in my private dark. I felt weighed down by the vision of millions upon millions of people working day in and out at these a-human tasks. At the same time, I had earned almost twenty-five dollars between the two jobs. My fortune was improving. I walked around downtown a bit, and feeling exceptionally flush, decided to go to the Stud Turkish Bath. I thought that a steam bath, and the possibility of some sex, would add a nice touch to the day.

I climbed the velvet corridor, paid my four dollars, and entered that equally, but differently, bizarre world. I paid for a room, and as I turned to go upstairs, I saw a sign on the wall: HELP WANTED. A number of things fell into place at once. I inquired about the job, and learned that it paid two dollars an hour to start, and involved scrubbing down the steam rooms, cleaning the johns, vacuuming the halls, and in general being available for odd assignments. I would be working under an old black cat who had been doing this for ten years. I filled out an application, was introduced to the manager, and, using the proper jargon, tone of voice, and seductive glances, got the job. I was to report in two days.

Now, visiting the baths is different from working in them, although I was to learn that the hard way. They are open twenty-four hours a day, and are the nearest thing we have in our times to the classic Roman model. Baths across the nation range from the utterly vile to the totally sophisticated, and the Stud fell somewhere in between. It stood near an S&M bar with whips and leather jocks hung over the liquor bottles. The Stud was considered kinkier than the other baths in the city, which appealed mostly to the straighter homosexuals.

One of the first things I noticed when I started working there was that there was no way to tell the time of day other than looking at a clock. The windows were painted black, and the lighting never changed. It had the ambience of Purgatorio. People walked up and down the hallways, peering into the open rooms, in a slow rhythm, as though bearing some great secret burden. Except for late weekend nights, when there were wild carryings-on in the mass public bedroom downstairs. There were three stories of hallway, and off each hallway were scores of doors, each opening to a little room, some six by ten feet, which had a cot, a closet, and a spittoon. Part of my job was washing down the rooms at specified intervals. The job level above mine involved changing the linen in the rooms after each client left; and the highest job was taking money at the door and assigning keys.

The work itself was bestial. We had two hours to scrub down three steam and shower rooms, using ammonia and a great, stiff-bristled brush. The man I worked with was muscled like a discus thrower, but by the second day I realized that the job was at the limit of my physical capacity. I had a flash on using the job as a weight lifter uses exercises, and might have stayed with the strain of it, but the psychic heaviness did me in. All day, up and down they walked. Lonely men, horny men, confused men, sexually charged men. Wearing red towels around their waists. Their feet made slapping sounds on the floor as they walked. Whoever gave the name "gay" to the homosexual world had a cruel sense of irony. For the gaiety was all superficial, all hysterical. Mostly, there was pain.

Previously, going to the baths, I had entered either to bathe or to fuck, and from my goal-oriented viewpoint, missed the larger sense of the place. Now I had a privileged position. It was house policy that none of the workers could have sex with the patrons, and it was strictly enforced. To get the job, I had to have mug shots taken for the police files, since the baths walked a thin line between respectability and illegality. The police knew what went on there, and were nervous about it, but since it was all discreet, and since everyone was "a consenting adult," they pretty much left the place alone. Of course, that there were pay-offs went without question.

So, the customers began to approach me, but not for sex; instead, they began to talk. And I learned many stories. The one thing which emerged most clearly is that there is no difference between heterosexuals and homosexuals. They have the same range of problems, from impotence to promiscuity, struggles with fidelity, guilt. They have the same joys, the same fears. And they completely share the general sexual sickness of the nation.

In one thing there is a difference. The homosexual community, by and large, is much more upfront about its condition. Especially in a place like the baths, where one thing is admitted right out. Everyone is there for sex, pure and simple. It was not unusual to have a three- or four-hour intense, intimate, and totally satisfying sexual encounter with another person with whom one did not exchange a word. In may ways, there was a greater honesty here, for in its essence, sex is not between personalities, and it is not necessary to know the name of the person one is fucking.

Of course, fucking gives rise to feelings of tenderness and warmth, and in the meat rack, these feelings are suppressed and ignored. But this is no different from the cruising that is done in heterosexual bars, at parties, in the suburbs, and up and down every stratum of our culture.

For the first time, I entered the gay social community. Up to then, my encounters had been only sexual. Even when I went to gay bars, it was only to cruise. And my observations were private ones. For example, it is possible to see the entire anthropology of the American male by spending an evening in a gay bar. Of course, as Gurdjieff notes, one can't understand another human being without *agreeing* with that human being. And that means, to know what it means to be homosexual, one has to be homosexual. Any psychologist attempting to deal with homosexuality who has not himself sucked a cock is a hypocritical liar, and ought to be arrested for malpractice.

My experience with Tommy that night in the Circle Hotel had been the first time I had cracked the barrier of mixing sex with friendship. Now, however, I began to get involved in the lives of my fellow workers. I began to enter into the affairs and marriages of these men. One of the men who worked at the Stud had been married for seven years, an unusual thing in the gay world, and when he spoke of his home, it was with all the love and fervor that any happily married heterosexual would show. I found myself going to private gay clubs, and discovering all the social roles which exist in a world of dancing, and loving, and living, and working, with one's fellowman. And within a short time, my chameleon personality being what it is, I became gay. That is to say, I assumed the ambience of a homosexual. My clothes changed, my way of talking altered, I even walked differently. Not that I wanted to become swish, but that all the soft, undulating aspects of my psychophysical self came to the fore.

It was then that I had to make a decision. I knew that if I continued to work there, I would soon make my way up the hierarchy, first to room boy, then to desk clerk, and on into the bar, and higher echelons of the organization, which embraced stag movies, bookstores, and branched into design, art, and all aspects of the civilization. And I decided against it. Not because I had any prejudice against the gay life; it was in many ways more gentle and humane than that offered by the straight world. But I couldn't accept having come so far, experienced so much, broken through so many barriers, to exchange the straight establishment for the gay establishment.

Already I could see that this world had its own mores, its own codes, its own taboos. The maverick in me was too strong. If I was to be homosexual or bisexual or heterosexual or orgiastic or celibate, it would have to be an ad hoc decision, based on the promptings of my instincts at any given time. I wanted to hang no social identification tags around my neck. Also, there was a horrible moment when, coming out of the S&M bar, I saw three young girls passing on the street, and my heart filled with dread at the idea that I would never have a woman again. To make a choice which sexually rules out half the human race seemed idiotic.

And so, I walked in one afternoon and tendered my resignation. It was met with regret by the men whom I had come to know as co-workers and friends and lovers. I had made enough money to tide me over for a while, and wanted to take a week or so to plan my next move. The letters from Georgia were getting frantic, and I knew that I had to find some way to bring her to the city, or else go back to Arizona, or else tell her to have an abortion and call the whole thing off.

That night, I dropped by to visit Leah and found her in bed with a dropout psychiatrist named Steve. I sat down and the three of us got stoned for a few hours and Steve began talking about some friends of his who were setting up a new psychiatric ward on the Peninsula. It was to be a blowout center, based on the type that R. D. Laing had set up at Kingsley Hall in England. I became interested at once. I had read Laing two years earlier, and had been much turned on by his words. He had dropped acid and come to see how rotten psychiatry is at its core, and set about doing something to change it. During the course of it, he flipped out a few times, and met with such resistance from his fellow doctors that his work remained limited to what he himself was able to accomplish.

Now a radical—radical, of course, only within the context of the Neolithic psychiatric community—wing was being opened, and the people running it were looking for staff members. They wanted people who had taken acid, or who were into an Esalen bag, or who had establishment credentials and wanted to do more than the establishment allowed. Steve told me a bit about it, and I felt the call. It sounded like just what I needed. It would pay about a hundred dollars a week, and give me a chance to get back into my relaxation work as well as use my knowledge of drugs. Also, it would allow me to come to terms with my own insanity.

"Give Al Feldman a call," said Steve. "He lived with me in Ukiah, and he'll be the ward psychiatrist there."

"I'll do that," I said.

The next day I called Al and with that began a trip which almost destroyed my mind.

9.

Al is a gentle Scorpio. Like many doctors who get bored with the routine of general medicine, he went into psychiatry. The way that scene is set up in this country, an MD has to know very little by way of formal psychological training, and needs absolutely no qualifications by way of sensitivity, warmth, humanity, or perceptiveness to start playing with people's minds. About the only formal requirement is an internship in a mental hospital, but this is usually spent filling out forms and walking through the wards at a rapid pace. A doctor, to be a psychiatrist, only has to hang out a shingle proclaiming himself one. And the one advantage these inept witch doctors have over their lay therapist cousins is that they can prescribe pills.

But like a number of other psychiatrists, Al had dropped acid, and got a flash on what a con game the whole business is. The professional posture, the mask of objectivity, the jargon, the rituals, the high fees. And he became concerned enough to want to actually help his suffering fellow human beings. Of course, the acid insights took him to a realm of compassion which his level of self-knowledge could not make effective. He saw more than he could handle.

He was living with Larry, another dropout shrink who sported long sideburns, a cowboy hat and boots, and a general air of insouciance. Harish was also there, an enlightened Pakistani who looks like Meher Baba; Carol, Harish's wife; and a constant stream of friends, crashers, well-wishers, and family. It was one of the warmest, most-together households I had ever seen.

I made an appointment to meet Al at the hospital. I arrived in the early afternoon and was charmed by the physical layout of the place. The weather was ideal, in the middle seventies, dry, with a slight breeze. The buildings were new and the grounds were immaculate. Almost everyone walking around was a patient or a staff member, the former practically all on Thorazine, and drifting about in a peaceful haze. At one point, a few weeks later, I saw two patients get into a fist fight, but they were so drugged on that horse tranquilizer that they fought in dreamy slow motion, making the whole scene unreal in the hot afternoon. If it weren't so pathetic, it would have been funny.

My interview was with Al, Harish, and Teresa, who was a research psychologist. I was somewhat apprehensive because I felt that this was the perfect place for me to be, and I didn't want to blow the chance. We chatted a bit, and then Al said, "What is your fantasy about working here?"

I thought a bit about it and answered very slowly. "I've been crazy a few times," I said. "I mean, I've been in a place where I was trapped in what felt like eternal suffering, where no other person could ever reach me, and which I couldn't communicate to anyone. And when I took acid, I realized that it was possible for me to go over that edge and never come back, I mean, to be in such anguish that my behavior would seem mad to everyone around me, and they would put me away. And then I read Laing, and he made sense. When he said, 'If a person has one human being to talk to, then he's no longer crazy,' I realized that he had put his finger right on the issue, without any bullshit. Because I'm convinced that insanity has no objective definition. In the East they say, 'The only difference between a schizophrenic and a holy man is that the schizophrenic doesn't realize that he's holy.'

"I heard about Laing's blowout center in England, and I wanted to go there. From what I can gather, a person who is having a psychotic break is allowed and encouraged to see it through to the end, and the therapist does nothing but stay with him, giving him someone to talk to, like a guide on an acid trip. And I thought, if I could blow out like that, really go crazy once, just let it all hang out, look at it, feel it and taste it, then I would be free of the fear, and there would be no places left in my mind that were dark corners.

"My fantasy about this place is that there won't be any difference between patient and staff, that we'll all be just people trying to help each other out of our pain and confusion. And that the people who work here will be able to freak out and get in touch with their own craziness. That we won't dull anyone's head with Thorazine, but really put our guts on the line to help one another through our bad trips.

"My ultimate fantasy is of a place where everyone understands that on the highest level there is no crazy or sane, no good or bad, but just this fact of life."

Harish eyed me thoughtfully. "Are you familiar with any esoteric work?" he said.

"I studied with the Gurdjieff Foundation in New York," I said, encapsulating that entire complex experience into a single sentence.

"Ah," he said, and closed his eyes. He said no more for the rest of the time that I was there.

"What do you expect you can do at the ward?" Teresa asked.

"I don't know," I said. "Mostly just be there, get into people's heads, let myself hang out, find out whether I can work with relaxation and massage as a means to getting people out of their bad trips."

There was a general nodding of heads, in proper interview style, and then we all rapped a bit more about the whole psychiatry trip and I told them something of what I had done and been doing. We talked about drugs and politics and in general got a sense of one another's psychic space.

Then Al laid the trip on me. "The hospital has received a grant to do a study on the effectiveness of new modes of therapy, something in the area of a quarter of a million dollars. We're setting up a wing in conjunction with Marvin Goldman, who's doing a research study. The trip is to find out whether patients improve more quickly using our approach."

"More quickly than what?" I asked.

Al looked a bit embarrassed. "Than if they are given Thorazine," he said. "Half the patients on the ward will be on the drug, and half won't."

Several things struck me as being out of joint. First of all,

Marvin Goldman was a research specialist for Esalen, and I had a deep mistrust of anyone from that organization. Secondly, he had the reputation of being a career hustler, and of being clinically paranoid. Third, the study was to last for five years, and I wondered whether there might not be more emphasis on it than on the actual condition of the people we would be working with.

But some of my fears were quieted when Al told me about the rest of the staff. A few would be straight nurse types from the hospital roster. About a third would be ward attendants who had had their fill of the way things were done at mental institutions, and had volunteered for this new program. And the rest would be acid heads, odd guru types, and assorted freaks. "I think we'd like to have you with us," said Al. "But first I'd like to introduce you to Richard."

He took me to meet Richard Kaprow, the project director. He was an extremely successful psychiatrist, working his way up into the higher echelons of California's hierarchy of mental hospitals. He had just enough humanity left to want to see a program like the blowout center succeed, for he truly understood the horror of the current treatments. But he was a most fearful man, afraid at every moment that some catastrophe would split the foundations of his career. He spent a good deal of time piloting his private plane to and from Sacramento to have conferences with state officials. When he spoke, his eyes were always gazing a little above the tips of his shoes. And when he got excited, his voice took on an unmistakable whine.

The first thing he said to me was, "We don't have the funds to pay you a salary yet. We're expecting them to be cleared through Sacramento any day, but we can't give you any salary until they come in." Three months later, the funds still hadn't arrived, but I was past the point of caring. I had other problems.

For now, it seemed that I had a job, something I would like, getting my head straight, and helping other people out of their own dark bags. I went back to San Francisco feeling high.

I moved into the Berkeley House a week later, and began going to the hospital regularly, to attend the many meetings which had to happen before the ward could open. I was on very good behavior, to the point of blinding myself to some obvious facts. The ward was to be in the very middle of the state hospital, with its window bars and police, its atmosphere of repression and debilitating drugs. The people I was meeting did not seem to be the types who would lay their hearts and minds on the line to help anyone out of a bad trip. And the project very early got mired in an immense bueaucratic tangle. But I didn't want to see any of this.

One of my excursions produced a meeting with Alistair Frazier, a prominent Jungian analyst with a list of books and papers to his credit. Alistair was a super-civilized man, thoroughly rational, with a dilettante's love for the pathological. He had a rich appreciation of insanity, and could talk for hours on the symbolism of madness. In fact, he and Marvin Goldman had worked up a two-man act which fetched a stiff fee at Esalen weekends, dealing with such fluff as "the poetry of madness," and "the science of madness." Still, I liked him immensely, for he was warm and charming and highly intelligent. He was going to act as a visiting father confessor to the ward, dropping in once a week to lay some sheets of wisdom on us from his storehouse of clinical experience. He had never taken LSD, a fact I found curious in a man who was supposedly involved in understanding the intricacies of the human mind. Like they say, he *talked* a good game.

My money was running out again, and the ward was coming together. Finally, the day of the big meeting came, and some fifty of us met to discuss our future. In that first meeting, as is usually the case, the entire outcome of the scene was projected, had any one of those supposedly therapeutic hotshots had the perspicacity to see it. Most of the people there were sincere, but not one of us had the presence of mind to call attention to the essential dishonesties which began from the very first moment. I saw them, but had no way to articulate them.

For one thing, the meeting was boring. We spent a good deal of time talking *at* one another and not *with* one another. Much of the talk involved schedules, pay rates ("Do I get listed as an Assistant Seven or Nine for this project?"), and administration. It followed the pattern of all such meetings, with the usual waves of inattention, irascibility, and ego-tripping.

And then the big question was asked: What of our relations with the hospital at large? How would the administration feel about a revolutionary ward on their grounds, a ward where there would be no locks on the doors? A tremor of insurrection ran through the crowd, for everyone here had the sense that we were participating in some form of radical activity. A true revolutionary is someone who understands all the ramifications of the condition in which he finds himself, from the economic to the psychologic to the cosmic, and who has made the inner decision that he has nothing to lose, having come to the conclusion that the existing order has no redeeming value whatsoever and must be destroyed. Yet, for all their pretty ways, most of these people were protecting their salaries, their apartments, their status. And those who weren't were worse, for they were the Kaprows, the Goldmans, the Fraziers, who were still climbing the ladder to greater power and prestige.

Now, however, everyone let out with great vocal complaints against the barbarity of the current treatment of the mentally ill, and on this issue the group found its cohesiveness. Within a few minutes, the place sounded like an angry PTA meeting. And then Marvin stepped in. "We are not at war with the hospital," he said. "In fact, we depend on them for a good many services, for food, for garbage collection, for linen. We need their goodwill, and our task will be to educate them to what we're doing." All of this was true, but seemed to sidestep the basic question which was, how to run a free ward in the middle of a mental concentration camp?

Marvin swept the meeting with his eyes. "I want to hear no further talk of revolution," he said. "The most important aspect of this project is the research, and nothing must stand in the way of that." He stood up. "I want to hear no wild language," he continued. "We must protect the research project, no matter what else happens."

Al and Harish exchanged knowing glances, but no one said anything.

And then Marvin told us what the scene would be. Each of us would be assigned to several patients for observation. We would be given forms on which to check off patients' behavior and attitude. We would have to write reports of what they did and how they seemed to be feeling.

"But that goes against the very nature of what the ward is about," someone protested. "How can we relate to them as equals if we are making out reports on their supposed progress?"

"I admit that's a problem," said Marvin with that oily smile which can be so disarming. "But we'll work on it. Just don't anyone forget that the research is what pays our salaries, despite any utopian ideas you may have."

In a flash I saw the dream of the blowout center go up in

smoke. The place I had pictured, a secluded house in the woods where the poisons of civilization wouldn't reach, disappeared, and suddenly I was in a dismal gray hospital room with a bunch of timid and confused people, listening to yet another petty dictator lay down the laws by which we would have to live. The vision was so horrid that I immediately squashed it and returned my attention to the mechanics of the meeting.

Which was degenerating into squabbles concerning the effectiveness of research done with paper and pencil techniques. But this was merely the mumbling of the troops; the essential point had been driven home. In a while, Richard smoothed things over with an appeal for us to all pull together and put this project over the top. "In three days," he said, "we open the ward. Ward Sixteen. And I'll see you all there."

At this point, my fantasy life and my objective condition were coming together in a weird way. As I began to get involved with the intricacies of insanity, my social existence began to fall apart. Without a car in California, I was like a man without a canteen on the desert. I began to watch each penny I spent. I had no basis upon which to maintain friendships, since I could find no center inside myself.

When the ward opened, I was put on the daytime schedule. Yet, the whole idea of schedule bothered me, for my image of a blowout center was that the staff members would more or less live-in, timing their hours with the needs of the patients. At the Berkeley house, we had had many discussions about breaking down the artificially constructed chronology on the ward. As it stood, three times a day, no matter what else was happening, an entirely new shift walked in at eight-hour intervals. Naturally, after a while, the people on the ward ceased paying attention to their inner flow and adjusted to the demands of the clock. Shift-change time. Feeding time. Recreation time. Play therapy time. And so on.

This is, after all, the essential sickness of the civilization, this trifling with schedules while life goes begging. We concern ourselves with the superficial, with the style, with the details, with the mere appearance of things, and miss the fact of being. If a person can hypnotize himself with some compulsive ritual which he calls his "daily routine," then he can excuse himself for all the things he does not perceive. Is this not the core of the Eichmann mentality, this ability to deal with life as though it were a series of reports on paper, and be purposively blind to the reality which these symbols supposedly represent. Jumping, as I always do, to the logical conclusion of any activity, I began accusing the staff of having a Nazi mentality, and already, in those early days, they began to think I was crazy.

There was not a person there who seemed ready to devote more than the compulsory eight hours out of every day. Such was my need and enthusiasm, and such was the real desire on the part of many of the people to do the best they could, that I didn't take the precaution of protecting my vulnerabilities. The notion of living-in was picked up by Dan Winters, an executive of Esalen. Dan had, myth told it, flipped out some time earlier, and spent a long time in seclusion in Big Sur, talking to whales off the coast. He was now billed as Esalen's official schizophrenic, or to put it in their own terminology, "a real heavy." He arrived a week after the ward opened, slept there one night, and spent the next day screaming at Al for what a poor job he was supposedly doing. He disappeared that afternoon and never returned. I asked Bill, the chief ward psychologist, what the story was. "Dan split," he said. "He said there wasn't enough action for him here." I was somewhat taken aback to hear the ward spoken of in terms of a gambling casino, but such was the way of it.

It became impossible to drive all the way in from Berkeley with Al every day because of our conflicting schedules. I wasn't ready to be the first person to move in on the ward; my mind was shaky enough as it was. At this point, a beautiful, tall, long-haired and bearded cat came up to me, a man by the name of Joel. And then things began to change. Joel said I could crash at his pad until my money came through, and then I might find a place in town.

Joel spoke little. He was a veteran of several hundred acid trips; he was so much on top of the drug and his own scene that he headed the East Bay Drug Rescue Center. This was one of the services offered by the city's underground *head* community, and involved being on call twenty-four hours a day to rescue people from bad trips. He described his work as the Giggle Patrol. "I go into a place where everyone is freaking out, and get everybody to giggling and then, when the vibes are up again, I ask what the trouble was." Singlehandedly, without education or training, he provided the most effective, rational, intelligent, and humane approach to the psychology of drug use that I had ever seen.

Joel and I soon came to form the hub of the radical elements on the ward. Al was sympathetic, but still hung up on his psychiatrist image. Also, he had a legal responsibility which kept him tied down. Harish was hip, but had his detachment bit going, which is to say, whenever it came down to really getting involved with another person's pain, he claimed cosmic indifference and removed himself. And most everyone else on the staff was hanging in, waiting for the scene to develop in one direction or another.

Develop it did. We got the ward set up, but with a few surprises. The head nurse, Donna, was presented to us by the hospital administration. The hospital wanted the ward to succeed because of the prestige of having such a huge grant, but they were extremely suspicious and wanted to keep their hand in. Donna was the middle finger of that hand, pointed straight up.

From the first, things went badly. We were to have had an open-door policy. That is to say, since all the patients were volunteers, theoretically they should be able to come and go as they pleased. If they split, they would just be returned to the wards they came from. But more importantly, having the doors open would give the patients a sense of humanity which is removed when they are locked in like prisoners. Also, it would remove from the staff the onerous task of being in charge of keys, and give the place a true sense of democratic equality. It was, in fact, the *sine qua non* for the success of a blowout center.

But the hospital said no. And at our first general meeting on the ward—we had two each day, with both staff and patients supposedly attending—the issue was discussed. The patients came in hopefully. For the first time in years many of them had a glimmering hope that their lives could be different. Here were people who, they were told, would not lock them up, shoot them up with massive doses of deadening dope, think they were crazy, or scream at them. And the symbolic proof of this was to be the open door. The open door! The simple freedom to step outside the confines of the building and breathe fresh air whenever one wanted! Such a simple thing, and so glorious!

And at the first meeting, the hope was squashed. They had come with a backlog of suspicion, for from the viewpoint of the mental inmate, society at large is brutal, deceptive, unperceptive, and unfeeling. It was vital, therefore, not to give fuel to that suspicion. And yet, at that very first crucial moment, Richard walked in and threw gallons of gasoline on the flames. There was much hemming and hawing and sidestepping, but finally one of the patients yelled, "Will the door be open or not?"

There was a long pause and then Richard said, "I'm sorry, but you will continue to be locked in."

All of the patients but three walked out of the meeting. Those who remained were Nick, a fifty-five-year-old professional psychotic who had been drifting up and down the insane asylum circuit for years, following the sun from Mendocino to Phoenix; Loren, a brilliant young paranoid with a cutting edge of cynicism; and Bruce, a hopeless ass-kisser. The staff was furious, and when the patients left, we began to vent our anger. Richard turned up his palms. "What can I do?" he said.

Marvin rose to his feet. "Anyway, it would interfere with the research to have them coming and going as they pleased. Maybe, once we have the schedule down pat, we can give them some more freedom.

Someone asked, "And when may that be, Marvin?"

He smiled, "We'll just have to wait and see."

Alice, usually a very mild-mannered woman, spoke up. "But what about these people we're supposed to be helping? They need help *now*. What will the research tell us that we don't already know?"

"Well," said Richard, "that all may be true, but the reality is that the doors will stay locked. And that's the way it is."

And indeed, that was the way it was.

Interestingly, since my money hadn't come through yet, I was still officially on a volunteer basis as far as the record was concerned, and as a volunteer, I wasn't allowed to have a key either. From the first, I was on a par with the patients in having to ask permission to be let out each time I wanted to take a walk or go to the snack bar. This put me in a mind-bending place. For one moment, I would be a staff member, sitting in the psychologist's office rapping with the brass, and the next I would have to go begging to be let out. There was one difference, however. When the patients asked to be "given grounds," they were often refused, but I was always let out. Very early I found myself formulating the thought, "What if I weren't so sure that I would be let out each time? What would it be like to be locked in here?" And from that moment, I began to change my viewpoint, I began to understand what it is like to be a patient in a mental hospital, to have one's liberties, one by one, stripped away, to be treated like an inferior human being. It was a split in perception that would be healed only when I had gone completely around the bend.

I busied myself with my work, thinking that the other problems were beyond my control, foolishly thinking that the central issue of freedom could, somehow, be swept under the rug. At times Al and I would rap about the ward, and get all liquored up on our visions of what it could be like. But he was as helpless in his way as I was in mine. Or Joel and I would get stoned and dream up visions of starting a Schizophrenic Liberation Front. Joel was very heavily into the revolutionary currents around the Bay Area. Like all true revolutionaries, he didn't belong to any group. He just did the good work wherever he found it needed to be done. From his experience in hospitals, I began to get some idea of what the scene was in the psychotic underground, and his reports were later corroborated by my own experiences.

For example, as with any subculture, the total society was mirrored. There were the dropouts like Nick who wandered from asylum to asylum. He would sit for hours, rolling cigarettes, not saying a word. And every once in a while he would look up and say, to no one in particular, "Fuck them, they ain't getting any from me." At first I didn't understand him, but when I realized that most of the people who worked on the wards were psychic vampires, sucking energy from the patients, I came to appreciate his refusal to get involved in any of the actually insane games played by so-called sane society. He never participated in psychodrama or music therapy or any of the other inane games provided for the inmates by people who would shit purple turds if they ever got the slightest flash on what it really is to be mad.

Then there were the "good patients," like Bruce, the broken product of a gently vicious Jewish mama. He was in constant inner pain, and continually hoped, somehow, that the doctors would cure him so he could go back to school and get a job and get married. He was thoroughly homosexual, but the only sex he ever knew was lonely masturbation late at night. Whenever any of the staff passed by, he would look up like a puppy, smiling, hoping for a gram of attention.

There were the radicals, like Loren. Loren had memorized most of Blake, and could zap a person's mind with unerring quotations at the apt moment. During our raps, he would spin out analyses of the American culture which made Marcuse seem like an infant in his understanding. The difference between Loren and any political philosopher was that Loren *was the living experience* of the way in which our society cripples people. He was it. He knew.

The only problem with Loren was that he was crazy. That is to say, his unhappiness would get past his ability to sustain it, and he would have to do things which seemed inexplicable to anyone who didn't understand him, which included almost everyone on the ward. Every once in a while, he would get up and methodically and calmly break every window-glass on the ward.

Once, in the middle of his act, I went up to him. "What's happening, man?" I said.

SMASH. Another pane of glass.

"Do you know that Donna is a witch?" he said.

"Sure," I said.

SMASH. Another window.

"People have the wrong idea about witches," he said. "They think a witch is a funny lady with a hooked nose and a conical cap."

"That's a historical error," I said. "People don't understand the notion of witch as a psychological model."

SMASH.

"Why are you breaking windows, Loren?" I said.

He turned and looked at me. "Well, you know, I have to," he said. "Do you understand?"

"Sure, I understand," I said, and did, because there were many times when I needed to break windows but just didn't have the courage to do it.

"But you know," I said, "they may put you back on Thorazine and throw you into your old ward."

He stopped for a moment. "That's too bad," he said. "I hate being on that stuff. It makes me feel like I'm buried alive."

SMASH. And he went on breaking windows.

I decided to give classes in relaxation. They were a qualified success. I couldn't give them outdoors because Thorazine makes one's skin ultrasensitive to sunlight. Indoors was difficult because there was always someone bustling around, some schedule to be met, some hassle to be dealt with. And there was the further problem of the delicacy of the condition.

As soon as a person lets go and begins breathing, the first thing he contacts is the anxiety he had been suppressing by holding his breath. And the last thing these people needed was to have their anxiety liberated in a scene where it couldn't be dealt with. The entire notion of blowing out had been shelved in light of the interpersonal and administration problems we were facing, and in light of the great open-door defeat.

I set up a small room to hold individual sessions, and was told that I was blocking a fire exit. With that, and the lack of continuity from day to day, my classes became less frequent.

Our daily meetings continued to get more acrimonious. Now that the first flush of beginning had died down, the staff settled into normal human relations, that is to say, suspicion, hostility, false civility, selfishness, and all the rest of it. The meetings got so terrible that not only the patients but even some of the staff stopped going. Our policy was not to force anyone to attend, so the staff was left to its own inner resources. It got like a badly run encounter group. We began attacking one another, highlighting one another's faults, bitching about the administration.

Once a week, Alistair Frazier came and gave little talks on the dynamics of insanity, illustrated with material from his private patients. Then, having collected his fee for his little performance, would dust off the chaos of the ward, and split.

Then Marvin arrived one afternoon with a great pile of forms. They were the behavioral-norm charts that we were supposed to fill out. Partially because his approach was so inhuman, and partially because the group was looking for a lightning rod for its pent-up frustration. Marvin received the full venom of the staff. We began to discuss the relevance of his research, and got him to the point where he admitted that the research was, "in a sense, meaningless." But, he insisted, it had to be done.

"That's all bullshit, Marvin," a voice shot out. "You're just interested in your own career."

Marvin leapt to his feet. "I know that," he cried out, "I have to live with that. Don't you think I'm tortured? Half of me wants to be down here with you, helping people, doing the real work. But half of me needs to support a house and a family and a style of living. That part of me is real too." And then he stretched out his arms like Christ on the cross and shouted, "I'm torn between two worlds!"

The humor of the demonstration and the pathetic honesty of his self-exposure let us overlook the fact that he had once again bypassed the basic question, which was, Why are we going through all the rituals of a research project when we all understand that it means nothing?

Then, drawing himself up to his full height, he eloquently said, "The work you people do is beautiful, but I want to quantify it, to bring it into the scientific community at large. Don't you see, if we can show that our method works, we have a chance of changing the attitudes of the entire scientific community."

God help me, his eyes grew moist. He actually believed it, at that moment, anyway. In face of the fact that the psychiatric community in this very hospital was showing unrelenting blindness and hostility to anything which would involve them past the point where they need only prescribe Thorazine and run an orderly internment camp. And in face of the fact that "our work" had not begun to get off the ground and was mired in our total inability to act in anything but a bestial fashion.

My money ran completely out. I began sleeping on the ward a few nights each week. My last pair of pants gave way at the zipper and I went into the stock room to put on a pair of hospital issue. Now I was broke, without keys, sleeping on the ward, and dressed like a patient. The transformation was taking place, but I still wasn't aware of what was happening.

Crushing news arrived. We would have to move out of Ward Sixteen. The hospital director, a man who like to shuffle people about on paper and then have the real people follow the plans, had decided, quite arbitrarily, that we would move to Ward Nineteen. The staff set up a howl of protest. Nineteen was a double ward. It was one of the old buildings on the other side of the grounds, and quite depressing. It involved using a shared dining room. It went even further against the notion of setting up an environment where restraint and fear didn't rule the roost. The move was to push us even deeper into the regular hospital setup, with old nurses who looked upon their patients as animals to be controlled. It was part of the scene which reeked of hopelessness and the stench of the chemical lobotomy, Thorazine.

We demanded that Richard come to our next meeting. He had stopped coming to the ward altogether. He was leaving the dirty work to the peons. The psychic proletariat felt crushed, the people like Irene, a beautiful black nurse who had a simplehearted belief that we might accomplish something on the ward, and the darkness of the mental hospital might see some light.

"I sympathize with you, of course," Richard said at the next meeting. "But the hospital director is a very difficult man to convince."

"Have him come to the ward," we said. "Let us talk to him."

That turned out to be impossible. Finally, we badgered him into letting Al go see the man. Al returned with an earful of double-talk that boiled down to a single message: NO. The move was scheduled.

Joel and I talked that night. We decided that the hospital strategy was clear. They would keep putting pressure on until we had stopped fighting. The more active staff members would leave, and, with the docile people left, they would set up a nice safe Thorazine study ward, with all pretences at a blowout center gone.

The current research schema called for putting half the patients on Thorazine, keeping half off, with no one to know which was which except for Marvin. Then, we were supposed to do our blowout scene, and see, via the behavior forms, which patients "improved." The trouble was that improvement was measured by inane external standards having nothing to do with a person's well-being or understanding of himself necessarily. Also, our "blowout thing" never came off, and each day on the ward was spent in a round of random behavior, punctuated by the routines imposed by the hospital structure.

The following day, I went with Al to a meeting of the general hospital staff and had all my fears confirmed. It was like a Republican convention. Everything was discussed in generalities. Perhaps a thousand people sat stiffly in the auditorium, listening to the director lay down a vague rap about dedication to the improvement of conditions at the hospital, and then enter into a round of discussions on rules and regulations, and "essential services," meaning everything but the actual state of the patients. Boredom reached cataclysmic levels; yawns were stifled; voices droned on in monotone.

Not once was there a hint of humanity, a wave of humor, a spark of awareness. There was not the slightest sense that what was being discussed was the condition of actual human beings, with as much existential worth as anyone in the room. These were the "doctors" discussing the "situation," these were the "sane" discussing the relationship to the "crazies."

When I left the meeting, I was suffocating. I got out onto the green lawn outside the building, and was swept up by the sunlight and air and trees, and in a burst of exuberance, jumped in the air a few times to get the circulation going in my limbs. I let out a loud exhalation to clear my lungs.

Suddenly, several people standing around me jumped back, and one man glared at me with heavy hostility. And then I realized. I was dressed in patient's clothing. As far as they were concerned, I was a "patient" and I was exhibiting "psychotic" behavior, that is to say, behavior which fell outside the accepted boundaries imposed by the strictures of the culture. After all, "normal" people don't jump up and down and breathe loudly. In a flash I saw the entire vicious cycle of the mental hospital scene. The doctors, by law, by definition, were sane; by the same criteria, the patients were insane. Therefore, whatever the doctors did, whatever they did, including sitting for two hours in a stultifying and dehumanizing conclave, was all right. But whatever the patients did, including exhibiting some simple physiological relief, was crazy; was sick. It was like the situation between teachers and children, between police and citizen; the masters ruled, the others had to obey.

But this was what Laing was talking about! This is what drove poor Ronnie to the brink, his insight into the way the cards are stacked, the way civilization breaks its members, the way the people internalize their sense of being malformed, and are then punished for their inability to conform. Visions of Reich and Jesus came crashing home, as well as of every other man who has seen once and for all the vicious trap of sleep which has captured almost every single human being in the world. The doctors and nurses were all mad, truly mad, but their madness had been controlled and compressed until they could walk around like automatons with a great semblance of self-control, all the while being the people who contributed to the wars, to the crises, to the general unhappiness of mankind. The only difference between them and the patients was that they had the guns behind them, they had the power. It became a political question after all.

I grabbed Al, but he was deep in some Scorpionic depression of his own. I got back to the ward and saw Alistair, and spilled my vision out to him. He puffed on his cigar. "Yes, it really is a vicious cycle, isn't it?" he said in the best Rogerian manner, and I recognized the tones as those he reserved for his patients. He was agreeing intellectually; that is to say, he was humoring me. I could have hated the man except that I realized that he had spent his entire life humoring himself.

The situation on the ward suddenly got to seem extremely grim. For one of the few times in my life, I was seized by a passion which put the suffering of others before my own. These people in the hospital were really in trouble. Not only were they burdened by a vision and a pain they couldn't sustain, there wasn't a single human being they could talk to who would listen to them with true understanding. The best they could hope for was an uneducated sympathy, a soft shoulder. For when they really started to talk about what they saw and felt, they were put into the category of crazy, even by those who wished them well. For who would believe a patient who said that the doctors were mad? I mean, truly mad? A great poet might say it, and get away with it, but some poor loonie locked in the asylum would only get himself deeper into trouble.

For, if the doctors were mad, what did that say about the priests and presidents and generals and teachers? The message was clear enough. The civilization is rotten to its core. The entire bag, all two thousand years of it in the Western world, and some six thousand years for as far back as there are written records in the East. In fact, man is malignant at heart, a broken spoke in the wheel of creation, a stupid bestial creature who is barely redeemed by odd moments of decency. And his quintessential madness, his wars, are so totally accepted as natural that one rarely considers them as the blasphemy that they are. Our history books are very little else but the record of our wars. And because, somehow, through some ironic joke on the part of nature, we attained to the use of language, we deign to consider ourselves as images of God.

We made the move to the new ward, and the situation got worse. Many of the staff members weren't even talking amicably to one another. Everyone was depressed. The art therapist, theoretically the lowest on the hierarchical flagpole, was doing the only creative work, hanging pictures, providing crayons and paints for people to use, trying to get the patients to express something of their inner states through paint.

No one could relax. There was always so much going on. Nurses were walking through. Phones were ringing. Research forms were being filled out. If only it could have been possible just to stop everything for a while, to allow us just to settle down and look at one another. If the place were only something like a home. I saw all this, and was as powerless as anyone else. The system was too strong, both inside and outside of us. The ward nurse began a personal vendetta against me.

Since I wasn't being paid, and since I practically lived on the ward, I decided I would just follow my own inclinations in regard to working with the patients. This involved mostly flowing with the vibrations on the ward, to be present with whoever needed me at any given time. This came as a challenge to her authority, and was the focal point for other resentments.

She had married into the upper middle class, and was working because it was a chic thing to do, and was having trouble with her teenage children, and really didn't like her husband all that much. She was physically attractive for her age, somewhere in the late forties, and from time to time I amused myself by playing sexual eye games with her, which both turned her on and put her uptight. A major blowup came during one of the meetings, when I let down my guard and let everyone know what I really thought of the way things were being run. I had written a two-page denunciation and circulated it among the staff, and almost gave Marvin a heart attack for fear it might be seen by someone in the administration. As in any encounter situation, when a person comes forward, he serves as a magnet for the accumulated feeling of the group, either love or hatred. This time, I got the negative reaction, and for a half hour was ripped into by the entire staff for sins both real and imaginary. Since I wasn't too stable anyway, I felt my personality disintegrate from under me, and at that point, Donna unleashed a vicious attack.

"You're a pig," she said. "You pick your nose. You don't wash. You're arrogant. You're always looking for a handout. You have no decency." And so forth. I had no recourse but to stumble out of the meeting.

Some form of retribution came to Donna, however, through Larry. He was a tall thin veteran who spent all his time walking around the ward, to the point where his feet got infected, and drinking coffee and mumbling to himself. As with so many other of the crazies, one had to spend a great deal of time with him and listen to his rap to learn what he was saying. In effect, he was giving a running commentary on his condition, including what was going on in the ward, exaggerating his perceptions. He was a superb mime, and when Joel and I sat and watched him, he would put on little performances that were invisible to anyone who didn't know what he was doing. His craziness came out most fully when he started rapping about how the ward was a concentration camp and that the Geneva Convention promised more freedoms that he was now allowed.

Donna was in the habit of massaging him. She would go over to him, get him to sit down, and rub his feet tenderly. It was, in her mind I am sure, a strictly humanitarian gesture. But the fact that she was so warm to him and to no one else indicated that there was a chemistry happening between them. Every once in a while, when he was in a playful mood, Larry would make a grab for her crotch. And she would turn, with that jocular anger women show when they are pleased but refuse to show it, and say, "Now, now, touching's not allowed." And once or twice he shot back, "Hubbie wouldn't like it, eh?" Which simply proved that insanity is a relative notion.

Then, one day, she came running into the lounge, claiming that Larry had "attacked" her. He had flown at her in a rage, threatening to do her in. There was a great deal of serious discussion as to whether or not he would be transferred to another ward. But when she told the story, she left out one detail. That she had been angry with him all morning for refusing to take his Thorazine, and at the time of the "attack" had been walking toward his bed with a hammer in her hand.

Of course, she was going to hang a picture. But if someone hadn't seen her with the hammer, and called attention to it, we would have had another instance in which the insane man was judged guilty because he was insane, and the nurse was put in the right because she was, by definition, normal. The analogy to black men and white women in the South is clear.

One afternoon, while things were particularly frazzled, Joel came up to me and said, "Let's take a ride." We drove around the hospital grounds and got pleasantly stoned. And when we returned, were much calmer.

But we came back to an almost unrecognizable ward. Peace reigned. The patients were sitting around, rapping, reading, looking out the windows. One was fixing a phonograph. Two were playing checkers. Even Larry was having a talk with one of the others. Joel and I sat down, and soaked up the vibrations. Within a few minutes, we became part of the milieu and sensed the deep feeling of order in the large room.

"What is it?" I asked.

Joel looked around. "Ain't none of the staff around," he said.

Sure enough, there was not a staff member to be seen. For the first time, the context within which the insane are judged as insane was removed, and lo and behold, the abnormal were normal. One imagined them having no more difficult problems of survival than any other group of people and, perhaps, if left on their own, would construct a whole new society. "Where are they?" I asked.

And then we heard them, faintly, from the small meeting room way in the back of Bill's office. Muffled shouts. We got up and went over. The voices got louder as we approached. And when we opened the door, we recoiled as from a blast furnace. The staff were sitting around in a circle, their faces distorted with hatred, their voices harsh and rasping, their bodies in the clenched attitudes of attack. As I stepped in, Marvin was screaming at Al, "I've never liked you, you motherfucker, and if you don't get off this fucking ward, I'll kill you."

The doctors were having a meeting.

Another week dragged by, and one day the hospital's assistant director visited us. He was a fuzzy old man who told us that we shouldn't get too excited by our work, because every five years someone comes along with a new theory or new idea, but in the end it's always the same; things don't get any better. The important thing, he reminded us, was to see that the buildings were maintained, and the fire laws obeyed. He was so senile, so feeble, so innocuous, that we didn't even bother mocking him or trying to talk to him. He was the final result of *homo administratus,* a pale shadow of humanity.

Loren went on another window-breaking spree and was transferred. I saw him a few days after his move to his old ward. He had been shot up with massive doses of Thorazine, and he was entirely changed. The light had gone out of his eyes, and he stuttered when he spoke. He told me to apologize to everyone for his behavior. He said he had seen the light and promised to reform. "I hope I can get well enough to get out of here and get a job," he said. "The doctor says that if I behave, he'll put in a good word for me." I couldn't bear to look at him. He had been utterly broken.

And then Sam flipped out.

There had been little bizarre behavior on the ward until then, unless one counted relatively minor things like Larry's running monologue, or Loren's window-breaking, or Julio's periodic dashes for freedom. Julio was a Mexican, born in California, who spent most of his time in a mildly catatonic state. He was mobile, but just didn't move very much. Every once in a while, when one of the ward personnel opened the front door, he would leap up and burst out of the ward with amazing speed. Once out, he would run for several miles, and then stop, and sit down until he was picked up again. Once, Irene and I followed him in her car as he jogged down the highway. He was physically magnificent, superbly muscled, and with a natural animal rhythm. No one ever got into his head, and I never got the slightest notion of what his scene was.

But one day, during a meeting, Sam came in shouting. He was completely naked and dripping wet. He had been taking a bath. "You fuckers!" he shouted. "Doesn't anyone see me?"

The grins that flushed the faces of many of the people there are such as I hope never to see again. It had finally happened; someone was freaking out. The blowout center had its first blowout. And after all the theoretical discussions, the preparations, the fights, the intramural strife, we were going to get a chance to "do" our first patient.

"You bastards. I'm talking to you!" he screamed.

He was about five feet ten inches tall, with a medium build, and a handsome face. He had an extremely small cock. "I'm impotent," he said more quietly. And then, screaming again, "I'M IMPOTENT!"

David, one of the ward doctors, went up to him. Sam jumped back. "Stay away from me," he warned. "You don't understand what I'm saying."

Al stood up, but Sam just ran away down the hall, whooping like an Indian, and disappeared in the bathroom, the place used to cool patients off. In a few seconds we heard a splash; obviously he had jumped into the tub as though it were a swimming pool. And then there was a long silence.

"Let him work it out," Al said.

And then everyone went right back to the details of the meeting, some vague and heated discussion concerning what we might do to make the patients more interested in attending the daily discussion groups.

I got up and went to the back. Sam was sitting in the tub. He seemed quite calm. He looked up at me.

"Bullshit," he said. "It's all bullshit."

I couldn't agree more. "That's right," I said.

Then the fury flashed again. "You're no better than the rest of them," he shouted.

"That's right," I said. "So what? Neither are you."

He hung his head. "I'm no good, I'm no good," he chanted

over and over again. There was no way to get into his space without doing him violence.

"You want me to stay?" I asked.

"STAY?" I heard him scream and he leapt up, rushed past me, and ran back into the meeting. "Stay where?"

One of the other patients went over and said something quietly to him, and he seemed to relax. The two of them went off into the side wing of the ward. I rejoined the meeting. David said to me, as I sat down, "What's happening with him?"

I got angry. "What's happening? He's freaking out, that's what. He's losing his fucking mind and you people are sitting around having inane discussions. That's what's happening."

Their guilt transformed into anger and came shooting at me. And for twenty minutes, as I sat, half the people in the room again lacerated me with long lists of grievances, dredging up almost everything I had said or done since I arrived. I listened less to the words than felt the waves of hatred washing over me. Their faces became biting masks, their voices cut like razors. The months took their toll, the scenes I had been in, the constant fear of madness, the long weeks of having no money, the corrosive quality of having to crash just to sleep, wearing hospital issue, having not a single person around who knew me well, the drugs, the historical context of my entire previous life being obliterated, the mounting hostility. I became comatose and sank lower in my chair, Donna leapt up and showered me with needles of invective. I was burned raw. I felt myself coming apart.

I made one last effort to preserve my ego, pulled out the last weapon of defense. I sat forward. "You may all be right," I said, "but I never wanted anything except for the ward to live up to its early promise." And I began recounting what our initial vision was, our early dreams, and contrasting that to what we had become. As I spoke, my voice fell into the hypnotic rhythm I use in relaxation workshops. I made an effort to steady and deepen my breathing. I used eye contact to center the group's vibrations. And within five minutes, I had almost regained everything. I had single-handedly climbed out of the psychic pit I had fallen into, and was now directing the group in the way that I wanted it to go.

I was just at the point of letting the reins I had on myself slip a bit; the world was barely coming back into focus; and I felt that I was all alone inside my head with what I was doing.

And at that moment, Sam, who had walked up behind me, leaned over and whispered in my ear, "Naughty, naughty." I turned around suddenly and found myself staring right into the pit of his crazed eyes. He smiled a smile of deep complicity and said, "It's not nice to cast spells."

For a moment I stood on the brink of the most momentous decision I had ever made in my life. I could, from this position, treat what he had just said as "crazy" and gather to me the approval and acceptance of the doctors and staff, of my civilization. Or I could cop to the fact that what he had just said was chillingly accurate, and showed the kind of perception with which schizophrenics are constantly frightening their doctors. And while my mind pondered the choice, my instincts made the decision, and, letting out a full throat-wracking scream, I leapt from the chair and ran from the room.

I had crossed the line.

Sam and I spent the next six hours in total psychic contact. His mind and heart opened to me as mine did to him, and we were locked in a deadly ride which promised to destroy both of us. And the more terrifying the ride became, the more we needed to hold on to one another. Yet, it was that very holding on which brought us closer to disaster. It was like a long marriage compressed into a very short time.

Since we were human beings, with all the fallibility that implies, we showered one another with as much hate as we did love, as much violence as we did gentleness. And since we could read one another's hearts perfectly, we had absolute power over the changes we put one another through.

There was one difference between us. Sam was a pro. He had been "crazy" for a long time, and he knew the ropes. I was stunned by the revelations which were pouring in, living at a height of intensity in communion with another human being that I hadn't conceived could be possible. I was trying desperately to integrate my experiences so I wouldn't be overwhelmed by them. And I had to give up. Too much came in too fast.

"You're selfish," he said to me. "You are the single most selfish human being in the world."

And I knew it was true. I examined my conscience and realized that I had never done a single thing which didn't take as its starting point the benefit it would bring me. Later, I came to understand that I was just for the first time getting an insight past the myth of altruism with which we are inundated since we are small. In that time, I lived the experience of the fact that we are born alone, and die alone, and during our lifetimes pretend to keep one another company.

But then, I knew only what struck me the hardest. And I was coming face to face with all the copouts of my entire life, all the times I refused to see what I was seeing, all the times I turned my fellow human beings into two-dimensional projections, because I couldn't admit that they were as real as I. In this state, this catacomb of echoing insanity, there was no place to hide. Pain was real. Existence was immediate.

And a strange thing began to happen. As I got crazier, that is to say, as I got more real in the awareness of my actual condition, others began to fade to the degree that they couldn't or wouldn't recognize me. Most of the staff began averting their eyes when I went past. A few, like Al and Harish, recognized me, but refused to see the dimensions of my trip. And astonishingly, the other patients emerged as real people in a way I had never seen them when I was "on the other side." For the first time I realized that I had been afraid of looking at them, and afraid specifically to see that they had, whether they were aware of it or not, more balls than me.

This is not to make a romantic myth about schizophrenics, but to point out that unless one has been trapped in their confusion and helplessness, which is actually only a different level of clarity; unless one has cut off all sense of acceptance by the world, one cannot deal with them as equals, for one is afraid. Laing saw this, and that is why he went crazy, to know what it was all about.

The ward became jumpy, like a cattle pen at shipping time. Four o'clock came, and the new shift arrived, but much of the day staff stayed on. Some of the other patients went into more quiet freak-outs, and generally there was an increase in the pacing and muttering and demands to be let out for fresh air. At one point, Sam began threatening people with physical violence. I went up to him and he punched me in the chest. Three of the staff came over to hold him and I could suddenly see in their grotesque postures the mixture of fear and bravado which had them put their heads forward while holding their shoulders back and bringing their lightly clenched fists up in front of their groins.

"Get away," I spat at them. And with that, two more of the

patients came over and moved Sam away, one of them saying, "Come on man, don't be such a fuckoff."

I saw the difference. The patients spoke to one another as human beings, while the staff set up an unbridgeable gap between themselves and their charges. I found myself going off with the patients, leaving the staff members to chatter among themselves, hitting their jargon back and forth like Ping-Pong balls, encapsulating the experience neatly into prestructured categories.

"Calm down, man," Adam was saying to Sam. Sam broke loose again and ran into the dayroom.

"DON'T YOU UNDERSTAND?" he screamed. "I'M TRAPPED IN TIME, I'M TRAPPED IN TIME."

And with that, I fell over the final edge, and plunged deep into eternal fear. For I understood precisely what he meant, what he was feeling. He was all at once understanding his own historical mortality as an ephemeral pattern against the screen of eternity, and the vision was so vast that it pinned him to himself like a butterfly on a mat. He was having the kind of insight which the mystics revel in, and which LSD makes potentially available to everyone. It was a profound moment, unbearably rich in its human and divine implications, and it came through a naked crazy standing on the blowout ward at the state hospital. And not a single other person there, not one of the educated doctors, or prominent analysts, or trained nurses, or well-wishing attendants, not one bowed to the moment and gave the man his due for standing so fearful and exposed in the searing light of Truth.

A mammoth fury boiled up in me, and I charged out to stand next to him. I swept the ward with my frenzied eyes. "YOU'RE ALL DEAD," I cried. "DEAD. YOU FRIGHTENED FOOLS. YOU STUPID MACHINES. YOU PLAGUE-RIDDEN SCUM. WAKE UP AND SEE. LOOK!"

They all stepped back from us. I ran into the art therapy room. I pulled out a giant sheet of paper and wrote, YOU'RE ALL DEAD, on it in large black letters and pasted it to the front door. I heard myself yelling, screaming, unintelligible things, mad things. From time to time, I would pass Sam, who was also freaking, charging in the other direction, and our eyes would meet in a flashing glare of pure freedom. For the time, we were brothers against the foe.

I heard music and ran to the stereo. It was the Airplane singing "Crown of Creation."…"You are the crown of creation, and you have no place to run to." Yes, I thought. I am finally outside the inside. I am standing where everything is pure becoming, pure being, pure appearance, pure thought, all at once. I have stripped myself of all convention, of all inner stricture, of all sham. I am ready to stand at the edge of the earth, with all life pulsing in my veins, and stare into the unknowing void of the universe and cry out in terror and joy. I have finally become a man.

I ran into the dayroom, and found it almost empty. The day shift had gone. Seemingly, they had become bored with the floor-show now that the novelty of it had passed. Sam crashed, and went into the side wing to sleep. And I stood there, with the shreds of my satori, trembling.

As always happens, the higher one gets, the farther one must fall. And in an instant, I went from the peaks of manic realization to the depths of depressive confusion. What was I doing here? Who was I? I cast about for some familiar and comforting fragment of my personality, but none was there. For the moment, I was sheer essence, inchoate and raw. The fear began to choke me. I felt an animal need to escape, to get out.

I went into the office and found Al sitting there. For a moment I was cheered by his face. Al was my friend. He had got me the job. I had stayed at his house and we had got stoned together. I went up to him. "Al," I said, "let me out." And the moment I said it, I knew he wouldn't.

He looked down at his desk. "I can't, man," he said.

I got very scared. "Al, please."

"I'd like to," he said, and I watched with horror as he psy-chically stepped into his role of psychiatrist. "But I can't." He meant legally. "Look at yourself," he said. "If you went out like that, they'd never let you get off the grounds. The cops would pick you up and bring you to Ward Seven."

Ward Seven! The Marat/Sade ward, where the crazies drooled all day long and hit their heads against the walls. "You're better off here, with us," he said.

I stepped back. He was speaking to me in the condescending tones I had heard so often when doctors were talking to patients. And then it hit me. Inside me, I was crazy with confusion and fear. Outside me, my behavior was grotesque. I was penniless, dressed in patient's clothing. And the ward psychiatrist wouldn't let me out. By any standard, the door had closed behind me. I was mad.

And the minute I thought that, an insane giggle came to my

lips. A giggle! Like a burst of sunlight, the face of Joel exploded in my mind. All at once, I relaxed. "Can I use the phone?" I said.

He looked at me a moment. "All right," he said. "Go ahead."

I dialed Joel's number, and in five minutes poured out the whole story. By the time I got to the part where Al wouldn't let me out, he began giggling, and suddenly everything was all right again. I had someone to talk to. *Someone to talk to.* Such a simple, such a rare, thing.

My perspective flooded back. I wasn't out of the water, but I was no longer drowning. "Can you come get me?" I asked. "I can't come tonight," he said, "I'm doing my drummer gig. But I'll come get you in the morning and we'll give you some coffee and grass. You'll be all right."

I hung up, and turned back into the ward, my eyes wet with tears. I still had dues to pay. The experience had to be regurgitated and eaten, again and again, in a thousand different flavors, before I would be though with it.

I got the chills. It was getting dark. And the nighttime routine on the ward was beginning. One of the most terrible aspects of schizophrenia is the way it often robs a person of his ability to sleep. And so, with my blanket wrapped around me, I began to pace the long floors of the ward.

Some of the people were huddled in front of the television set. Larry made endless trips to the coffee urn. I went to the window and peered helplessly at the stars. I lay down and closed my eyes. Immediately, paranoia flared. I became convinced that someone would come up and slit my throat.

At midnight, the graveyard shift came on duty. And from outside their office I watched them. They looked like MP's guarding a military prison. They were brisk and efficient. They signed numberless forms, and filled log books with notations. From where I stood, they seemed pale and nervous, while those of us outside were dark and weary. It was the same story all over again, the white men and the niggers, the Germans and the Jews, the bosses and the workers.

Tim came up to me and stood by my side as we peered into the room where, just yesterday, I had sat, stupidly thinking that by going through the routines of schedule I was in some way helping the suffering of the poor madmen who were outside. And now I saw, clearly, once and for all, that the same sickness which produces schizophrenics insures that they will never be cured. For the cure is measured by a standard that any truly sane man would have to reject.

There is too little understanding of the nature of things, and those who understand are too few to be of any help, or too battered to care any more.

"Do you see them?" I said to Tim.

"Yeah," he said, "I been seeing them for a long time."

"Well, what…" I began, and then didn't know what to say.

"Oh fuck, man," he said. "Don't even think about it. Let's go get some more coffee."

The next morning, shortly after daybreak, Joel came to get me. By then I had pulled myself enough together to present a face to meet the faces I would meet. I shaved and put on clean issue. I spoke calmly. And when no one was noticing, Joel opened the back door and spirited me out. We drove back to the warmth of his home.

"What about them?" I said. "The ones still in there, who can't get out so easy?"

He gave me one of his beautiful stoned sad looks. "So," he said, "go make a revolution."

10.

"... *goin' back to New York City, do believe I've had enough...*" sang Dylan over and over again as I sat in Rita's San Geronimo pad. As always, when I had nowhere to turn to, Rita appeared as if miraculously and gave me the stability I needed to make it to the next cycle. Georgia had called and told me she wasn't really pregnant and was going back to Mexico for a divorce. My string in California had run out. I felt the need to go home, even though home was a polluted, snarling, criminal city with all the ills of our time concentrated in its zoo-like buildings. I needed, more than anything, people who had known me a long time, people who would just let me be, and among whom I could relax and let the scars of the trip heal. I needed, desperately, although I couldn't articulate it at the time, to put the wildness of this year and a half in perspective, and the best way to do it was to tell its stories to old friends, to integrate through sharing.

I had no money; the snafu at Sacramento had never been cleared up and the funds which were to have paid me didn't come through. So I hit the odd-job trail again, and wound up working for a gardener who kept all the trees and flowers which grew in the islands of the shopping-center parking lots in Marin

County. He had spent fifteen years as a Canadian Mounted Policeman, and during his long isolated rides through the northern winters, had become a strict Christian fundamentalist. He believed the world was created in 4004 B.C. I teetered on the brink of hysteria every time I just spoke to him. In the condition my mind was in, I was ready to be imprinted by anything I heard, and when he started on his rap, I would have to bite my inner cheeks to the point of making them bleed so the pain would distract me from what he was saying. And I had to be polite; I needed the money.

The job itself was a horror. It involved, each day, tearing up hundreds of flowers by the roots, because the supermarkets wanted the floral display rotated every few weeks. They treated living things like so much scenery, to be moved around at will. For almost a week I hunched over the islands of earth as cars rumbled past my heels, watching the hordes of housewives do their shopping, and methodically killing flowers.

I had to get out. I didn't know what was awaiting me in New York, or how that city would appear to me now after all my changes, but I was certain it couldn't be worse than my situation at the moment. I picked up my first paycheck and counted a little over eighty dollars. A plane ticket was a hundred and fifty. But that night I came across a notice for a half-price fare, which turned out to be the return portion of a half-used round-trip ticket. I bought it, threw my things into my knapsack, and went to the airport as M. Carpenter. I said good-bye to Rita, perhaps for the tenth time.

A nervous six hours later, at seven in the morning, the jet touched down at Kennedy Airport. By the time I paid for the buses to Manhattan, I stood on the corner of Seventy-second Street and Broadway with five cents in my pocket. I walked over to Zelda's apartment, and woke up my lover-friend of seven years. She looked at me once, smiled, and said, "You're back. Come in. Have some breakfast. You need a place to sleep? You need some money? Come in. Sit down."

And with the first breath of relief I had taken in a very long time, I sat down and let myself be ministered to in classic prodigal son style.

I delayed calling my parents. My mother would immediately have wanted to know "What have you been doing?" and the thought of being confronted by that question right now boggled my mind. Zelda laid some bread on me. Now that she had decided she didn't want to be an actress after all, she was racking up a high salary at an ad agency. And then she went off to work.

For a few days I just prowled the streets, letting the city vibrations wash over me. The one comforting thing about New York is its utter imperviousness to individual madness. The city's population had reached such a convoluted and intense pitch of constant anxiety that I found it restful simply by contrast. Of course, I realized that if I stayed in it too long, I would be absorbed into its movement and find myself drawn into that tense, headlong rush to oblivion.

I decided to plug back in to the New York action, and gave Francis a call. During the time I had been away, he had undergone a radical change in temperament. In the old days, he was strictly a private person, and spent most of his time in his fortress loft, without telephone or doorbell. He was involved in an effort to paint, abstractly, the AHA! experience described in Gestalt psychology. His canvases emerged as dense swirling drifts of subtle pigment, absolutely monochromatic, which kept enticing the eye, challenging it to discern shapes. His technique involved getting very stoned, climbing to the top of a twelve-foot ladder, and leaning down into the canvas, painting precariously, while Mozart played for twelve or fourteen hours. He was hyperthyroid, with a metabolism about three and a half times faster than normal, was skeletally thin, and slept about two or three hours a night. He has perhaps the world's only *head* library.

Now, his metabolism had reverted to normal, he had become sociable, and had given up painting for videotape. He had met some video freaks who gave him acid and had him watch a screen for three hours, looking at the white noise patterns. As anyone who has tried that knows, one gets stoned on the infinity of possible perceptions. One is watching pure energy, the random dance of electrons across a magnetized screen. And in a while, it becomes the ground upon which any possible figure may appear. For a while, one writes the effect off to hallucination, and then one realizes that standard television is merely the arrangement of these same electrons into patterns which, through conditioning, are "recognizable." The line between perception and hallucination is quite thin, and from the subatomic standpoint, the difference between reality and illusion is merely a matter of prejudice. When one takes the further step in realizing that what we call physical reality is also the configuration of electrons into familiar patterns, the psychological revolution is complete. One understands that television is the art form of our epoch, standing in relation to our renaissance the way painting stood in relation to the Italian Renaissance.

Francis was involved with people whose notion was that the counter-culture, the worldwide society of *heads,* might build an actual alternate network, which would begin with the mailing of tapes and continue to the use of satellites. Since the misuse of technology by power- and money-hungry bandits has brought the world to the brink of ruin, and since it is too late to go back on our technology, the technology itself could be used to extricate ourselves from the peril it helped get us into.

I was swiftly swept up into this latest phase of the revolution, this wave which called itself media ecology. I began to meet the media freaks, and spent many weeks, very high, talking about international networks, and computer interfacing, and the new consciousness which the children of the television age are manifesting. Everything fit into place. And I got lost in the folds of the conception, which put together all the aspects and pieces of the human problem, cosmically, and historically, and psychologically.

As the title for this gathering of forces, Francis chose the name: RAINDANCE, which implied that the electronic exo-skeleton had to be understood as a real part of the earth's ecology before it could be intelligently used.

Stoned on images, I forgot to check my internal meters, and found myself on another trip before I was aware of it. Still, I grew strong on the energies which were being unleashed, until the fatal error was made. Francis and Barry, a reporter whose ambition was to become the electronic Henry Luce, got infected with dreams of wealth and power. Raindance stopped being an activity of friends and revolutionaries, and attempted to become a business.

From then on, everything got ugly. For to do business, one had to deal with businessmen. And it took some three months before the message filtered through our enthusiasm that there is only one principle in all business dealing: Profit is good, everything else is bad. Already CBS was coming out with a system for distributing home cassettes. But in their usual totalitarian mode, they were going to manufacture tapes for which they had the sole printing process. They were not going to allow the people to make their own tapes, their own art, to record their own history. The very improvement in technology which might have signaled a revolution in the human spirit was to be used to further enslave that spirit. All the ideas we had were being had by the businessmen who run the country, but they were interested in extending their own empires, not making the world a saner, healthier place to live.

The enthusiasm for videotape came from the evenings we spent using the equipment with one another, to create portraits, and modes of psychological insight, and sheer technological art. I suppose we all had our first flashes of power through those sessions, the realization that if one had access to the technology, he had as strong a voice in shaping the destiny of the world as the politicians and generals. And yet, how often need the old saw be repeated that power corrupts.

Ultimate corruption came in the form of a pleasant and friendly man named Edward who was a lawyer for a Wall Street investment firm. He volunteered to act as our attorney and advisor in return for a share of stock. And within days the air was redolent with talk of futures and options and raising millions of dollars and keeping an eye on competitors, and all the rest of the vicious jargon of our commercial civilization. The death stroke came when we ceased being Raindance, and became: Raindance Corporation (RDC). The last three letters were included for any business we had to do with large companies; it was felt that "Raindance" might sound too far-out, wheres "RDC" would make us sound *respectable*. This was perhaps the first instance in which a revolutionary force sold out before it even had anything to sell.

One of our group happened to be a millionaire through inheritance, and he put up thirty thousand dollars seed money for equipment and salaries. And so, for a few months, I was content, learning about video, getting a pad on East Eleventh Street, and reintegrating myself into city life.

But the euphoria couldn't last. After a while, the initial investment began to run out, and we weren't bringing in any money. Francis was totally erratic, disappearing for weeks and then showing up with a series of brilliant tapes which had, of course, no commercial value. Otto, our accountant, finally admitted that he didn't know how to keep books. Barry kept spinning more and more grandiose schemes which had less and less relevance to real conditions. Hugh, who provided the money, got bored with the project, and since he was independently wealthy, felt he could drop it at any time whatsoever. And I became more and more unhappy because the group was committing the very sins it was put together to eradicate.

We stopped understanding ourselves as comrades in a common venture and became business partners out to make a buck. We stopped exploring the joys of videotape and began drawing up proposals which we thought would show quick financial return. In attempting to solve the problem we became part of the problem. We had become too venal to continue as artists and revolutionaries, and were too inept to succeed as businessmen.

Finally, the pressures began to mount to the breaking point, and the most intense friction occurred between Francis and myself. Filled as I was with the West Coast philosophy of euphoria-at-all-costs, I kept calling attention to the fact that Raindance had stopped being pleasurable, and that nothing good could come of an organization where the people were unhappy in what they were doing. From Francis' point of view, I was creating obstacles to the smooth functioning of the group. Also, since I was in a privileged position to him, he saw me as a distinct threat. I became RDC's first Trotsky. Also, our business commitments were forcing us to see one another more frequently than our natural rhythms would have dictated. And nothing will destroy a friendship or a marriage faster or more thoroughly than enforced contact. In the early days, after three weeks of being locked in his loft, he would come roaring out, hungry for companionship, and seeing him then was always a joy. Or when, after a particularly rocky trip, I would go in search of someone to allay my paranoia, Francis was a perfect one to visit. Now, with the scheduling of conferences, business dinners, and all the rest of that vapid ritual, contact became deadly. Slight irritations grew into mammoth resentments. Love turned to hate. And the explosion came.

Francis was the group's leader, but didn't really want to lead. He wanted to be the brilliant innovator, and have others follow through on his ideas. He chose people that he liked to work with, but none of us was the type who knew how to follow through either. To follow through means to take away something from spontaneity, and we were enjoying the theater of our condition too much to worry seriously about the details of our plans.

I began to rant and rave, changing my role to that of Savonarola. I proclaimed that we were sliding into ruin, that we were playing into the hands of the forces of evil. And time and again I took Francis aside to remind him that our friendship was worth more than any empire, for if the friendship failed, there could be no sound foundation for any empire to be built upon. This was the same problem that has faced every organization that has ever been formed. In the beginning, the bond is the shared vision of its members, but then the organization develops a life and momentum of its own, and the members become subservient to its currents and directions. The group becomes the monster, swallowing its parts. I had been through this at the state hospital, and I could see the same patterns emerging. But as usual, I was helpless to do anything but point frantically at the reality. As my frustration grew, my pointing became more annoying to the others. I was becoming a drag on the daily functioning, while everyone was trying to grab the golden ring of wealth.

Finally, Francis went to tape a seminar at Princeton which was arranged by a sociologist who saw Raindance as a possible means to up his income to six figures a year. It included twenty of the world's top scientists in some eight disciplines, and concerned the growing ecological crisis. They came to the sober conclusion, based on things like a three-year study of carbon content in the atmosphere, that life on earth has from thirty to fifty years left.

I should have thought that this would make a perfect Raindance tape, disseminating this news to the world. But, in that odd way people have, the scientists refused to have any of the tapes shown. In the face of their own findings that the world was coming to an end, they were afraid that such controversial material might damage their careers.

I couldn't accept it. This was a betrayal on the scale of anything General Motors might be doing. But the others were of a different mind. We got a thousand dollars for doing the taping, and Francis and Barry got very high, rubbing shoulders with eminent men. The tapes were to be sealed and kept in the sociologist's office, not even to be referred to.

When we had our next meeting, Francis and I clashed. I accused him of failing his own vision, of not being able to hold Raindance together, of not knowing how to use the equipment either to make a revolution or an honest dollar, and of being such a megalomaniac that he couldn't see that his newfound peers were shitty cowards.

The five of us sat for four hours and exchanged unpleasantries. It all peaked when I challenged him to get off the level of general issues and discuss his own emotional immaturity.

At which point he stood up and declaimed, "If this is going to degenerate into an encounter group, I quit."

And with that, he wrote out a letter of resignation, signed himself a severance check, and walked out, not to be heard from for two weeks.

The spirit went out of the place. One more dream had fallen through, and in the process, I seemed to have lost a friend. The revolution was a farce, mankind was lost, everywhere there was greed and deception and misunderstanding. And even here, among allies, among those who were trying to make a final effort to save the species from destruction, we were at one another's throats. I couldn't even blame anyone. It seemed simply to be part of the human condition.

While I mucked about the office, haphazardly going through the motions of running a videotape company, Francis consolidated his forces, and one night, about three weeks later, came marching back in with Barry, Hugh, Edward, and two others he had swept into the fold. He was clearly back in control, so I decided to leave.

I wrote a check for two thousand dollars, my first bit of embezzling. With that much money, I could go to Spain and live for over a year. Let the world perish, let the civilization collapse, let my friends go fuck themselves, let the entire insane dance of mankind come to its crashing end. I would go smoke dope and lie in the sun and watch the waves roll in. There seemed to be no other purpose in life worth living for.

I stood at a place where there seemed not the slightest hope for love or decency or peace. Everywhere I looked, there was blight. I became sick with the history of my people. Nothing would work, nothing could work. I scanned our path over the past six thousand years. It was always the same. The strong got into power and drove the weak into one or another form of slavery. There were revolutions, and a new set of strong men came into power. And the people continued, ignorant, sexually crippled, frightened, ill. This, then, was life, a series of disasters, punctuated by occasional moments of relief, and for the fortunate, brief periods of joy. I sank into deep pessimism. We are born in trauma, we die in solitude, and in between we stumble about causing damage.

I suppose any psychologist might have found the proper series of labels to pin on my condition at the time, as might the articulator for any school of philosophy or simple street knowledge. But where to find help? Just to walk down Second Avenue in the morning was a struggle. Before my eyes there lay the fact of existence, once again appearing as this mysterious and indifferent jig, this grotesque accident out of the womb of nothingness, with mankind the living abortion to mock it. Meaning drained from perception the way alertness drains from a sleepy mind. The words from Gurdjieff came back to haunt me again. "Everyone is asleep." And so it was. Even those I had once considered intelligent, most aware, were but another form of sleepwalker, doing another kind of absurd play. All the interests of man paled to insignificance, its politics, its art, its religion, its science, its senescent philosophy. "Look," I wanted to shout, "being IS!", and yet, the minute I put words to it, I sounded like another nutty mystic, another freak-out acid head.

I went into the Raindance office to get some things I had left in the desk, ready to split to the nearest airlines office. But Otto was there, sucking at his pipe, turning his quiet exasperation into clouds of blue smoke. He is a phlegmatic cat who had been a teacher of philosophy before dropping out and trying to make it as a hippie businessman. We had spent many long hours rapping about time, and whether numbers had an objective existence, and now, in a burst of weakness, I told him that I had taken the money and was splitting.

"Very foolish," he said. "Barry will call the cops. You know how he is."

"What about Francis?" I said.

"He'll probably come after you with a knife."

I thought about it. "Sure enough," I said.

And in that, there was a kind of relief. The notion of some real action, having to dodge police and knife-wielding associates, snapped me out of the funk I was in.

I sat down. "You don't think I should do it then?"

"Well," he said, "you're my friend, and anything you want to do is cool with me, but I hate to see you do it. You'll be cutting yourself off from all your other friends." "What friends!" I shouted. "We started as friends. But everyone has become so fucking money-mad and power-hungry that it's impossible even to talk to them without an appointment. They're becoming just like the people they want to overthrow."

Otto puffed philosophically. "Sure. You knew that before you got into Raindance. It's always like that. The minute the good guys define themselves as good guys and decide to fight the bad guys, they enter the same arena as the bad guys, and before you know it they're bad guys too. But the interesting thing is that they still think they're good guys. Nobody believes that he's a bad guy."

"So what's the point? Why not just take the money and run?"

"You'll only have to take yourself with you," he said. "And if you can't manage living with your friends, what will you do among strangers? Besides, this is only temporary. You know that you and Francis will get it together again. Why make the split any worse than it is?"

My resolve seemed to drain out of me. "So, I'll give the money back. Then what?"

"You ought to go out more," he said. "Find yourself some chicks, go to parties. Why don't you get into the literary circuit? You can make witty conversation."

"Otto, you go from the profound to the inane with greater ease than anyone I know."

"Let's go see a movie," he said. And off we went to see *The Damned,* which threw my own problems into relief.

I put the money back, and formally resigned from the organization. But the restlessness inside me would not be assuaged. I was filled with inchoate visions and unarticulated notions and undigested experiences. And there seemed to be no outlet for me that didn't point to another round of confusion. There was no doubt about it; the civilization was coming apart at the seams and to be involved with it at all ran the risk of total contamination. Yet, what was the alternative?

Of course, the first thing which came to mind was suicide. It had not yet occurred to me that death merely relieves the ego of its burden of self-consciousness, but solves no problems. For the first time in my life I lay down to seriously and soberly consider whether killing myself might not be preferable to this endless round of conflict.

But within seconds I had drifted off into a cinematic reverie concerning the melodramatics of my death. I would go off to the Grand Canyon, carrying a capsule of hemlock. A few of my dearest friends would accompany me, only those who could be counted on not to become maudlin, not to lose their sense of humor. We would spend a long time discussing the ramifications of the void, and then, watching the sunset fill that awesome space with light, I would pop my last pill and become One with the All.

The phone rang. It was Aaron Woodbridge inviting me to dinner.

I discarded the notion of suicide. The death of the physical body was the one sure thing in the world and would come sooner or later. Everything being equal, there was no point in rushing it. And so my existential decision was made on the twin pillars of banal coincidence and ennui. I recalled Wittgenstein's serious joke: "I am committed, but I do not know to what.

That night, I went to visit Aaron and his wife, whom I hadn't seen since returning to New York. I thought of his tale of flipping out in Morocco, and lying on a bed for an entire night, deciding whether to live or die, after his most recent love affair had ended with the chick's committing suicide. It was around that time that he had had his "religious experience," and had stormed into his therapist's office demanding to be labeled insane. "I feel like a saint," he had yelled. "Can you tell me that I'm crazy?" And when his poor doctor couldn't get around the fervor of Aaron's trip, he quit all notions of therapy on the spot, coming out with a conviction that it is no different to be holy than to be crazy.

I had met him shortly after that, when I was working at a literary agency, grinding out ten letters a day to would-be writers who paid up to fifty dollars to be told that their style was reminiscent of Hemingway, but that they didn't know how to create plot structure, and would they please try again, sending along another manuscript and another fee. He later married, this time to a chick who never quite made it past the nineteenth century, one of those girls who leave the Midwest and come to New York and graft on a patina of sophistication which, luckily, never quite masks their actual simplicity and beauty.

He retreated into a rigid life-style, getting to appear more and more like the Henry James he had done his master's thesis on. He and his wife now lived an oddly tasteful life, capable of working up great circular delight over the trivia of daily occurrences, such as the expressions on their dog's face. Rebecca is the only woman I know who is still afflicted by the vapors, and regularly takes to her room to lie for several pillow-tossing hours, periodically bringing lace-edged hankies to her nose.

Like so many sensitive and intelligent people trapped on the margin of a culture they cannot exorcise and cannot assimilate, they have taken refuge in routine, trading orgiastic outbursts of joy for steady minimal pleasure. Subliminally they served as symbols of what I most needed right now, a solidity which was still hip enough to laugh at itself. When I went over in my nylon jumpsuit and beard, with an aching need to be heard, I was like a lock about to close in over an obvious key.

Aaron was a little stouter than when I had seen him last, and now sported a bushy moustache. The two of them greeted me in their upper Fifth Avenue pad, complete with stultifying Spanish hardwood furniture and crystal glasses. As I stepped through the door, all the fragments which whirred through me came together and formed a stained-glass mosaic.

Through their window I looked down on the streets of East Harlem, now a snarling slum, while around me glowed the cameo comforts of that middle class to which my entire childhood had propelled me, and which had been at the core of all my revolt, all my search. This was my historical destiny, and I could accomplish nothing else until I accepted it. This is what I had been conditioned for, through my mother's fears and my father's failures. And all the twistings and turnings I tortured myself through were helpless to make me other than I am. With a shudder, I donned the garb of my sociological karma.

Aaron had invited a woman over, an editor from one of the chic publishing houses, and after a beer and some grass, he began to disentangle the knot of my experiences with gentle questions. And in a while, I found myself talking freely, letting the tales spill out.

Suddenly, it was good to be here again, with two years wiped out in an instant, relegated with a literary flourish to the realm of the past. In the familiar setting of a New York apartment, amid cultivated people, the screaming vision of my trip took on the coziness of an adventurer's story told by the fire at a comfortable club. And from time to time Aaron would interject an "Egad...you don't mean..." or, peering into his own past, would remark, "Yes, I remember well, when I had my Experience," referring to the time he flipped out, still calling it *the* experience, as though it were the fulcrum upon which his life before and after was once and for all balanced.

By the end of the evening, I had completed reentry into the fabric of consciousness I had torn loose from when I headed west. I felt like I do after a high fever has passed, drained but sound. And yet, a disquieting grayness had seemed to settle over everything, a distance between myself and all other entities in the universe. A cold shadow passed over me and I grew afraid.

"After that night," Aaron was saying, "I realized that I am dead, and that everyone around me is dead, and that every breath I take is pure miracle, and I should never expect another. But it makes it so hard to live in the world, because so few others understand that, that we are all dead already."

At that point some essential tension which I had carried with me since the moment the cold steel of the forceps clasped my skull and pulled me from my mother's womb, relaxed, and I was set free.

We went out to walk his dog, and we continued to talk, shifting to the war and the chaos in the nation. "I've become totally apolitical," he said. "As far as I can see, they're all mad, all the rulers and the revolutionaries. I've come to find satisfaction in my work, in my writing. It's the only thing that means anything to me anymore."

I looked up at the sky, the clouds, the brilliant moon. Two lovers were leaning against a tree. But Central Park seemed sinister, unsafe. Aaron's voice spun out on the air like a leaf doing somersaults in the breeze.

"What happens with you now?" he said.

"I don't know," I said. "I'll find something to work at; there's still the rent to be paid. But there seems to be no point to anything anymore, just a sense of futility pervading everything."

"Keep in touch," he said.

And shortly thereafter I plugged in to the current of sexual flow which increases in intensity and volume in inverse proportion to the level of conscious freedom in the nation. I added a new mask to the theater of identifications which has been my life, and became a pornographer.

I watch with detached interest now as I go through my days. I breathe in, I breathe out. Who am I becoming? I see lines in the winds of time, leanings which congeal into the contours of the future.

A new trip begins to write itself in. Another voyage into knowing. But with a single difference from all the others before it. This time I cannot deceive myself into thinking that the trip has some destination, that there is some final act which will draw everything together into a bow of understanding. Never can I forget that everything I know, or do, or think, or feel, or create, or understand is but a brief poignant gesture into the supercilious face of the unknown.

There is only what is, and that is mute.
I have stopped searching.